PURR-FECT CRIME

Edited by
Carol-Lynn Rössel Waugh,
Martin H. Greenberg,
and Isaac Asimov

MJF BOOKS

NEW YORK

Published by MJF Books
Fine Communications
Two Lincoln Square
60 West 66th Street
New York, NY 10023

Library of Congress Catalog Card Number 95-81603
ISBN 1-56731-084-2

Manufactured in the United States of America

MJF Books and the MJF colophon are trademarks of Fine Creative Media, Inc.

10 9 8 7 6 5 4 3 2

Acknowlegments

John D. MacDonald—Copyright © 1959 by John D. MacDonald. Reprinted by permission of George Diskant Associates, Inc.

Allen Kim Lang—Copyright © 1966 by Fiction Publishing Company. First published in *The Saint Magazine*. Reprinted by permission of the author.

Ellery Queen—Copyright 1934; renewed 1962 by Ellery Queen. Reprinted by permission of the agents for the author's Estate, the Scott Meredith Literary Agency, Inc., 845 Third Ave., New York, NY 10022.

Randall Garrett—Copyright © 1958 by Columbia Publications, Inc. Reprinted by permission of the Scott Meredith Literary Agency, Inc., 845 Third Ave., New York, NY 10022.

Betty Ren Wright—Copyright © 1958 by H.S.D. Publications, Inc. From *Alfred Hitchcock's Mystery Magazine*. Reprinted by permission of Larry Sternig Literary Agency.

Edward D. Hoch—Copyright © 1972 by Edward D. Hoch. First published in *Ellery Queen's Mystery Magazine*. Reprinted by permission of the author.

Contents

Introduction

Cats

ISAAC ASIMOV

About ten thousand years ago, human beings invented agriculture. They learned to grow grain and to
spend the growing season in the back-breaking work of
plowing, sowing, watering, weeding, harvesting and so
on. The reward was that, in the end, much more food
was available, *much* more food, than would have been
obtained by mere hunting and gathering. The new farm-
ing communities grew in population, therefore, built
cities, invented writing, formed specialized groups—
and, in short, became civilized.

There was a price to be paid for all this. If the harvest
failed, there had come to be too many people to be
supported by emergency hunting and gathering, so that
the failure meant starvation. Again, if the food were
stored away to last the winter, and if there were enemy

raids that carried off the stores, that meant starvation, too.

Well, with a good network of canals and levees about some unfailing stream like the Nile; a reliable annual flood to bring in fresh, fertile soil; a well-equipped force of soldiers to beat off any invaders; all was well. Surely all was well.

Ah, but there was another enemy. Human beings and large animals could be fought off and killed, but mice, swarming by the uncounted millions, were difficult to track down and kill, and those which were killed were quickly replaced. These small animals must have ruined enormous quantities of grain and, in bad years of infestation, must surely have threatened the farmers with starvation.

What to do? In Egypt during the early centuries of the development of its agricultural civilization, the cat was domesticated. It was small enough not to be a danger to human beings, but it was an efficient predator that was lip-smackingly fond of the little rodents. When there were cats on the farm, the mice population decreased and the crops were saved.

It is no wonder that the ancient Egyptians were grateful to cats, considered them divine, and made the killing of cats a capital offense. It was the cat that stood between the Egyptians and starvation.

In medieval witch-hunting centuries, cats fell upon hard times. It was usually old women on whom suspicion of witchcraft fell, and old women then, as now, tended to keep cats.

Why not? Old women were lonely and wanted company. Cats were quiet, peaceful, gentle, and loyal (as long as they were fed) and made ideal pets. Unfortunately, the theory was that witches kept familiar spirits that acted as intermediaries in their dealings with the devil and these spirits could take any shape they wished.

What better shape than that of a cat, so apparently harmless?

In particular, it was a black cat that was suspect. Black was the color of evil and of the devil. Besides, a black cat at night was hard to see and could be tripped over. Its eyes, gleaming greenly, in the dark seemed menacing. As a result, cats were slaughtered senselessly wherever the witch-hunting mania passed.

Fortunately, that particular insanity died down. It has left its marks, of course. A black cat is still considered "bad luck" if it crosses your path, and in animated cartoons, mice are perversely considered heroes and cats villains.

Nowadays, cats are enormously popular again and cat-lovers abound. I know. I'm one of them. I never tire of listing the virtues of cats. They are beautiful. They are quiet. They are clean. They do not smell, and if their litter boxes are kept clean, they do not cause smells. They are easily housebroken, and need not be taken for walks. (In fact, they scorn to be taken for walks—they walk where they darn well please.) They live with dignity and treat you with a quiet condescension that is soothing. (I dislike animals that jump all over you and slobber at you.) On the other hand, when they are at peace with the world, they will sit on your lap and sing softly to you. And at night they do not scorn to sleep in your bed with you.

Cats always know which member of the family is most enamored of their presence and carefully share the bed of that member only. When there has been a cat in my family, it always spent the night in my bed, watching carefully for any sign of my bare toes creeping out from under the covers. If the toes appeared, they were attacked at once, tooth and claw, and you can bet they disappeared under the covers quickly. When there is no cat in the family, it takes me years to relax to the point where I can allow a foot to emerge from under the cover.

My daughter, Robyn, is even more extreme a cat-lover than I am. At the moment, she has two cats, one that is entirely black (Satan) and one that is a weird mixture of colors (Angel). Although Robyn loves me dearly, I hope I am never in the position where she has to choose between saving the cats, or me, but not both, from some enormous danger. I'm certain she'll save the cats.

In fact, Robyn has a recurrent dream that she is trying to save the cats from danger and, invariably, can't find one of them, and, when it is found, then the other at once disappears. She wakes up in a miserable panic, and chirrups. Naturally, the two cats at once appear, inquiringly, and jump onto the bed; whereupon Robyn hugs them to the point of asphyxiation.

What will happen when one of them comes to the natural end of its days? To tell you the truth, I fear the consequences.

Now, then, how can we think of these sweet, soft-furred, four-legged animals in connection with crime and mystery, even with murder? It seems impossible, and yet it has been done.

There is Edgar Allan Poe's "The Black Cat," which we all know and have all read at one time or another, but there are others as well—mysteries in which cats, or the rumors of cats, are somehow involved. Here, Carol-Lynn, Martin, and I have tracked down fourteen such stories (including Poe's, of course) for your pleasure and delectation.

I'd suggest you read the book with your cat purring at your side, and if some of the stories present the dear animal in a rather grim light, I would advise you to stroke the cat lovingly until all evil thoughts depart.

Black Cat in the Snow

JOHN D. MACDONALD

When I got the phone call from the State Police Barracks that Trooper Jerry Jackson was on his way to pick me up, I cut old Mrs. Agnew off in the middle of a symptom and told Alice to let the folks in the waiting room know that they could take their chances in sticking around, but I didn't know just how soon I'd be back.

"Accident in the woods?" Alice asked.

"Not this time. Martin Wadaslaw got himself shot."

I saw a little gleam of satisfaction in Alice's eyes. She certainly wasn't hypocrite enough to make any noises of regret. And I was pretty certain that gleam would be repeated in most of the eyes in the village. Up here in Pattenberg, in the wildest part of the Adirondacks, there's only nine hundred of us in permanent residence, and we get to know each other pretty well. In the summer the influx of campers keeps things stirred up, but after the hunting season is over and the snow stands deep on the hills that ring the town and the ice is as blue and hard as steel on our three lakes, we live in each other's pockets.

I am as charitable toward my fellow man as anybody, but I'd never been able to find a trace of good in Martin Wadaslaw. He was born mean and he lived mean. He had been a lumberjack, and when a chain broke about twelve years ago, he lost a leg and got a pension from the lumber company. At that time he had a bunch of halfgrown kids and a wornout wife. Before his accident he drank heavy enough to keep his family on short rations, and so the kids old enough to work were doing what they could. Good kids. Bright and hardy and energetic. The accident should have killed Martin—would have killed a normal man—but he was too mean to die. There's some say that the men who had to work with him had something to do with the chain breaking, but maybe that's just gossip. After Martin began to spend all his time home, his wife lasted about two years before she died, and then the kids began to scatter.

I knew there was just six people living in the home place. Martin, and one of his older boys, Stanley, and the only unmarried girl, Rose. Then there was Stanley's wife, Helen—she was one of the Ritter girls—and Stanley and Helen's two small kids. I'd delivered both of them. And Helen too.

The Ritters didn't go much for Helen marrying a Wadaslaw. Thought it beneath her or something. But she got one of the best in town. Stanley owns and operates the big fishing lodge on Crossbow Lake. During the winter he closes up and they move back into the home place, and in between building boats in the barn, he works on the County snow plow, the one they keep here in Pattenburg.

I'd heard the old man was getting worse, if anything, and that things were pretty tense out there at the Wadaslaws. I knew the old man had beat Rose up pretty bad because I took care of her. And I'd heard that Stanley had changed his mind about wintering at the lodge just so Rose wouldn't be left alone with the old man.

I had what I thought I'd need in the bag and when I saw the trooper car coming, I went out to the curb. The tires squeaked on the snow and Jerry swung the back door open for me. Trooper Dave Devine was in the front with him.

"How bad is he hurt?" I asked.

"Don't know, Doc," Jerry said. "We just got the call from Stanley Wadaslaw saying he'd shot the old man."

"It's time somebody shot him," I said, "but that's a hell of a mess."

We went into town, fast, and turned onto the Little Karega Mountain Road. When we pulled into the driveway some neighbors were there, and Deputy Sheriff Bob Trable was there, and it was a good thing he was, because he'd kept anybody from trampling on the marks in the snow in the side yard.

They hadn't wanted to move old Martin much. You could see where he'd fallen, just outside the side door to the kitchen, and the footprints where they'd picked him up and lugged him inside the door and put him on a blanket on the kitchen floor. They'd unbuttoned his shirt and the front of his long johns. He was so hairy it was hard to see the small hole, just under the rib cage and dead center. His color and his breathing were bad. They said he'd been like that ever since the bullet hit him twenty minutes ago. While I was fudying around opening my bag the hoarse shallow breathing stopped.

I lay my head on his chest and listened to dead silence. I gave him a shot to try to jolt the heart back into action, but he was dead and gone. I folded the loose part of the blanket over him, and Rose gave a little whimper, but her eyes were dry.

Stanley, as big as his father had been, stood with his feet planted, face completely expressionless. There was just Bob Trable, the troopers, Rose, Stanley and me in the kitchen. I could hear a kid crying so I guessed Helen had herded them to another part of the house.

"What happened, Wadaslaw," Jerry Jackson asked.

"It was an accident."

"You shot him."

"Yes, I shot him, but it was an accident."

"You better tell us about it."

Stanley Wadaslaw told us, and he showed us. He had a Winchester .22, a bolt action. He said he'd been in the kitchen and seen crows out in the side lot, beyond the barn. So he'd put on a jacket, taken the rifle and gone out. We were able to follow his footsteps in the snow to the fence. He said the crows had moved out of range. So he had started back to the house.

"I had a shell in the chamber. Our black cat ran from the corner of the barn there over toward that shed." We looked and saw a lot of cat tracks back and forth. It seemed to be a regular winter route for the cat.

"For no reason at all," Stanley said, "I decided to fire close behind her. You know. Startle her a little. I was aiming toward the house, of course, but into the snow. I'm a good shot. The old man came out of the house just as I shot. The cat jumped up in the air and ran twice as fast. The old man gave a funny kind of grunt and sat down in the snow and rolled over on his side. I didn't know what happened. I thought maybe he had a heart attack. After we got him in the kitchen then

I saw the hole in his shirt and a little blood. So I phoned right away.''

"Why didn't you call the doctor first?"

"I tried, but I couldn't get the line."

"You aimed pretty high, didn't you, Wadaslaw?"

"No. I saw the snow kick up from the slug. It must have ricocheted."

Jerry Jackson stared at him. "Off snow?"

"Off snow," Stanley said stolidly.

The troopers and Bob Trable checked exactly where Stanley had been standing. Midway between his footprints and the back door, near the cat tracks, they found the foot-long mark of disturbed snow.

"Let me see that rifle," Dave Devine said.

He checked the clip and he walked over until he was about the same distance from the side of the barn as Stanley had been from the side door of the kitchen. He aimed at the snow halfway to the barn. We saw the snow kick up, and we heard the after-crack of the slug smacking into the side of the barn. He emptied the clip. We walked and looked at the side of the barn. Of the five slugs, three had tumbled and kicked out big splinters, and two had hit square and bored through. All were in a pattern about as big around as a bushel basket, and about where a man's chest would be had he been standing against the side of the barn.

"I'll be damned," Jerry said softly.

"The autopsy will check it out for sure," I told them. "If the slug ranges upward from point of impact."

Rose verified Stanley's story. He had been looking out the kitchen window and spoke about the crows, and gone out. She hadn't seen the crows or the cat. She had heard the shot and heard Martin Wadaslaw grunt. Helen and the kids hadn't been in the kitchen.

Harvey Burnbridge took the body to his place in his combination hearse and ambulance. I went back and finished up my office calls and went over to Harvey's place in the evening and opened Martin up. The nippers wouldn't handle those big ribs so I had to saw. The entrance wound was a little raggedy as though the slug was starting to tumble. It had ranged on an upwards course, ripping a hole in the heart sac and coming to rest snug up against the left side of the spinal column. A normal man wouldn't have lasted five minutes.

So that was the end of it. There was no B.C.I. investigation called for. They said Stanley had been pretty damn careless. The old man was buried, artificial leg and all, next to his wife and two of the kids who hadn't lived long enough to grow up. I didn't attend, but I heard that even the Reverend Dudley Simeon had an awkward time putting in a good word for Martin Wadaslaw.

I guess one of the penalties of a country practice is that you get too much time to think, and you get too curious about people and the way their minds work. I spent a lot of time last winter with a book open in my lap, just staring into the fireplace and thinking about Stanley Wadaslaw. Stanley had been trapped. He couldn't arrange to get the old man put away. Rose had no place to go, except move in with Stanley, and that would have left the old man alone, unable to care for himself.

And the little facts kept adding up. Like Helen bringing the three-year-old boy in saying he fell. But if he fell, he must have bounced, and neither Helen nor Stanley nor Rose would have pummeled a little guy like that.

And I remembered that when Stanley came home from Korea, he was still in uniform and he wore a distinguished marksman's badge. He was known as a dead shot, but the only hunting he ever did was for meat.

Then I remembered another thing about Stanley. He got pretty upset about unnecessary cruelty. There was a story about him knocking some kid off the dock at the fishing lodge when the kid kept right on skinning a smallmouth bass while it was still alive, after Stanley had told him to kill it first.

I couldn't see Stanley firing at a cat just to scare it. Or firing in the direction of the house.

On one of the first warm Sundays last spring, I knew I had to get it out of my system. It used up nearly the whole day to find what I was looking for. But I found it in the late afternoon, a mile beyond the Wadaslaw place. It was a big billboard set back from the road, so weathered that you couldn't make out what it used to advertise. On the back of it I found three places where it had been struck repeatedly by small caliber slugs. Some of them had tumbled and torn the old wood. All three groups were pretty well centered, at chest height. I guessed about three hundred rounds had been used up. All had apparently struck at an upward angle.

After Alice had washed up and gone home that night, and I was alone in the big old lonely house, I tried to think it out.

So how had Stanley arranged to have the cat in the right place at the right time.

Then it struck me. The cat didn't have to be there. Just the tracks.

The house was getting chilly. I went over and stirred the fire up and put another log on. Stanley was working hard to get the lodge in shape for the new season. Helen was looking happy. Rose was going to help out at the lodge this season.

And I was a busybody. I was just an old man with too much time on my hands and too much curiosity. It wasn't any of my business. I would put it out of my mind.

But I looked into the flames and I saw the kitchen in the Wadaslaw house. I saw Rose at the sink. She looked out the window and she saw Stanley where he said he would be.

And above the hiss of the flames I seemed to hear Rose say, "Poppa, will you please step out and call Stanley."

The old man grumbled, hoisted his great weight out of the kitchen rocker.

He opened the door slowly and stepped out into the snow.

Murder is a Gas

ALLEN KIM LANG

I parked the unmarked Indiana State Police sedan and walked over to the gatehouse of Loki Laboratories, carrying a brief case fat with autopsy reports and a half-gallon Thermos of black coffee. Behind the forty-foot hurricane fence, six buildings curved about a lawn set with circular beds of tulips, marigolds and scarlet phlox. The structure farthest to the right—wooden, window-less, and painted heavy-duty red—looked like an Amish farmhouse. The central building spiked the bell tower I'd sighted far down the highway. For one dizzy instant, I thought that someone standing behind that tower was peering around its green copper cupola, like a squirrel reconnoitering from the top of a tree trunk. By the time I'd blinked my eyes, he'd disappeared.

A uniformed guard stood at the gate. "Pass?" he asked.

I flipped open my wallet to display my credentials. "Sergeant Felix Himmel, Indiana State Police," I announced. I stared past the guard at the girl who sat beside his desk. "I believe that I'm expected."

"So you are, Sergeant," he said. "If you'll just sit over there in the catbird seat, I'll introduce you to the boss."

"Rough!" I hardly noticed the pop-eyed pup, so fetching was the girl who held him. A brunette in her middle twenties, she turned to regard me with eyes of cobalt blue.

"Miss Michelle Kelly has been assigned as your secretary," the guard explained.

"Thank you, Sergeant Himmel, for rescuing me from the Pool Room," Miss Kelly said. "The secretarial pool, that is." She took my hand. "This is Bem," she said, introducing her cornsilk-colored Pekingese. "He's authorized himself to nip the ankles of all strangers, so you'd better shake hands with him right away."

"Bem?" I asked, taking the tiny beast's right paw.

"For Bug-Eyed Mouser," Miss Kelly explained. "Bem was Dr. Heinemann's dog until poor Hans got blown up in that awful shower-room accident. I adopted the little orphan."

The dog, abandoning his role as menace, loosed half an inch of pink, upward-curling tongue to lick my hand. "Sit down, please, so that you can meet Mr. Luger," the girl said, pointing to the plastic contour chair that was bolted to the floor. Checking to see that it wasn't plugged into the wall, I sat.

The guard picked up the red telephone on his desk. "Security One Here," he said. "Connect me with Lucky."

A halo of lamps flashed on in the corner of the room. I saw that the metal-sheathed eye of a TV camera was aimed through the lights at me. A screen blinked to life beneath the camera. It flickered through the spectrum, then settled down to a picture of a Vandyked young man seated on a deck chair against the rail of a boat. Behind him, clouds scudded and a sea gull swooped toward the water. "Howdy!" the bearded fellow said. "I'm Lucky Luger. You must be the state cop they told me was comin' out to visit my outfit."

"Where are you?" I demanded, my curiosity overwhelming courtesy.

"Just down the pike a ways," Lucky Luger said, grinning. "About eight hundred miles due east as the electron flies, aboard my *Midas Touch* in Buzzards Bay, Massachusetts."

"Sergeant Felix Himmel," I told him, and unfolded my wallet to let the camera scan my ID.

"I've let out orders that you've got the run of my place," Luger said. "You'll get all the assistance the Loki Laboratories staff can provide."

I shook my head. "Assigning Miss Kelly as my girl Friday will hardly help me keep my mind on police work," I said.

"Shelly can type, introduce you to my eggheads, and run down to the cafeteria to fill up that coffee jug you got cuddled under you arm," Luger said. "Coffee's good stuff—squeezes sugar out of your liver to perk up your brain cells." He reached out of the picture to get his own stimulant, a glass of gin-and-tonic with a bright green half of lime floating in its ice. "I want you to find out what's been happening, Sergeant. I can't afford to lose any more help. My motto always was to give the best men I could hire the best tools I could buy and run to the bank with what they thought up. When a string of accidents picks off three of those best men— the whole danged Cosmos Project team—I feel a twinge, and it ain't just my wallet. I liked those fellas, Sergeant Himmel. So dig in. Anything I can do, you just hop on the phone and give me the word." The owner of Loki Laboratories gave me the thumbs-up sign for luck, then switched off the viewphone. The lights dimmed. I was off-camera.

"Even on vacation," I observed, "Luger runs a tight ship."

"Lucky Luger is never on vacation," Miss Kelly told me. "He's working around the clock out there off Martha's Vineyard. The *Midas Touch* is his research ship. He's got tanks of a special resin down in her holds, chelating gold out of sea water."

"Ridiculous," I said. "That's like the old scheme of squeezing sunbeams out of cucumbers. It'll never work."

"Of course it won't," Miss Kelly agreed, stepping to the lab-side doorway of the gatehouse. "On your way out, Sergeant Himmel, be careful that you don't trip over our doorstop. It's a forty-four-pound block of Lucky Luger's Atlantic Ocean gold, and it might mash your toes."

"Oh." I reverently stepped across the brick that blocked open the door, and followed the girl out onto the grounds. She dropped Bem, who trotted several times around my ankles, barking, then took off ahead of us down the sidewalk.

"Forgive me for needling you, Sergeant," Miss Kelly said, "but the word *impossible* is in bad taste at Loki Laboratories."

"Three stripes are frail armor to carry into this arena," I mused. The sidewalk ducked under an old-fashioned rose arbor, arched over with pink-and-cream blossoms. "Even the flowers here have their doctorate."

Shelly Kelly halted at the far end of the arbor of Dr. Nicholls roses. "Right here is where Dr. Hoyotoko Nakamura was stung by a bee," she told me. "It killed him. He was hypersensitized—allergic to bee venom.

Nakamura was the motivational research associate on Project Cosmos, Sergeant.''

"Call me Felix," I suggested.

"I'm Shelly," she said. "Felix isn't a common name.''

"My father was a Latinist," I explained, "and he called me 'most happy fellow,' which I am, except when some lardwit twits me for being named after a comic-strip cat. Tell me more about Project Cosmos," I suggested, easing over toward the park bench set beneath a flowering redbud tree. Bem hurtled up to sit between us like a conscientious chaperon. Shelly stroked the fur on the pup's belly. He closed his eyes in ecstasy.

"There were three men working on Project Cosmos," she said. "But I suppose you've got everything I know, and more, right there in your brief case.''

"I'm a cop, not a nibby neighbor," I said. "Fill me in.''

"All right, Felix." Shelly got a filter cigaret from her purse, and I lighted it for her. "Drs. Heinemann, Nakamura and Wilson all died last month," she said. "All of them were here at Loki Laboratories when their fatal accidents occurred." She paused. "Do you know who Loki was, Felix?''

"The Nordic marplot," I said. "The delinquent juvenile of Valhalla, who made eternity tough for Odin, the boss god of Norse mythology. It's an odd name for a think-works.''

"Not really," Shelly said. "*Loki* is a pun on Lucky Luger's nickname. Loki Laboratories makes a business of shaking the world up with research-and-development, of inventing new things for Americans to buy and making buggy whips out of what they were buying yesterday.''

I was staring toward the brick campanile, that facsimile of Venice transplanted in our Hoosier heartland. "Hey," I said, grabbing Shelly's arm. "There he goes again!'' Someone forty feet tall was promenading behind the tower, wearing a red baseball cap and look of extreme concentration.

"One of our R-and-D programs is the pedipulator," Shelly said. "If you'll forgive my saying so, they're making great strides with it."

"Magnify, if you please, that last remark."

"Manipulator comes from *manus,* hand; pedipulator from *pes,* foot: surely that should be obvious to the son of a Latin fan," Shelly said. "I imagine that you've seen these master-slave devices they have in radiation laboratories, gimmicks that allow a man to handle radioactive materials from a distance of thirty feet, standing behind a radiation-shield wall and window. Well, just as that operator wears a glove that activates the slave 'hand' in the hot-room, the giant who's walking toward us wears mechanical legs that multiply his natural walking movements."

A jeep raced around the corner of the building, towing a trailer on which was supported a hairnet thirty feet across. "Sometimes the pedipulator pilot stumbles," Shelly said, explaining the net. "Generally, the jeep driver is able to catch him."

The Brobdingnagian pedestrian strolled toward us on his mechanical stilts. "Hi, Shelly!" the operator called. Bem vaulted from our bench and set off after the intruder, barking at the yard-long, jointed feet that settled down, one after the other, on the soft grass. "I thought I might run into Bem," the stilt-walker shouted. He rained a handful of dog biscuits down on the Peke. "Watch out, kid," he cautioned Shelly's pup. "I'd hate to have to scrape you off my instep."

"Bingo, this is Sergeant Felix Himmel, of the State Police," Shelly yelled up. She explained to me, "Dr. Bingo Lane is the development chief for the pedipulator."

"I'd shake hands," Dr. Lane shouted at me, "except

I'm afraid to lean forward that far. Miss Kelly, may I have the next dance?'' He executed a waltz step over the red bud tree, looking down at his feet anxiously as any Arthur Murray drop-out. ''Watch it!'' he cried. One stilt-knee clashed against the other. The forty-foot man leaned to the left, struck the other leg out for balance, and fell with the majesty of a Douglas fir. His jeep driver gunned the vehicle and raced around to field Dr. Lane in the glove of his net.

''It ain't the gettin' up that brothers me, it's that long step down,'' Bingo Lane said, taking off the baseball cap and blotting his forehead. He disengaged his bare feet and knees from the straps of the follower-rack, a sort of control box in which he'd been standing to walk his machine. Wearing Bermuda shorts, he clambered down the net and dropped to the grass. We shook hands. The two-man crew of the catcher-jeep got to work with a hydraulic hoist, getting the pedipulator legs strapped under the net of their trailer. ''Take you up for a spin sometime, Sergeant,'' Dr. Lane volunteered. ''It's like skiing, only warmer and higher.''

''I seldom have to pick any coconuts,'' I said. ''Anyway, I'm clumsy enough at ground level.''

''My pedipulator is as easy to walk in as a pair of elevator shoes,'' Lane said. He rubbed a bruise on one bare knee. ''Almost as easy,'' he amended that. ''You here to look into those Cosmos Project accidents?''

I admitted that the State's Prosecuting Attorney had exhibited interest in that cluster of exotic deaths.

''Find out what those three men were working on, Sergeant,'' Lane advised me, ''and you'll have found out why they were killed. Unfortunately, the Cosmos Project is a bit of a mystery. They were all pretty close-mouthed about what they were aiming at. My game, well, I stick out like a City College basketball center in a Japanese teahouse. Let me strap you into my follower-rack, Sergeant; I mean it. You can get higher than a dozen martinis will take you, and no headache after, if you land right.'' He jumped into the back of the jeep, waved, and rode off, towing his seven-league boots behind him.

Bem had gulped the veterinary cookies and was bounding toward what had once been a tennis court, now surrounded by wire and populated by a bedlam of chickens. The dog scampered around the enclosure, terrorizing the hens with his sharp-edged barks and lunges toward the wire. ''Chickens?'' I asked Miss Kelly.

''You're a whiz at descriptive zoology,'' she said. ''Those Leghorns are guinea pigs in one of DeeGee Nova's programs. He added a teaspoonful of aspirin to each hundred pounds of their feed. The chickens who got the aspirin averaged seven percent heavier after three weeks than their sisters who didn't eat the pills. Multiply that weight gain by the number of orders of southern-fried served every Sunday, and you've got one reason Lucky Luger can afford to spud around on a yacht.'' She intercepted the Pekingese as he vaulted in an attempt to high-jump the chickenwire, and patted the pup calm as we walked on toward the towered building. ''What do you personally think about those three accidents, Felix?'' she asked.

''The coroner couldn't pinpoint what was wrong with them,'' I said, ''but my colonel and the doc agreed that three fatal accidents, one right after the other, suited *Hamlet* better than Hoosierland.'' I held open the main door, then jumped aside. ''What the hell?''

A miniature tank, clustered with waving tools, rolled past us. A turret swiveled, and a pair of glass eyes inspected me as the tanklet ground toward the rose arbor. ''Make way, make way,'' it announced from its loudspeakers. ''Lady with a baby . . .''

''That's Kitten,'' Shelly said. ''Lucky Luger's prize project. She's a cybernated, servomechanical cat. Kitten's brains are mostly upstairs in the tower, in Lucky's laboratory. His idea was to build a robot that was self-supporting, that had intelligence enough to plug itself into a wall outlet when its batteries ran down, that could avoid hitting people and dogs, and that could find its way around. Kitten has free run of the grounds. She's something of a pet at Loki Laboratories.''

Like a ceramic Chinese figurine, Bem was frozen in attack position, pointed toward the robot and gurgling deep-throated growls. ''The furred pet doesn't seem to care for the steel one,'' I remarked.

''Bem can't stand Kitten, and Kitten purely hates Bem,'' Shelly said. ''I think Lucky programed a little malice into that machine. One day I caught Kitten carrying off Bem's water bowl. I'd swear she was chuckling as she ran down toward her den in the basement.''

''You say Kitten's brains are in the tower?''

''It wouldn't be practical to program a robot as complex as Kitten without making her too big to run around,'' Shelly explained. ''The tower computer works with her through telemetry. Once, during a lightning storm, Kitten went crazy, and tried to stand on her head on a stairway. Static had commanded her to play yoga.''

''I wish,'' I grumbled, ''that I was back in my quiet MP car, chasing speeders. The colonel didn't tell me I'd be visiting the funhouse.''

''It's hardly ever dull at Loki Laboratories,'' Miss Kelly agreed. She shooed Bem through the door, and he pattered down the hall with all the aplomb of a chief of research.

''What was the Cosmos Project all about, Shelly?'' I asked. ''That's one piece of information I don't have in this brief case.''

''I don't know.'' She gazed at me with those deep-blue eyes and shook her head. ''I mean that literally, Felix. I was secretary for the Cosmos team for half a year, and I didn't get the faintest hint of what they were up to. Secret? The Manhattan Project was a brass band by comparison. Nothing was filed in our office beyond scientific journals and laboratory-equipment catalogues. The lab was used mostly, it seemed to me, as a coffee kitchen. Any notes that may have been in our safe disappeared the day Woody—Dr. Wilson—had his fatal heart attack.''

''Perhaps some Federal agency, CIA or FBI, sneak-footed in to pick up the confidential notes before the Albanians got 'em,'' I suggested.

''No, Felix,'' Shelly said. ''Project Cosmos had nothing to do with the government, except as a possible means of increasing Lucky Luger's income tax. Our secrets here are mostly drugstore, supermarket, filling-station stuff; not outer-space or Pentagon-type mysteries.''

Bem, pausing at the open doorway of a brightly lighted laboratory, barked a note that ended on a banshee howl, the most succinct piece of music criticism I've ever heard. Through that doorway came a sound that would have set an Arab's teeth on edge: the shrill, fruity tones of a clarinet doing violence to the memory of Wolfgang Amadeus Mozart. ''Is snake-charming another of your projects here?'' I asked my pretty secretary.

''Doc Greene's degree was not in musicology,'' Shelly said. We went on into the lab.

The gray man in the white coat put his instrument aside and stood to learn my name. ''Einstein had his violin, Sergeant,'' he explained, ''and I have my clarinet.''

''I blow a little French horn, myself,'' I confessed, shaking his hand. I glanced around the laboratory, recognizing only the most obvious items of equipment. There was an electric furnace in which Volkswagens could be baked. Over a kitchen sink hung a spice cabinet, whose glass-stoppered bottles were labeled in chemical shorthand. Near one wall a doughnut of steel was mounted on enormous gimblas, an electromagnet large enough to serve as pot-holder for those hot Volkswagens. On another wall hung several dozen copper cooking pots. "I give up," I confessed. "Is this the cafeteria, or the room you bring competitors to for coaxing out their secrets?"

Dr. Greene picked at the yellow-headed map pin that was stuck into the lapel of his lab coat. "This is a metallurgical research laboratory," he said, somewhat primly. "I am working toward a process for keeping copper kitchenware, among other things, bright as a new penny. Got it, too," he added, a brief smile lighting up his gray face. "A sixteenth-inch coating of Johnson's wax does the job fine." He frowned. "Stinks up the kitchen some, though, when you put the soup on the fire."

"All this alchemist's nightmare just to keep frying pans shiny?" I asked, waving my Thermos jug around the crowded room.

"Don't trivialize my dream, Sergeant," Greene cautioned me. "I'm really onto something: a magnetic altering of the copper-air interface that seems to inhibit oxidation. What's more, with the bonus I'll get once the kinks are smoothed out, I intend to buy myself a symphony orchestra to conduct. You may audition, if you like." He sat and picked up his clarinet. "Right now, there's a gap betwixt theory and practice. If you'll excuse me?"

The woeful music commenced again, something, I believe, by Bloch. We tiptoed out, Bem eager to leave the woodwind's wail. "What's the yellow pin Doc Greene is wearing?" I asked Shelly.

"That's the emblem of the Mensa Society," she said. "It's an organization of brain buffs, people who flaunt their IQ's the way other folks do sports cars. Only the top two percent of the population is smart enough to join. The three Project Cosmos men wore the yellow pinhead, too; but they joked about it.''

Behind us, down the hall, another musician was whistling ''Jingle Bells'' with fearful concentration, hitting each note hard as a steam calliope, and rattling as accompaniment something that sounded like sleigh-bells. ''That's Red Cowhage,'' Shelly said. ''You'll meet him soon enough, Felix. In the winter he whistles 'In the Good Old Summertime.' ''

''Red Cowhage sounds like a welcome relief from the company of giant brains,'' I remarked.

''That he is,'' Shelly said. ''Here's the animal room.''

There was no smell of zoo in the place, no odor beyond that of damp animal feed. Peering at us through the walls of transparent, flexible vinyl plastic hutches were several generations of white rabbits. ''Dr. DeeGee Nova, I'd like you to meet—don't panic—Sergeant Felix Himmel, of the Indiana State Police,'' Shelly said, introducing me to the man in charge.

''Germ-free animals?'' I asked him.

''These bunnies are, strictly speaking, gnotobiotes: infected with selected organisms,'' Nova told me. His words had the streetcar clatter of Chicago accent. ''I'm trying to find out just how aspirin, added to their chow in almost homeopathic doses, fats 'em up fast. You may have seen my Leghorns out on the old tennis court. If not, you'll meet 'em at lunch, once I'm done.'' Nova grinned down at Bem, who was dancing around his feet like a nephew petitioning a fond uncle for chewing gum. ''Here, beast,'' he said, opening the household refrigerator behind him to get out a sandwich. He dangled a circle of ketchup-smeared baloney above the Peke's nose. Bem arfed, jumped, and swallowed the meat. A lipstick trace of ketchup remained on the pup's nose. Bem thoughtfully licked the upper part, then let Shelly blot the lower, which his tongue wouldn't reach, with Kleenex.

"Back there in the silicon jungle is Dr. David Ilf, the rabid Russian," Nova said. I looked through a forest of glassware toward the far side of the lab, where a bear in a white coat was peering into a funnel of filter paper, pushing some sort of greeny-yellow fluid through it by sheer force of will. "Ilf has no time for the social whirl," Nova explained to us, "working, as he is, on the most profound problem of our generation. He's trying to develop a lining for beer cans that won't taint the brew."

"What poet has done as much to promote human happiness?" I inquired.

Dr. Ilf smiled at me through his distillation columns. "Heh, heh," he said.

"What say, Sergeant Felix, shall we run a little test right here and now?" DeeGee asked me.

"Fine." We sat down at a dissecting table, pulled the zippers on three cáns of beer that Nova produced from his refrigerator, and tilted them up. "Good stuff," I remarked. "I can't taste degradation-product one."

"Dey are dere," Ilf growled. "Dey will poison you, give dem time."

"A case a day for ninety years, and your liver will look like a coral sponge," Nova promised. "If I may make so bold, beer-drinkin' buddy, what's a state cop doing here in Disneyland Central?"

"Snooping," I said. "What do you know about Project Cosmos, DeeGee?"

"Heinemann, Nakamura and Wilson used up herds of germ-free mice," Nova said. "Heinemann was the bacteriologist, Nakamura a hidden persuader of the most dangerous sort (although I liked the man), and Wilson was a pretty fair cookbook chemist. Bright men, all of 'em. What were they doing, though?" DeeGee Nova shrugged his big shoulders. "This place is run on a

need-to-know policy. It isn't considered graceful to ask
unsolicited questions, lest Lucky Luger suspect you of
wanting to tote off our know-how to General Mills to
claim a spy's ransom.''

"You're not wearing your yellow-headed pin,
DeeGee," I noticed. "I thought it was part of the uniform at Loki Laboratories."

"The costume jewel of the Mensa gang? Nope,"
Nova said. "These IQ-nuts round here remind me of
little boys comparing their equipment behind the barn,
begging, Miss Kelly, your innocent pardon. All this
emphasis on raw intellect bores me. There are facets of
personality that bear more weight. Honesty, say. The
grace to wince at another man's misfortune. Brains are
like a bank account, Sergeant. They're to use, not to
brag on."

"Jingle Bells" sounded outside the door.

"That's Red Cowhage," Nova said. "There's a fellow uncontaminated by reason, but a nicer guy you'll
never want to know."

The rattle I had interpreted as sleighbells proved to
be the supermarket shopping cart loaded with mail that
Red Cowhage pushed through the door. The pilot of
this craft was redheaded, red-faced and round. "Hey,
there, Miss Antarctica!" he bellowed at Shelly Kelly.
"Love letters, DeeGee," he told Nova, piling our table
with professional journals, lab-gear flackery and books.
"Got a can of juice for this thirsty, wing-footed Mercury?" He checked DeeGee's reefer, found himself a
can of beer, and joined us. "Call me Red," he told
me, sticking out a freckled hand. "Nothing political
about my name, either, understand?"

"I'm Sergeant Felix Himmel," I said.

"Felix? Like the cat?"

"Very like," I sighed.

"So bottoms up!" Red Cowhage emptied his can at
a single draught, took it between the heels of his hands,

and crushed it flat. "You an Army sergeant?" he demanded.

"State cops."

"Good you're a sergeant, and not a doctor, like
DeeGee and the mad Russian and that crazy flute player
down the hall," Cowhage said. "We got more doctors
in this lash-up than the Mayo Clinic, and ain't one of
'em fit to paste a Band-Aid on a sick cat. What you
doin' here?"

"I'm looking for the cause of the plague that killed
three men," I said.

"That wasn't no plague," he said. Cowhage reached
down to scratch the back of Bem's neck. "Doc Hans
got blew up in the shower room. The Jap guy was killed
from a bee—can you feature a little bug biting a man
to death? Doc Wilson had an ordinary heart attack. No
plague."

"I've got to tie up some loose ends, that's all," I
said.

"They say that on TV all the time," Red Cowhage
observed, "and some joker always ends up with a rope
around his neck, all the same. Well, anything I can help
with, Felix, let me know." He wiped the back of his
hand across his mouth, removing a blond mustache of
beer foam. He jumped up and seized the tiller of his
shopping cart. "Back to carrying billy-dues to the cells
of this prison compound," he said. "See you all." He
winked at me. "Meow!" Whistling the top tune of his
warm-weather repertoire, Red Cowhage shoved his cart
out the door and headed down the hall. "Watch your
feet, you darned Frankenstein!" he yelled.

"Lady with a baby . . ." Kitten cautioned, rumbling
past the mailman on an errand of her own.

"We'd better get on with our sightseeing tour, Felix," Shelly suggested. "Fifteen minutes is all the
morning beer break we're allowed."

"I intend to organize a union to fight that sort of

sweatshop regulation," DeeGee Nova vowed. "Well, I've got to do a colostomy on a bunny. See you at lunch, Sarge."

Shelly Kelly, Bem and I stepped out into the hallway. "We could visit the Diamond Mines, out in Building B," she mused. "They're hunting for a catalyst to ease the process of squeezing graphite into diamonds. It costs as much now to produce a handful of synthetic industrial diamonds as it does to dig the real thing out of the ground. A cheap diamond would sell well. Or we could visit the Radiation Lab, down in the basement next to Kitten's cave. But maybe I'd better show you where we live, first, so you can drink some of that coffee you've been carrying around." We were outside Doc Greene's copper foundry, where the clarinet still climbed up and down the scales in weary search of elusive theory. "We're in here," Shelly said, opening a door.

Bem skittered in, and headed under the desk for the petri dish of water that sat there to wash down his recent snacks. "There's not much equipment in our lab, since I have no idea of what a policeman needs; but you can draw on the Glass Shop for anything from a cyclotron to a can of beans." Shelly pointed to the desk Bem was sprawling under. "You can use that if you want to, Felix. Woody Wilson was sitting there when he had his heart attack."

"You are, Miss Shelly Kelly, a regular little sunbeam." I dropped my brief case on the desktop, got a couple of 500-ml. beakers from the lab, and poured us each a shot of coffee from my Thermos.

"I was fond of the Cosmos bunch," she explained. She dragged her Pekingese from under my desk and smoothed the fur down over his ears. The pup came as close to purring as his dignity would allow. "The word you haven't said yet, Felix, is murder."

I sat at Dr. Woodrow Wilson's fatal desk. "If I could say that word," I told her, "I'd still need more than your blue-eyed intuition to make it stick on a warrant. What I really want is a picture of the big McGuffin.''

"The huh?''

"It's a technical term used in the science of flatfootery,'' I said. "It means the boodle, the loot, the bait that coaxed a person or persons unknown to detonate one scientist, stop another's heart, and sic a lethal bee on the third. What was in the Cosmos Project lockbox? Ten years' salary in unmarked bills? A blank check on all the drugstores in North America? Or the blueprints for a hotline to Mars? What the devil was that project all about?''

"All I know,'' Shelly said, sipping her coffee, "is that my three doctors felt they had something big. They felt sure that they'd make a fortune for Loki Laboratories, and win for themselves bonuses big enough that they could quit and go into pure research. That's the applied egghead's equivalent of a fallen woman's return to the church, Felix—abandoning the marketplace for the sanctity of pure research.''

"Hans Heinemann was the first to die.'' I tipped back my beaker of brain stimulant. "Did Nakamura and Wilson go ahead with their project afterwards?''

"After Doc Hans died, the other two scientists acted like a four-man basketball team—busy, but not getting much work done. Then Hoyotoko Nakamura was beestung, went into convulsions, and died. I wasn't here at Loki Laboratories the day it happened; but when I got back to the office, Woody Wilson sat at that desk, staring at the wall. It wasn't a week later that he bowed over his blotter and died.'' Shelly scooted the dog off her lap to get a Kleenex from her purse. "Don't worry, Felix,'' she said. "I'm not going to go all weepy on you. Murder makes us Kellys grim, not giddy.''

"You sound convinced that the Cosmosmen were murdered,'' I said.

"They died in the same month, Felix,'' Shelly said,

lifting one finger. "All of them were working on the mysterious Cosmos Project." Another finger went up. "All their notes disappeared the day the last of them, Woody Wilson, died." She held up the "W" of her fingers, then inverted it. "*M* is for Murder most foul," she whispered.

"Pretty, Shelly; but your demonstration will convince neither my colonel nor a jury. And without a suspect, it would be an empty victory to prove those deaths were murders." I popped my brief case open. "Here are the postmortem reports on your three doctors," I said, fanning out the typewritten forms. "Woody Wilson was born with a damaged heart. When he was twelve years old, a surgeon went into his chest to perform one of the first successful open-heart operations, implanting an artificial mitral valve. The pathologist who opened him up on the autopsy table found Wilson's heart torn to bits, as though it had been hit by a steel-jacketed bullet. Nothing, though, had perforated his skin."

I picked up the second report. "Hoyotoko Nakamura, although his physician confirms that he has long been sensitive to bee and wasp venom, had at death a peculiar scratch at the right angle of his jaw. Razor bite? He shaved electrically." I glanced through the final report. "We've nothing at all on Hans Heinemann. Not much of him was left. Heinemann stepped into the shower room down the hall and exploded. Sewer gas, that's what the sheriff said caused the explosion. Luger had a firm of plumbers tear up all the pipes here in Building A. All the drains were wholesome."

"Dr. Hans was a fat man," Shelly said. "He perspired, wearing his shirt and tie and white lab coat. Every day, before he went home to his bachelor apartment with Bem, he'd take a shower and change clothes." She cuddled the Peke. "Poor little pup," she crooned. "He can't understand what became of Papa Hans."

"Neither can I," I complained. I held up my hand. "Someone's fumbling with our door," I whispered. Getting up quietly, I reached over and tugged the door open.

"Thank you kindly," Kitten said. She rolled into the room on her six fat-tired wheels. The robot came to a halt in front of the desk and tilted its brain-listening cup-antenna toward the tower, above and to the left of the machine. "I thought I'd stop by to see if there's anything I can do for you, Sergeant Felix Himmel," Kitten said.

"Lucky Luger taped Kitten's voice-bank," Shelly said.

"Could I, perhaps, run down to the cafeteria to fill your coffee jug?" Kitten asked me.

I felt self-conscious about talking back to this rolling toolshed; it was like holding conversation with a Cadillac. "You're a clever machine, Kitten," I said.

"Clever? Why, I should say!" Kitten raised one of her half-dozen paws—this one a three-tonged plier—and tapped the front of her optical turret. Between her "eyes," I saw, was welded the yellow-head map pin that identified Kitten as a member of the Mensa Society.

"Gruff!" Bem oozed out from under my desk and leaped onto the robot's back, a cornsilk David taking on steel Goliath.

A whiplike tentacle wrapped itself around Bem, lifted him with a hydraulic surge, and dropped him onto Shelly's lap as gently as a handkerchief. "Dirty dog," Kitten said. "I would delight, were it permitted, to eviscerate, decorticate, maul, fray, and depilate hair-by-particular-hair the obnoxious, egregious, excrementitious small mammal. Blood and stink in a bag . . . ugh!" Kitten wheeled out of the room like a goosed dowager.

"Wow," I said. "Who'd think I'd ever meet a pile of junk that drops tag-lines from the *Meditations* of Marcus Aurelius?"

"Drawing on her tower full of brain tapes, Kitten could rattle off the technical catechism from *aardvark* to *zymurgy*," Shelly said, "and if there was anything she didn't know, she could call up Lucky Luger to fill her in. But let's get back to our murders, Felix. What makes you so sure that I'm not the Lady Macbeth behind all the bloodshed? No one else worked as closely with the Cosmos team as I did."

"You're innocent," I said.

"What makes you so certain?"

"Masculine intuition, my pretty, added to which is the fact that you were visiting your sister in Omaha, down with infectious mononucleosis, poor girl, the day that Dr. Nakamura was killed."

"If I hadn't taken that three-day vacation . . ."

"I'd have had to ask Luger to assign me the second-loveliest girl from the Pool Room," I said. "For now, I'm going down to look at a shower room."

"Scene-of-the-crime?" she asked.

"Exactly. Can you find me a screwdriver?" I asked.

"Surely." Shelly got one from a cabinet in our laboratory. "If you're going to be wandering around here, Felix, you might as well disguise yourself in a scientist-suit," she said, holding out for my inspection a white, knee-length laboratory coat. I slipped off my jacket and hung it on the coat tree. Shelly stared at the .38 revolver snugged into my blond-leather shoulder holster. "Do you really have to wear that awful thing?" she asked me.

"It comes in handy for fending dragons off raven-tressed maidens," I explained, buttoning up the white coat. I walked out, snapping my fingers for Bem to follow me. Surprisingly enough, the Pekingese fell in at my heels.

In keeping with the general air of luxury displayed in Lucky Luger's money factory, the john was equipped with a locker room that would have done a country club credit. A small gymnasium adjoined for the convenience of the *mens sana* who wished to maintain his *corpus sanum.* The locker room boasted forty combination-locked wardrobes and a faint odor of athletic endeavor.

Bem stuck his nose into the shower room, sniffed, and backed out whining. I patted his head, then stepped around the pup to look into the room that had become Dr. Hans Heinemann's death chamber.

The shower room had been rebuilt since the explosion, which had brought the ceiling down onto Heinemann after spreading him across the floor. The coroner's physician had reassembled him with tweezers.

Bem barked for my attention. The punching bag back in the gym was rattling on its hook, massaged by a pair of well-synchronized fists. "Hi, Red," I said, looking in to the Lab's mail clerk.

"Howdy, Felix." Cowhage grinned, keeping the bag skittering off his fists. "You want to keep some change-of-clothes here, the end locker's your'n. The combination works 20-right, 15, 20."

"How do you know?" I asked.

"All the combinations are the same," Cowhage said, dropping to his knees to pet Bem. "These brain-types can't seem to keep three numbers straight in their heads; so I set the locks simple, and all the same. Forget your combination, you just ask the next guy what it is."

"You do more, then, than hustle around the mail," I said.

"All kinds of stuff," Red said. "I'm the factotum."

I nodded recognition of his field. "The mail comes in twice a day, and I trundle it around in my baby buggy. Between mail calls, I change light bulbs and weed flowers and bring up sandwiches to the brass. They make

me mad, I run in here and pound at 'em on the punchin'
bag." He left-handed the bag one more time. "See ya
'round, Felix. *Meow!*"

Forty lockers. I began at the right end and worked
my way down the line, trying on each the combination
Red Cowhage had given me. All the first twelve opened.
Lacking any reason to snoop on my hosts, I didn't so
much as glance inside the lockers, just snapping each
one shut again and going on to the next. Number 13
didn't open to the all-purpose combination. The next
twenty-six lockers did.

Interesting. Was locker 13 the cache into which the
thief of the Cosmos Project papers had dumped them?
Had the murderer stored his killing tools, whatever
those might have been, in locker 13 until he'd seen his
opportunity to use them? Never having worked burglary
detail, I'm a dub at lock-picking. Tomorrow I'd bring
along a set of soft-copper keys, with which I could feel
out the tumbler patterns of the slot-lock at the center of
locker 13's combination dial.

I hefted my screwdriver and went again into the
shower room. Choosing a four-by-four tile above eye
level, I slipped the blade beneath it and pried it off the
wall. It went into the pocket of my lab coat. Time for
me to play scientist.

Dropping Bem off to keep Shelly Kelly company in
my office, I went down to the basement. The Radiation
Lab at Loki is marked, of course, by the purple-and-
yellow rosette that means for your genes' sake, wear
your film badge. I pinned on the badge, and the pencil-
type personal dosimeter Dr. Lily Fredericks, chief
radiation physicist, handed me. "I'd like to have a
neutron activation analysis run on this," I told the
handsome Dr. Lily, giving her my vandalized shower-
room tile.

"What are you looking for, Sergeant Himmel?" she
asked.

"Iodine has been suggested to me," I said. "Can do?"

"Can do," she replied briskly, taking the tile. "This is about Dr. Hans Heinemann's death, is it not?"

"Yes."

"Murder?" She fitted a chip off my tile into the slide that would carry it into the hotspot of Loki Laboratories' most expensive toy, their TRIGA Mark-F pulsing reactor.

"Iodine would suggest foul play," I admitted.

Dr. Lily Fredericks smiled. " 'If this paper remains blue, all is well. If it turns red, it means a man's life.' Like that?"

I nodded. "My dear doctor, it's clear that you and I grew up in the same literary neighborhood, breathing an ecstatic yellow fog and thrilling to the rattle of cabriolet wheels. What a pleasure it is to meet an alumna of the Baker Street Irregulars in this unlikely place."

"Call me Lily." She activated the device that transported my shower-room shard into the inferno of her reactor. "Do you understand the principles of neutron-activation analysis?" she asked, keeping an eye on the stopwatch that was ticking off the seconds above us.

"Only in tales-for-tiny-tots terms," I admitted. "As I get it, neutron-activation analysis consists in causing a bit of material to absorb radioactive energy, after which one measures the nuclear 'heat' that oozes back from it. The various elements show themselves by the character of their induced isotopes, which can be identified by the monstrous clever computers you no doubt have at your disposal."

"Capital, Sergeant!" Dr. Fredericks said. "The last policeman I had business with presented me an undeserved pink parking ticket. I had nearly come to despair of the detectival breed. You have renewed my faith. I have no doubt that you, like The Master, can differentiate the ashes of all one-hundred-forty varieties of pipe, cigar and cigaret tobacco. While we await results, Sergeant, would you care to have another cup of coffee? I observe that you're addicted to that innocent juice."

"Elementary," I said, glancing at the coffee stain that marred the exposed cuff of my shirt. "Yes, indeed."

Over our coffee, Lily sang the glories of NAA, the technique that had sniffed out scandalous arsenic in a lock of Napoleon's hair; that had proved King Eric XIV, dead 400 years, to have been the victim of a northern Borgia who'd served him a broth spiced with (most likely) corrosive sublimate.

It was with a sense of betrayal, therefore, that I received the verdict of the jury of computer read-out charts. No iodine had been blasted into the pores of that bathroom tile. "What had you in mind, Sergeant Himmel?" Dr. Fredericks asked me.

"I wanted an explosive that could have been spread on the shower-room floor in solution, which, upon drying, would be fulminated by Dr. Hans Heinemann's bare and unfortunate feet," I said. "Crystals of nitrogen tri-iodide, which fits the bill admirably, can be set off by shouting at 'em. You've just ruled that out."

"I can supply you with an understudy for your Enn-Eye-Three," the physicist volunteered. She stepped into her office and returned with her finger marking an article in the British *New Scientist*. " '. . . a violent explosive, of power about equal to that of TNT,' " she read aloud.

"Excuse me, Lily." I grabbed the magazine and read on: " 'The explosive nature of xenon trioxide, leaving no traces of solid materials, may find use—not, it is to be hoped, by criminals, as detection of the explosive used would be difficult.' "

"At present, impossible," my savant interjected.

"This may be it," I said, uncrossing my superstitious fingers. "It appears that any clever high-school boy could cook up a batch of this xenon trioxide, once he got hold of the groceries required. He'd pipe xenon and fluorine gases through a hot nickel tube, bubble the escaping xenon tetrafluoride through water, and spread the resulting solution of xenon trioxide on the shower-room floor to dry. The game, Doctor, is afoot."

"What will you do now?" she asked.

"I'll find out who ordered supplies of xenon and fluorine from the Glass Shop," I said. "The killer didn't pick that stuff up at his friendly corner Walgreen's."

I took Bem along to the Glass Shop to check the records. Both gases were kept in stock, the attendant told me, amused that I should suppose that his inventory lacked any imaginable resource. His amusement vanished when he discovered that his shelves were short a peck of calcium fluoride and a tank of xenon.

Only moderately elated, I led Bem back to the office, where we could confer with our friend and secretary. "Poor Hans," Shelly said. "Finding out what killed him does no more good than pointing to the bullet hole. You still don't know who held the gun."

"With Lily Fredericks' help, I've found one invisible weapon," I said.

"Lily, eh?" Shelly asked. "First-naming lady physicists now, Felix?"

I ignored her. "Something of the same sort, far-out, fingerprintless and fatal, was used on Nakamura and Wilson."

"And will be aimed at you, if the killer feels your caffein-scented breath on the back of his neck," Shelly observed.

"Since you mention danger," I said, "you'll have to take precautions, too, Shelly."

"I'm always circumspect in the company of strange men, Sergeant," she said.

"Shut up and wear this," I said, handing her a pocket

dosimeter I'd got from Lily Fredericks' stock. "Radiation is the sneakiest killer of them all."

"Do you suspect anyone yet, Felix?"

"I don't even know everyone here, yet," I protested. "All I know about our murderer is that he had free access to lab goodies, can go pretty much where he pleases, and wanted the Cosmos Project papers badly enough to kill for them." I gazed at Michelle, her hair the color of coffee unmarred by cream, her arms tanned to the tint of claro cigar leaf.

"What's the matter, Felix?"

"I'm contemplating the wondrous structures that can result from piling amino acid on amino acid, tying peptides into polypeptide chains, weaving skeins of protein molecules into lacework of helixes and nets. . . . You're a beautiful girl, Shelly. I'd rather not tell you everything I find out from here on in. You'll be in danger if the murderer thinks you suspect his name."

"This is the first time I've been complimented as an organic compound," Shelly said. "Thank you, Felix. And thanks for the warning. I'm with you, all the same. Those three men who died were my friends, not just entries on a coroner's report."

"I wish we had a canary in this office," I mused. "A bird of the sort coal miners used to carry with them underground, to warn of noxious gases. Lacking such a sensitive bird, though, I'm glad I wear hardware under my white coat." I patted the .38. "How about dinner this evening, Shelly?"

"You'll get bored with me," she protested, "seeing me on duty and off."

"If I do, I'll get my Smokey Bear hat back, put on blue whipcord again and return to the job of terrorizing motorists on the Toll Road," I promised.

The next morning, Bem and I adjourned to the men's locker room with the set of copper keys I'd requisitioned. After some jiggery-pokery with a file, I got locker 13 open. A black jacket hung inside, with a yellow-headed Mensa pin on its lapel. A chessboard sat on the floor, the pieces arranged in a pattern that awoke no insight in ignorant me. Laundry ink inside the neckband of the jacket spelled out COWHAGE. For some reason, Red was hiding his light under a bushel. I leaped to no obvious conclusions. A murder investigation typically turns up tangential bits of hanky-pank.

Shelly and I had fried chicken with the gang in the cafeteria, refused DeeGee Nova's offer of a postprandial beer, and went back to our office to try the Mycroft Holmes bit. "It's strange," I said, pouring warm water over Bem's grubby-looking chow, "that Lucky Luger shouldn't know what Project Cosmos was aimed at."

"That's the way he organized his shop," Shelly said. "Lucky gives his researchers their heads. Paper work is anathema. He expects loyalty from his staff, and that's the end of his rule book."

"What devices did Cosmos employ, Shelly?" I asked. "Any hint would help."

"Hans Heinemann had a row of bac-tee incubators over there in our lab," she said. "He and Woody Wilson did a lot of work with DeeGee's germ-free white rats, too. Not even Nova knew what they were up to. When people hinted, little Nakamura would grin and shake his head. The project seems to have been originated by the other two. Nakamura came along later, adding, I'd guess, some sort of motivational-research-type hooker."

"How many people knew about Dr. Nakamura's allergy to bee stings?"

"I did. I suppose everyone did," Shelly said. "Hoyotoko would walk way out across the lawn to avoid the flowers when they were in blossom, this to lessen his chance of being ambushed by a peevish bee.''

"Heinemann's penchant for showers was no secret either, was it?'' I poured us out some coffee.

Shelly smiled. "Hans had a deep-dish Dutch accent,'' she remembered. "The other fellows had one joke they repeated time and again: about how Hans would go take his shower and feel Rosie all over. He'd laugh each time they told that, and slap his belly; a three-hundred-pound Katzenjammer kid.''

Someone fumbled at the door. I opened it for Kitten, who rolled in like she'd had a hard night and headed for the wall socket next to my desk. Bem padded out the open door, muttering canine curses over his shoulder. "Thirsty,'' Kitten whispered. She reached out her power-tentacle and plugged it in. "Aaah!'' she sighed. "Delicious alternating current. You meat-things don't know what you're missing. Don't mind me, now.''

It is difficult to ignore half a ton of iron in the middle of the floor, especially when it persists in purring and scratching at its back with half a dozen arms, rejoicing in recharging. "How long have you been here, Kitten?'' I asked the robot.

"Since the Greeks first stroked amber with a woolen cloth,'' she boasted.

Unable to resist the invitation of our open door, Red Cowhage wheeled in his shopping cart to join us. "Got any more of that coffee, Sarge?'' he asked. I got another beaker from the lab and poured him a shot. "I saw Bem hot-pawing it down the hall, and I kinda figured old Kitten had shooed him out,'' Red said. "How's the big murder case shaping up, Felix?''

"I'm drinking lots of coffee,'' I testified. "How much time does that tin cat generally spend sucking at the electric teat?''

"Kitten just sips, a little here, a little there,'' Red said. He patted the three-foot-high turret.

The robot brushed Cowhage's hand aside with her whip-tentacle. "Human perspiration," she growled, "is very corrosive." Rather pointedly, Kitten unplugged and rolled out the door.

"Snob," Cowhage hissed. "If she wasn't the boss's pet, I'd put sand in her gears."

"Red's afraid that Kitten will swipe his job of delivering the mail," Shelly explained.

"She's too darned lazy to work," Cowhage said. "She just runs around the halls, tracks through flowerbeds like Ferdinand the Bull, plays catch with folks that got nothing better to do, and makes wisecracks." Red jumped to his feet. "No stupid threshing machine is gonna automate me out of a job," he vowed.

After Red Cowhage left, I closed the door. "Kitten plays catch?" I asked Shelly.

"As a gag, Lucky Luger programed *The Rules of Baseball* into her," she said. "Kitten could pitch a marshmallow through a brick wall, and she fields like an acre of flypaper. At our last Fourth of July company picnic, Lucky let her pitch him. He held his bat out horizontal. Kitten broke it in two with a pitched ball. There was talk for weeks afterwards about selling her to the Mets." Someone, again, was scratching at our door. I admitted Bem, who stalked around the presumably oil-scented patch of floor where Kitten had stood and spread himself out to glower at us. "If Pekingese could swear, we'd get an earful," Shelly said.

"Do you hear something, Shelly?" I asked.

She sat silent for a moment. "No," she said. "What was it—Doc Greene's wistful clarinet?"

"Something here in our office," I said. "The sort of noise a mouse might make. Maybe in my desk drawer?" I tugged the center drawer all the way open.

The thumbtacks and paper clips that normally rested in the tray at the front of the drawer were clustered now at the back, squirming as though they wanted to burrow through the wood. "Get back into the lab, Shelly," I ordered.

"What's happening?" she demanded, backing away from the desk.

"That's what I'm going next door to see." I drew my gun and rounded the corner from our office into Dr. Greene's music room.

The door was open. The lab was empty. The huge electromagnet with which Greene plotted victory over copper oxide was tilted back, aimed through the wall at the spot where I'd been sitting. I tugged my gun back into its holster through a magnetic field sticky as quicksand, then switched off the big machine.

Who had turned the magnet on? Why?

I glanced over the spice bottles ranged above Greene's kitchen sink. Powdered aluminum, in one of the glass-stoppered jars, looked like just what I needed. I spilled a little of the dust onto my palm, then went over to puff it onto the control box of the electromagnet, around the scarlet ON button. A few smudged prints appeared, outlined in the silvery metal. "Shelly!" I shouted out the door. "Bring over a roll of Scotch tape."

"May I ask," Dr. Greene asked, pointing at my middle the gun he held in his right hand, "what you're doing with my 1000,000-gauss magnet?"

It was a showdown. Fortunately, before I attempted a Hollywood draw with my revolver, I saw that the gun in Greene's hand had a cord at one end and a soldering tip at the other. "What happens to people exposed to a 100,000-gauss magnetic field?" I asked. Shelly handed me the transparent tape, and I set to work lifting the prints I'd found on the switch.

"My field is metals, not mammals," Greene protested. He put down his soldering gun and peered over my shoulder. "Powdered aluminum?" he inquired.

"Yes. We call it a developing powder," I said.

"Did you stop to think that your lavish use of pow-

dered aluminum will have short circuits flashing around
this laboratory every time I throw a switch?''

"No," I admitted.

"Let's see what sort of prints you picked up," Greene
demanded. He glued down the scotch tape with its
shadow of fingerprints, procured a four-inch magnifier,
and stuck his right fingertips beneath it, beside the tape.
"Match, don't they?"

"Afraid so."

"Thus I stand convicted of operating my own electromagnet," Greene said. "I swear, Himmel, if you
weren't a French-horn player, I'd bust you one right in
the embouchure." He glanced toward his magnet. "Did
you tilt it toward the wall that way?"

"No."

"Aimed right at you, eh?"

"Got me square in the breadbasket," I said. "My
paper clips were crawling through the wall."

"I don't wonder," Greene said. "Now, I don't want
to be quoted—what I'm about to tell you is outside my
specialty—but several investigators have reported that
squirrel monkeys, subjected to a high magnetic field,
responded with a change in heart rhythm, a slowing of
the beat, and blackouts. Mice in the same fix lost a
quarter of their white blood cells and showed an increase in red blood corpuscles. Since I read all this,
I've been having the old peripheral blood checked every
single week."

"Dr. Greene, is nickel a magnetic metal?" I asked.

"You could say so," Greene admitted.

"Dr. Woodrow Wilson, who used to sit where I was
sitting ten minutes ago, had a nickel ball bearing built
into his prosthetic mitral heart valve," I said. "I don't
suppose the killer counted on that additional help, but
I'm sure he tore Wilson's heart out with this monstrous
electromagnet of yours."

"Oh, my goodness," Greene groaned. He slumped

down into the chair beside his music rack and shook his head. "I'll never feel the same about her again," he said, staring at the magnet. "It's as though you were to learn that your best silverware had been used to cut up babies."

"I'm sorry," I said.

"No fault of yours, Sergeant Himmel. Will you hand me my clarinet case, please?"

To the opening bars of Aaron Copland's *Clarinet Concerto,* Shelly Kelly and I tiptoed out of his laboratory. I glanced at my wristwatch. Unlike my heart, it had stopped. "When day is done, and shadows fall," I told Miss Kelly, "I feel the need for alcohol. Join me?"

"If I do, I'll miss the bus back to Connorsville," Shelly said.

"If you do, I'll guarantee you a State Police escort," I promised. "Get Bem and the coffee jug and we'll cut out." I hung up my white coat.

Shelly ransacked the office. "Can't find your Thermos, Felix," she said.

"Skip it," I said. "Let's go eat us some olives."

Bem trotted ahead of us out the building, down the walk, and into the gatehouse. He sniffed at Lucky Luger's gold brick, then led us on to the parking lot. Shelly glanced in the window of my car as I leaned over to unlatch the door on her side. "There it is, on the floor in back," she said. "Your Thermos bottle."

"How'd it get out here?" I asked. "No matter."

Bem seated himself between us, cheerfully confident that my plans included a steak for a Pekingese. I headed for the Constellation Club, a bar-restaurant at Sundown, a town so small that it seems to have been incorporated only to circumvent the Indian law that prohibits roadside pubs. "So far as method goes," I said, talking shop, "it's two down and one to go." I rolled up my window. "Chilly."

Michelle scooted as close as Bem would let her. I

freed my right hand from the wheel to warm her shoulder. "Somehow it seems more decent to bludgeon a man to death, or to shoot him, than to brew up exotic bombs and stop his heart with a magnet," she said.

"When we nail our man, it's gonna be Murder One," I predicted. "Premeditation is implicit in this nasty-science-project of his." Bem scooted down onto the floor. "Pick up the darned dog, will you?" I asked. "He'll get in the way if I have to brake."

"What?" Shelly asked me.

The highway ahead of us was shimmering. Mirages danced up from the pavement. I slumped down as far as my seatbelt would give and squinted my eyes. Somehow, anticipating that first martini had made me a little bit drunk. . . . "Shelly?"

"Mmmm?" She seemed half-asleep.

Some idiot, tooling along on my side of the pavement, hooted as I swerved to the right to let him pass. Suddenly I realized that I'd been driving on his side. "Hoo, boy!" I said.

Shelly was snoring, a mellow and ladylike sound I found rather appealing. I chuckled. "Hey, Shelly-baby, get that rug off'n my feets, will ya?" Bem was lying against my right ankle, inert and silent.

The Monon Railroad saved our lives, and the red blinkers that called attention to the freight that was crossing the road. I realized that I was being urged toward some mechanical decision, and wheeled down the window to watch those dancing spots ahead.

Clean air blasted against my face. Something wrong. I lead-footed the brake pedal, skidded, then started stabbing at it. The flickering wall ahead of us loomed up fast. A fog of hot rubber fanned out behind us.

We rocked to a halt. My front bumper was no more than spitting distance from the orange refrigerator cars that were rattling off to our left.

"Shelly!" I reached across her to open the door. I patted her face.

"Stobbit, Felix," she said, shaking her head.

Ahead, the caboose clattered over the crossing, and the red blinkers went dead. The cars behind me started hooting.

I pulled off to the berm, beyond the tracks. "Coffee," I told myself. I reached back to get the Thermos jug from the floor in back. "Damn!" The can was so cold that my sweaty fingers had stuck to it. Opening the back door, I swaddled the jug in my handkerchief and lifted it out. The top was loose. A boiling fluid streamed out into the roadside ditch as I upended the Thermos. I held my breath. Then I corked the bottle and tossed it back into the car, reciting every rude word boyhood on the farm and service in the Navy had taught me.

"Rough!"

"You said it, buddy." Bem was on Shelly's lap now, his pop-eyes reflecting suspicion.

"I didn't spike your drink," I told him.

"Somebody did," Shelly moaned. "Did I say anything I shouldn't have?"

"We haven't had the first sip yet," I said. My hands were trembling. Whether this was a symptom of carbon monoxide poisoning or simple nervous shock, I didn't know. "Let's get to Sundown and correct that lack."

Both of us innocently hungover, we had coffee with our steaks. Bem guarded the car, beside which he wolfed his very-rare. "Poison gas in the Thermos jug," Shelly said. "Your program of coaxing the rats out of the wainscoting seems to have borne fruit."

"We were very nearly killed." I told her about the car I'd almost hit, and the train we had very nearly cut in half at sixty miles an hour. "Not having much experience with liquefied carbon monoxide," I said, "I'll have to guess. But we're on the murderer's heels, Shelly.

He tried to turn us off this evening. There wouldn't have been any evidence of this killing, either; not unless the coroner thought to test our blood at autopsy. Even then, with the car chewed up by half a mile of fast freight, there wouldn't be any way to prove that we hadn't been gassed by a leaky muffler.''

"Put some silver in the juke box, Felix," Shelly said. "Punch several cheerful buttons."

I hired Al Hirt to trumpet at us, and returned to our table. "Shelly," I said, "I want you to take the rest of the week off."

"The game's getting too rough for you, eh?" she demanded. "Well, my answer is no. I'm not a quitter."

I took her hand, slowing up her progress with the steak. "Shelly, I have in mind a formal ceremony for you and me. It's not a double funeral." Hirt triple-tongued his way through "Trumpeter's Holiday," music roughly romantic as an ice-water shower.

Shelly Kelly smiled. "My college roommate said I snore," she reported. "I think I should tell you that before you make any rash commitments."

"You snore, I play the French horn," I told her. "Noisewise, that leaves us one-all."

Shelly frowned down into her coffeecup. "We'll be drinking oceans of this stuff together," she predicted. "Let me wash your offer down with something a bit more lively, Felix; and I'll give it the benefit of my best thought."

"If you'll give me a hint of the outcome, I'll bang on the table and yell for champagne," I said.

"Very well, Felix," she said. "You have my definite Let's See."

Al Hirt goes well with champagne. Later, when the Constellation Club's combo made its gig, we invited Bem in to dance with us. Much later, awash with enough coffee to assure that I could drive, but never sleep again, we hustled down to Connorsville, where I grudg-

ingly let Shelly say goodnight. Bem plodded up the steps
to the apartment they shared, glaring daggers at me for
having kept him out carousing till dawn.

I walked through the Loki Laboratories gatehouse later
that morning with a feeling I'd known before only while
watching GI movies on the late-late show: it was the
scene where the squad leader is advancing easy-footed
through a field spiked with antipersonnel mines. Someone in this crazy place wanted me dead. A feeble ray
of sunshine eased through my inner gloom. If I was
important enough to bump off, it could only be because
I was probing near a nerve. Remembering then that
Shelly would have gone with me, smeared across a
cornfield by a westbound freight, I felt a surge of anger
that washed though my sleep-denied brain.

"Aaah-Ooo-Gah!" A diesel horn blasted through my
head. I crawled up the hall's right wall. Kitten wheeled
past at twenty miles an hour. "Be alert at all times,"
she said, adding what sounded like a chuckle.

I added several salty phrases to the tin cat's vocabu-
lary, then went on into the office to brood through my
notes.

"Item one," I told my audience, Shelly and Bem.
"Red Cowhage wears a Mensa Society pin on his jacket,
and is a solitary chessplayer. If Red's not stupid, he's a
fraud; if he's a fraud, he could be a killer, too."

"There's a weak link in that logical chain," Shelly
observed. "Why need a con man be a murderer?"

"Better him than nice people like us," I explained.

"I hear Cowhage whistling down the hall with the
morning mail," Shelly reported. "If you want to interview him, now's your chance."

"I suggest that all girls and dogs leave the room
first," I said.

"Both Bem and I can claw and bite," Shelly said.

She seated herself like a statue of an Egyptian king, defying me to budge her.

Cowhage came in of his own accord. "No mail, Sergeant Himmel," he said. "There's something I want to tell you, though."

"About your owning a Mensa pin and brains to match?" I inquired.

Red sat on the edge of my desk. "You've heard the quatrain that goes, 'Behold the happy moron, he doesn't give a damn . . .' "

" '. . . I wish I were a moron: My God! Perhaps I am!' " I finished it.

"They had me on the books as a brilliant student," Cowhage said. "I was grinding away at my work—toward a Ph.D. in philosophy, something rare as gloves in a glove compartment—when I felt myself sinking into that slough of despond the medieval saints named anomie. So I retired for a year, got myself the dumbest job I could find. I'm with it again, Sergeant Himmel. I'm heading back to Columbia in the fall."

"How nice for you," I said. "But why brief me on your intellectual *Wanderjahr*?"

"Because I had to talk to you about this." Red Cowhage took from his shirt pocket a green metal wheel, a sharp-pointed asterisk some four inches in diameter. "Your problem, to find the man who killed the Project Cosmos team, is the first puzzle outside chess that has exercised me since I retired from thinking," he said. "I know that I'm your prime suspect. Who can go everywhere? I can. Who's below suspicion? The whistling moron. Right?"

"You come most carefully upon your hour," I said.

"I found this wheel on the lawn, out by the rose arbor, three weeks ago," Cowhage said, turning the green artifact in his hands. "Why was it painted green? I wondered. To hide itself in the grass, I decided. What was it for? I've opened books again, and I've discovered the answer.''

"That thing killed Nakamura?'' I demanded.

"A splendid inductive leap, Sergeant,'' Cowhage congratulated me. "Children in Japan, as you may not know, don't play cowboy any more; they play at Ninjutsu. The Ninja, invisible skulkers, bloody bawdy Robin Hoods, are invulnerable to poison. They can kill their enemies in a hundred ways, one of which,'' he said, taking one tine of the sharp-spoked wheel between the index finger and thumb of his right hand, "is this poison-tipped *shuriken*.'' He flipped it. I had my gun out faster than you could say "Channel Fifteen,'' and the sound of my shot bounced off the walls before the disk hit the floor, hopelessly bent out of shape.

"I was only going to nail it into the calendar over there,'' Cowhage said. "The bee venom that killed Dr. Nakamura has long since been washed away by dew and rain.''

I pulled a scrap of paper across the desk and lettered the message: HOW CAN I TURN OFF KITTEN?

"All you can do,'' Cowhage announced aloud, "is cut the power to the whole lab complex, and let her run out her batteries.''

"The hell you say!'' Kitten crashed through the office door, filling the air with confetti kindling. She headed toward me as though she intended to leap into my lap.

I stepped aside. *"Olé!''* Cowhage shouted.

"Get out to the car, Shelly,'' I yelled. I squeezed three shots into the robot's optical turret, then sprinted from the office, down the hall in the opposite direction to that Shelly Kelly (carrying Bem) and Red Cowhage had taken. I was headed to the tower to cut off Kitten's brains.

A steel stairway led past a window, up to Lucky Luger's laboratory in the bell tower. Kitten hummed along behind me.

"Aah-Ooo-Gah!" she bellowed. Three cans the size of spray-foam shaving-cream containers bounced down the stairs, sputtering. White fire flashed. The cans melted, welded themselves to the steel stair, burning it through. Thermite grenades, the robot's home-defense device. The stairway sagged like a sandcastle caught by the tide.

Kitten whipped out a tentacle to catch me around the neck. I cuddled my head in my arms and fell through the window. Outside, I was off and running without having time to check myself over for shrapnel wounds. Unable to scale the casement, Kitten turned to take the long way around. I had a very thin edge of seconds to get to the red Amish barn run by Dr. Bingo Lane.

Lane was, as usual, displaying bare feet and knees. His pedipulator was hitched to a hoist, ready to go up into walking position. "I'm commandeering this vehicle," I shouted.

"No need to take it over at gunpoint, Felix," Land told me, shoving aside the revolver I was brandishing.

"Kitten has gone crazy," I explained. "I've got to shoot up her computer, in the tower."

"Take off your pants, then, and your shoes," he directed.

"Eh?"

"The feedback mechanism in the follower-rack feels the movements of your feet and knees," he explained. Something over in the main building crashed.

I stripped off my shoes, socks and trousers and stepped into the control box of Lane's pedipulator. The whole affair fit itself to me tightly as a pair of wet boots. "Don't think about driving it," Lane said. "It does the thinking; you just walk."

"Roger," I said. Lane triggered the hoist switch, and I eased up toward the ceiling of the barn. I stepped out of the building.

"Catcher crew!" Bingo Lane shouted. I heard their jeep start up.

I walked on. It was a dream of glory, looming high above the world, striding ten yards with my most indifferent step. I saw Kitten, scrambling through the brick rubble she'd rammed through the wall. She saw me, too, and was rolling across a bed of tulips.

The slit windows of the campanile were five paces away. Two shots would have to do the job—two bullets to puncture Kitten's brain, to cut her off from her yachtsman master 800 miles east of us.

The windows were smashed with the butt of my .38. I rested my elbows on the pigeon-redolent ledge outside. Where to aim? Panels of lights flashed in the laboratory, feeding Kitten instructions from the *Midas Touch*. Whatever I hit, IBM would never forgive me. I chose a red light that seemed especially excited, and punched it out.

I glanced back over my shoulder. The jeep with the net was backing into fielding position behind me. Pessimists.

Kitten rolled on, waving all six arms in promise of mayhem. "Kill! Kill!" she bellowed.

My State Police sedan, as though eager to join in the glorious confusion, was headed my way, too; bearing in its teeth an eight-foot strip of hurricane fence. Shelly was at the wheel, and I saw Bem flash up behind the windshield as he leaped to watch.

No time to choose my target from the rich display before me. Kitten was gnawing at my right calf, and I was having trouble taking aim. An oscilloscope screen was writhing with green worms. I mashed 'em with my last shot.

I fell backwards. My sedan rammed dead Kitten in her right flank. Bem sprang from the car to leap upon his enemy. Then I was up to my ears in grass, with

Shelly purring into one of them. "They missed me," I groaned.

"You bounced out of the net," she said. "Clumsy, are you all right?"

"I'll be fine." I hitched myself deeper into the pedipulator holster. "I'll be better, once you've brought me my pants."

"I'm sorry that I wrecked your car," she said.

"No problem," I told her. "I'll invite my colonel to be best man, and as his wedding present he'll write off the sedan."

It was Bingo Lane who ran up with my trousers. Panted again, I accompanied Shelly to look at Kitten.

Poor beast. Wedged between the cop car and the catcher-jeep, she was silent as any anonymous pile of scrap. "I'd better call the Coast Guard," I said. "Get them to detain the *Midas Touch*. She's probably steaming into international waters this very moment."

"I doubt it," Shelly said. "I called the Coast Guard's Boston District office before I rammed Kitten. Let's get some coffee, Felix."

"Coffee, hell," I snapped, taking her arm. "We're going to buy ourselves a couple of blood tests and a license."

The colonel was all smiles, like cupid carved in granite. "Three murders solved and two aborted repay the state for the cost of the car you smashed, Miss Kelly," he told Shelly. He turned to me. "Felix, you've talked with Lucky Luger. What the devil was Project Cosmos?"

"That doesn't really matter, sir," I said. "The reason Luger killed the three doctors was that he'd overheard their plans to leave Loki Laboratories. Kitten carried his long-distance ears, as well as his murdering hands. Luger demanded loyalty. He couldn't let those men leave him."

"Tell me about Cosmos, Himmel, or I'll strip your stripes," he said.

"Toothpaste, Colonel," Shelly said.

"You jest," he said.

"The formula will license for some ten million dollars a year," I explained. "Heinemann and Wilson, working with germ-free rats, discovered an enzyme that inhibits tooth decay. One hundred percent fewer cavities, Colonel."

"Hoyotoko Nakamura supplied the huckster's touch," Shelly said. "He had his associates work up a colorless chemical that turns dirty yellow when exposed to saliva. It will make the consumer feel that his toothbrush is doing him good."

Bem looked toward us, toward the door, and wagged his tail.

"May I inquire, Sergeant Himmel, where you two . . . you three . . . are going on your honeymoon?" the colonel asked me.

"Yes, sir," I said, opening the door and leading Shelly out. "You may inquire."

The Adventure of the Seven Black Cats

ELLERY QUEEN

The tinkly bell quavered over the door of Miss Curleigh's Pet Shoppe on Amsterdam Avenue, and Mr. Ellery Queen wrinkled his nose and went in. The instant
he crossed the threshold he was thankful it was not a
large nose, and that he had taken the elementary precaution of wrinkling it. The extent and variety of the
little shop's odors would not have shamed the New York
Zoological Park itself. And yet it housed only creatures, he was amazed to find, of the puniest propor-
tions; who, upon the micrometrically split second of
his entrance, set up such a chorus of howls, yelps,
snarls, yawps, grunts, squeaks, caterwauls, croaks,
screeches, chirrups, hisses, and growls that it was a
miracle the roof did not come down.

"Good afternoon," said a crisp voice. "I'm Miss Curleigh. What can I do for you, please?"

In the midst of raging bedlam Mr. Ellery Queen found himself gazing into a pair of mercurial eyes. There were other details—she was a trim young piece, for example, with masses of titian hair and curves and at least one dimple—but for the moment her eyes engaged his earnest attention. Miss Curleigh, blushing, repeated herself.

"I beg your pardon," said Ellery hastily, returning to the matter at hand. "Apparently in the animal kingdom there is no decent ratio between lung-power and— ah—aroma on the one hand and size on the other. We live and learn! Miss Curleigh, would it be possible to purchase a comparatively noiseless and sweet-smelling canine with frizzy brown hair, inquisitive ears at the half-cock, and crooked hind-legs?"

Miss Curleigh frowned. Unfortunately, she was out of Irish terriers. The last litter had been gobbled up. Perhaps a Scottie—?

Mr. Queen frowned. No, he had been specifically enjoined by Djuna, the martinet, to procure an Irish terrier; no doleful-looking, sawed-off substitute, he was sure, would do.

"I expect," said Miss Curleigh professionally, "to hear from our Long Island kennels tomorrow. If you'll leave your name and address?"

Mr. Queen, gazing into the young woman's eyes, would be delighted to. Mr. Queen, provided with pencil and pad, hastened to indulge his delight.

As Miss Curleigh read what he had written the mask of business fell away. "You're not Mr. *Ellery* Queen!" she exclaimed with animation. "Well, I declare. I've heard *so* much about you, Mr. Queen. And you live practically around the corner, on Eighty-seventh Street! This is really thrilling. I never expected to meet—"

"Nor I," murmured Mr. Queen. "Nor I."

Miss Curleigh blushed again and automatically prodded her hair. "One of my best customers lives right across the street from you, Mr. Queen. I should say one of my most *frequent* customers. Perhaps you know her? A Miss Tarkle—Euphemia Tarkle? She's in that large apartment house, you know."

"I've never had the pleasure," said Mr. Queen absently. "What extraordinary eyes you have! I mean— Euphemia Tarkle? Dear, dear, this is a world of sudden wonders. Is she as improbable as her name?"

"That's unkind," said Miss Curleigh severely, "although she *is* something of a character, the poor creature. A squirrely-faced old lady, *and* an invalid. Paralytic, you know. The queerest, frailest, tiniest little thing. Really, she's quite mad."

"Somebody's grandmother, no doubt," said Mr. Queen whimsically, picking up his stick from the counter. "Cats?"

"Why, Mr. Queen, however did you guess?"

"It always is," he said in a gloomy voice, "cats."

"*You'd* find her interesting, I'm sure," said Miss Curleigh with eagerness.

"And why I, Diana?"

"The name," said Miss Curleigh shyly, "is Marie. Well, she's *so* strange, Mr. Queen. And I've always understood that strange people interest you."

"At present," said Mr. Queen hurriedly, taking a firmer grip on his stick, "I am enjoying the fruits of idleness."

"But do you know what Miss Tarkle's been doing, the mad thing?"

"I haven't the ghost of a notion," said Mr. Queen with truth.

"She's been buying cats from me at the rate of about one a week for weeks now!"

Mr. Queen sighed. "I see no special cause for suspicion. An ancient and invalid lady, a passion for cats—

oh, they go together, I assure you. I once had an aunt like that.''

"That's what's so strange about it,'' said Miss Curleigh triumphantly. "She doesn't *like* cats!''

Mr. Queen blinked twice. He looked at Miss Curleigh's pleasant little nose. Then he rather absently set his stick on the counter again. "And how do you know that, pray?''

Miss Curleigh beamed. "Her sister told me.—Hush, Ginger! You see, Miss Tarkle is absolutely helpless with her paralysis and all, and her sister Sarah-Ann keeps house for her; they're both of an age, I should say, and they look so much alike. Dried-up little apples of old ladies, with the same tiny features and faces like squirrels. Well, Mr. Queen, about a year ago Miss Sarah-Ann came into my shop and bought a black male cat—she hadn't much money, she said, couldn't buy a really expensive one; so I got just a—well, just a cat for her, you see.''

"Did she ask for a black tomcat?'' asked Mr. Queen intently.

"No. Any kind at all, she said; she liked them all. Then only a few days later she came back. She wanted to know if she could return him and get her money back. Because, she said, her sister Euphemia couldn't stand having a cat about her; Euphemia just *detested* cats, she said with a sigh, and since she was more or less living off Euphemia's bounty she couldn't very well cross her, you see. I felt a little sorry for her and told her I'd take the cat back; but I suppose she changed her mind, or else her sister changed *her* mind, because Sarah-Ann Tarkle never came back. Anyway, that's how I know Miss Euphemia doesn't like cats.''

Mr. Queen gnawed a fingernail. "Odd,'' he muttered. "A veritable saga of oddness. You say this Euphemia creature has been buying 'em at the rate of one a week? What kind of cats, Miss Curleigh?''

Miss Curleigh sighed. "Not very good ones. Of course, since she has pots of money—that's what her sister Sarah-Ann said, anyway—I tried to sell her an Angora—I had a beauty—and a Maltese that took a ribbon at one of the shows. But she wanted just cats, she said, like the one I sold her sister. Black ones."

"Black. . . . It's possible that—"

"Oh, she's not at all superstitious, Mr. Queen. In some ways she's a very weird old lady. Black tomcats with green eyes, all the same size. I thought it very queer."

Mr. Ellery Queen's nostrils quivered a little, and not from the racy odor in Miss Curleigh's Pet Shoppe, either. An old invalid lady named Tarkle who bought a black tomcat with green eyes every week!

"Very queer indeed," he murmured; and his gray eyes narrowed. "And how long has this remarkable business been going on?"

"You *are* interested! Five weeks now, Mr. Queen. I delivered the sixth one myself only the other day."

"Yourself? Is she totally paralyzed?"

"Oh, yes. She never leaves her bed; can't walk a step. It's been that way, she told me, for ten years now. She and Sarah-Ann hadn't lived together up to the time she had her stroke. Now she's absolutely dependent on her sister for everything—meals, baths, bedp . . . all sorts of attention."

"Then why," demanded Ellery, "hasn't she sent her sister for the cats?"

Miss Curleigh's mercurial eyes wavered. "I don't know," she said slowly. "Sometimes I get the shivers. You see, she's always telephoned me—she has a 'phone by her bed and can use her arms sufficiently to reach for it—the day she wanted the cat. It would always be the same order—black, male, green eyes, the same size as before, and as cheap as possible." Miss Curleigh's

pleasant features hardened. "She's something of a hag-
gler, Miss Euphemia Tarkle is."

"Fantastic," said Ellery thoughtfully. "Utterly fantastic. There's something in the basic situation that
smacks of lavenderish tragedy. Tell me: how has her
sister acted on the occasions when you've delivered the
cats?"

"*Hush,* Ginger! I can't tell you, Mr. Queen, because
she hasn't been there."

Ellery started. "Hasn't been there! What do you
mean? I thought you said the Euphemia woman is helpless—"

"She is, but Sarah-Ann goes out every afternoon for
some air, I suppose, or to a movie, and her sister is left
alone for a few hours. It's been at such times, I think,
that she's called me. Then, too, she always warned me
to come at a certain time, and since I've never seen
Sarah-Ann when I made the delivery I imagine she's
planned to keep her purchases a secret from her sister.
I've been able to get in because Sarah-Ann leaves the
door unlocked when she goes out. Euphemia has told
me time and time again not to breathe a word about the
cats to any one."

Ellery took his *pince-nez* off his nose and began to
polish the shining lenses—an unfailing sign of emotion.
"More and more muddled," he muttered. "Miss Curleigh, you've stumbled on something—well, morbid."

Miss Curleigh blanched. "You don't think—"

"Insults already? I *do* think; and that's why I'm disturbed. For instance, how on earth could she have hoped
to keep knowledge of the cats she's bought from her
sister? Sarah-Ann isn't blind, is she?"

"Blind? Why, of course not. And Euphemia's sight
is all right, too."

"I was only joking. It doesn't make sense, Miss Curleigh."

"Well," said Miss Curleigh brightly, "at least I've

given the great Mr. Queen something to think
about. . . . I'll call you the moment an Ir—"

Mr. Ellery Queen replaced the glasses on his nose,
threw back his square shoulders, and picked up the stick
again.

"Miss Curleigh, I'm an incurable meddler in the affairs of others. How would you like to help me meddle
in the affairs of the mysterious Tarkle sisters?"

Scarlet spots appeared in Miss Curleigh's cheeks.
"You're not serious?" she cried.

"Quite."

"I'd love to! What am I to do?"

"Suppose you take me up to the Tarkle apartment
and introduce me as a customer. Let's say that the cat
you sold Miss Tarkle the other day had really been
promised to me, that as a stubborn fancier of felines I
won't take any other, and that you'll have to have hers
back and give her another. Anything to permit me to
see and talk to her. It's mid-afternoon, so Sarah-Ann is
probably in a movie theatre somewhere languishing after Clark Gable. What do you say?"

Miss Curleigh flung him a ravishing smile. "I say
it's—it's too magnificent for words. One minute while
I powder my nose and get some one to tend the shop,
Mr. Queen. I wouldn't miss this for *anything*!"

Ten minutes later they stood before the front door to
Apartment 5-C of the *Amsterdam Arms,* a rather faded
building, gazing in silence at two full quart-bottles of
milk on the corridor floor. Miss Curleigh looked troubled, and Mr. Queen stooped. When he straightened he
looked troubled, too.

"Yesterday's and today's," he muttered, and he put
his hand on the doorknob and turned. The door was
locked. "I thought you said her sister leaves the door
unlocked when she goes out?"

"Perhaps she's in," said Miss Curleigh uncertainly.

"Or, if she's out, that she's forgotten to take the latch off."

Ellery pressed the bell-button. There was no reply. He rang again. Then he called loudly: "Miss Tarkle, are you there?"

"I can't understand it," said Miss Curleigh with a nervous laugh. "She really should hear you. It's only a three-room apartment, and both the bedroom and the living room are directly off the sides of a little foyer on the other side of the door. The kitchen's straight ahead."

Ellery called again, shouting. After a while he put his ear to the door. The rather dilapidated hall, the ill-painted door . . .

Miss Curleigh's extraordinary eyes were frightened silver lamps. She said in the queerest voice: "Oh, Mr. Queen. Something dreadful's happened."

"Let's hunt up the superintendent," said Ellery quietly.

They found *Potter, Sup't* in a metal frame before a door on the ground floor. Miss Curleigh was breathing in little gusts. Ellery rang the bell.

A short fat woman with enormous forearms flecked with suds opened the door. She wiped her red hands on a dirty apron and brushed a strand of bedraggled gray hair from her sagging face. "Well?" she demanded stolidly.

"Mrs. Potter?"

"That's right. We ain't got no empty apartments. The doorman could 'a' told you—"

Miss Curleigh reddened. Ellery said hastily: "Oh, we're not apartment-hunting, Mrs. Potter. Is the superintendent in?"

"No, he's not," she said suspiciously. "He's got a part-time job at the chemical works in Long Island City and he never gets home till ha'-past three. What you want?"

"I'm sure you'll do nicely, Mrs. Potter. This young

lady and I can't seem to get an answer from Apartment 5-C. We're calling on Miss Tarkle, you see.''

The fat woman scowled. ''Ain't the door open? Generally is this time o' day. The spry one's out, but the paralyzed one—''

''It's locked, Mrs. Potter, and there's no answer to the bell or to our cries.''

''Now ain't that funny,'' shrilled the fat woman, staring at Miss Curleigh. ''I can't see—Miss Euphemia's a cripple; she *never* goes out. Maybe the poor thing's threw a fit!''

''I trust not. When did you see Miss Sarah-Ann last?''

''The spry one? Let's see, now. Why, two days ago. And, come to think of it, I ain't seen the cripple for two days, neither.''

''Heavens,'' whispered Miss Curleigh, thinking of the two milk-bottles. ''Two days!''

''Oh, you do see Miss Euphemia occasionally?'' asked Ellery grimly.

''Yes, sir.'' Mrs. Potter began to wring her red hands as if she were still over the tub. ''Every once in a while she calls me up by 'phone in the afternoon if her sister's out to take somethin' out to the incinerator, or do somethin' for her. The other day it was to mail a letter for her. She—she gives me somethin' once in a while. But it's been two days now. . . .''

Ellery pulled something out of his pocket and cupped it in his palm before the fat woman's tired eyes. ''Mrs. Porter,'' he said sternly, ''I want to get into that apartment. There's something wrong. Give me your master-key.''

''P-p-police!'' she stammered, staring at the shield. Then suddenly she fluttered off and returned to thrust a key into Ellery's hand. ''Oh, I wish Mr. Potter was home!'' she wailed. ''You won't—''

''Not a word about this to any one, Mrs. Potter.''

They left the woman gaping loose-tongued and frightened after them, and took the self-service elevator back to the fifth floor. Miss Curleigh was white to the lips; she looked a little sick.

"Perhaps," said Ellery kindly, inserting the key into the lock, "you had better not come in with me, Miss Curleigh. It might be unpleasant. I—" He stopped abruptly, his figure crouching.

Somebody was on the other side of the door.

There was the unmistakable sound of running feet, accompanied by an uneven scraping, as if something were being dragged. Ellery twisted the key and turned the knob in a flash, Miss Curleigh panting at his shoulder. The door moved a half-inch and stuck. The feet retreated.

"Barricaded the door," growled Ellery. "Stand back, Miss Curleigh." He flung himself sidewise at the door. There was a splintering crash and the door shot inward, a broken chair toppling over backward. "Too late—"

"The fire-escape!" screamed Miss Curleigh. "In the bedroom. To the left!"

He darted into a large narrow room with twin beds and an air of disorder and made for an open window. But there was no one to be seen on the fire-escape. He looked up: an iron ladder curved and vanished a few feet overhead.

"Whoever it is got away by the roof, I'm afraid," he muttered, pulling his head back and lighting a cigaret. "Smoke? Now, then, let's have a look about. No bloodshed, apparently. This may be a pig-in-the-poke after all. See anything interesting?"

Miss Curleigh pointed a shaking finger. "That's her— her bed. The messy one. But where is she?"

The other bed was neatly made up, its lace spread undisturbed. But Miss Euphemia Tarkle's was in a state of turmoil. The sheets had been ripped away and its mattress slashed open; some of the ticking was on the floor. The pillows had been torn to pieces. A depression in the center of the mattress indicated where the missing invalid had lain.

Ellery stood still, studying the bed. Then he made the rounds of the closets, opening doors, poking about, and closing them again. Followed closely by Miss Curleigh, who had developed an alarming habit of looking over her right shoulder, he glanced briefly into the living room, the kitchen, and the bathroom. But there was no one in the apartment. And, except for Miss Tarkle's bed, nothing apparently had been disturbed. The place was ghastly, somehow. It was as if violence had visited it in the midst of a cloistered silence; a tray full of dishes, cutlery, and half-finished food lay on the floor, almost under the bed.

Miss Curleigh shivered and edged closer to Ellery. "It's so—so deserted here," she said, moistening her lips. "Where's Miss Euphemia? And her sister? And who was that—that creature who barred the door?"

"What's more to the point," murmured Ellery, gazing at the tray of food, "where are the seven black cats?"

"Sev—"

"Sarah-Ann's lone beauty, and Euphemia's six. Where are they?"

"Perhaps," said Miss Curleigh hopefully, "they jumped out the window when that man—"

"Perhaps. And don't say 'man.' We just don't know." He looked irritably about. "If they did, it was a moment ago, because the catch on the window has been forced, indicating that the window has been closed and consequently that the cats might have—" He stopped short. "Who's there?" he called sharply, whirling.

"It's me," said a timid voice, and Mrs. Potter appeared hesitantly in the foyer. Her tired eyes were luminous with fear and curiosity. "Where's—"

"Gone." He stared at the slovenly woman. "You're sure you didn't see Miss Euphemia or her sister to-day?"

"Nor yesterday. I—"

"There was no ambulance in this neighborhood within the past two days?"

Mrs. Potter went chalky. "Oh, no, sir! I can't understand how she got *out*. She couldn't walk a step. If she'd been carried, *some one* would have noticed. The doorman, sure. I just asked him. But nobody did. I know everythin' goes on—"

"Is it possible your husband may have seen one or both of them within the past two days?"

"Not Potter. He saw 'em night before last. Harry's been makin' a little side-money, sort of, see, sir. Miss Euphemia wanted the landlord to do some decoratin' and paperin', and a little carpentry, and they wouldn't do it. So, more'n a month ago, she asked Harry if he wouldn't do it on the sly, and she said she'd pay him, although less than if a reg'lar decorator did it. So he's been doin' it spare time, mostly late afternoons and nights—he's handy, Potter is. He's most done with the job. It's pretty paper, ain't it? So he saw Miss Euphemia night before last." A calamitous thought struck her, apparently, for her eyes rolled and she uttered a faint shriek. "I just thought if—if anythin's happened to the cripple, we won't get paid! All that work . . . And the landlord—"

"Yes, yes," said Ellery impatiently. "Mrs. Potter, are there mice or rats in this house?"

Both women looked blank. "Why, not a one of 'em," began Mrs. Potter slowly. "The exterminator comes—" when they all spun about at a sound from the foyer. Some one was opening the door.

"Come in," snapped Ellery, and strode forward; only to halt in his tracks as an anxious face poked timidly into the bedroom.

"Excuse me," said the newcomer nervously, starting at sight of Ellery and the two women. "I guess I must be in the wrong apartment. Does Miss Euphemia Tarkle live here?" He was a tall needle-thin young man with a scared, horsy face and stiff tan hair. He wore a rather rusty suit of old-fashioned cut and carried a small handbag.

"Yes, indeed," said Ellery with a friendly smile. "Come in, come in. May I ask who you are?"

The young man blinked. "But where's Aunt Euphemia? I'm Elias Morton, Junior. Isn't she here?" His reddish little eyes blinked from Ellery to Miss Curleigh in a puzzled, worried way.

"Did you say 'Aunt' Euphemia, Mr. Morton?"

"I'm her nephew. I come from out of town—Albany. Where—"

Ellery murmured: "An unexpected visit, Mr. Morton?"

The young man blinked again; he was still holding his bag. Then he dumped it on the floor and eagerly fumbled in his pockets until he produced a much-soiled and wrinkled letter. "I—I got this only a few days ago," he faltered. "I'd have come sooner, only my father went off somewhere on a—I don't understand this."

Ellery snatched the letter from his lax fingers. It was scrawled painfully on a piece of ordinary brown wrapping paper; the envelope was a cheap one. The pencilled scribble, in the crabbed hand of age, said:

Dear Elias:—You have not heard from your Auntie for so many years, but now I need you, Elias, for you are my only blood kin to whom I can turn in my Dire Distress! I am in great danger, my dear boy. You must help your poor Invalid Aunt who is so helpless. *Come at once.* Do not tell your Father or any one, Elias! When you get here make believe you

have come just for a Visit. Remember. Please, please
do not fail me. Help me, please! Your Loving Aunt—
                                          Euphemia

"Remarkable missive," frowned Ellery. "Written
under stress, Miss Curleigh. Genuine enough. Don't
tell any one, eh? Well, Mr. Morton, I'm afraid you're
too late."

"Too— But—" The young man's horse-face whit-
ened. "I tried to come right off, b-but my father had
gone off somewhere on a—on one of his drunken spells
and I couldn't find him. I didn't know what to do. Then
I came. T-t-to think—" His buck teeth were chattering.

"This *is* your aunt's handwriting?"

"Oh, yes. Oh, yes."

"Your father, I gather, is not a brother of the Tarkle
sisters?"

"No, sir. My dear mother w-was their sister, God
rest her." Morton groped for a chair-back. "Is Aunt
Euphemia—d-dead? And where's Aunt Sarah?"

"They're both gone." Ellery related tersely what he
had found. The young visitor from Albany looked as if
he might faint. "I'm—er—unofficially investigating this
business, Mr. Morton. Tell me all you know about your
two aunts."

"I don't know m-much," mumbled Morton. "Haven't
seen them for about fifteen years, since I was a kid.
I heard from my Aunt Sarah-Ann once in a while, and
only twice from Aunt Euphemia. They never— I never
expected— I do know that Aunt Euphemia since her
stroke became . . . funny. Aunt Sarah wrote me that.
She had some money—I don't know how much—left
her by my grandfather, and Aunt Sarah said she was a
real miser about it. Aunt Sarah didn't have anything;
she had to live with Aunt Euphemia and take care of
her. She wouldn't trust banks, Aunt Sarah said, and had
hidden the money somewhere about her, Aunt Sarah

didn't know where. She wouldn't even have doctors after her stroke, she was—is so stingy. They didn't get along; they were always fighting, Aunt Sarah wrote me, and Aunt Euphemia was always accusing her of trying to steal her money, and she didn't know how she stood it. That-that's about all I know, sir.''

"The poor things," murmured Miss Curleigh with moist eyes. "What a wretched existence! Miss Tarkle can't be responsible for—"

"Tell me, Mr. Morton," drawled Ellery, "it's true that your Aunt Euphemia detested cats?"

The lantern-jaw dropped. "Why, how'd you know? She hates them. Aunt Sarah wrote me that many times. It hurt her a lot, because *she's* so crazy about them she treats her own like a child, you see, and that makes Aunt Euphemia jealous, or angry, or something. I guess they just didn't—don't get along.''

"We seem to be having a pardonable difficulty with our tenses," said Ellery. "After all, Mr. Morton, there's no evidence to show that your aunts aren't merely off somewhere on a vacation, or a visit, perhaps." But the glint in his eyes remained. "Why don't you stop at a hotel somewhere nearby? I'll keep you informed." He scribbled the name and address of a hotel in the Seventies on the page of a notebook, and thrust it into Morton's damp palm. "Don't worry. You'll hear from me." And he hustled the bewildered young man out of the apartment. They heard the click of the elevator-door a moment later.

Ellery said slowly: "The country cousin in full panoply. Miss Curleigh, let me look at your refreshing loveliness. People with faces like that should be legislated against." He frowned as he patted her cheek, hesitated, and then made for the bathroom. Miss Curleigh blushed once more and followed him quickly, casting another apprehensive glance over her shoulder.

"What's this?" she heard Ellery say sharply. "Mrs. Potter, come out of that— By George!"

"What's the matter now?" cried Miss Curleigh, dashing into the bathroom behind him.

Mrs. Potter, the flesh of her powerful forearms crawling with goose-pimples, her tired eyes stricken, was glaring with open mouth into the tub. The woman made a few inarticulate sounds, rolled her eyes alarmingly, and then fled from the apartment.

Miss Curleigh said: "Oh, my God," and put her hand to her breast. "Isn't that—isn't that *horrible!*"

"Horrible," said Ellery grimly and slowly, "and illuminating. I overlooked it when I glanced in here before. I think . . ." He stopped and bent over the tub. There was no humor in his eyes or voice now; only a sick watchfulness. They were both very quiet. Death lay over them.

A black tomcat, limp and stiff and boneless, lay in a welter and smear of blood in the tub. He was large, glossy black, green-eyed, and indubitably dead. His head was smashed in and his body seemed broken in several places. His blood had clotted in splashes on the porcelain sides of the tub. The weapon, hurled by a callous hand, lay beside him: a blood-splattered bathbrush with a heavy handle.

"That solves the mystery of the disappearance of at least one of the seven," murmured Ellery, straightening. "Battered to death with the brush. He hasn't been dead more than a day or so, either, from the looks of him. Miss Curleigh, we're engaged in a tragic business."

But Miss Curleigh, her first shock of horror swept away by rage, was crying: "Anyone who would kill a puss so brutally is—is a monster!" Her silvery eyes were blazing. "That terrible old woman—"

"Don't forget," sighed Ellery, "she can't walk."

* * *

"Now this," said Mr. Ellery Queen some time later, putting away his cunning and compact little pocket-kit, "is growing more and more curious, Miss Curleigh. Have you any notion what I've found here?"

They were back in the bedroom again, stooped over the bedtray which he had picked up from the floor and deposited on the night-table between the missing sisters' beds. Miss Curleigh had recalled that on all her previous visits she had found the tray on Miss Tarkle's bed or on the table, the invalid explaining with a tightening of her pale lips that she had taken to eating alone of late, implying that she and the long-suffering Sarah-Ann had reached a tragic parting of the ways.

"I saw you mess about with powder and things, but—"

"Fingerprint test." Ellery stared enigmatically down at the knife, fork, and spoon lying awry in the tray. "My kit's a handy gadget at times. You saw me test this cutlery, Miss Curleigh. You would say that these implements had been used by Euphemia in the process of eating her last meal here?"

"Why, of course," frowned Miss Curleigh. "You can still see the dried food clinging to the knife and fork."

"Exactly. The handles of knife, fork, and spoon are not engraved, as you see—simple silver surfaces. They should bear fingerprints." He shrugged. "But they don't."

"What do you mean, Mr. Queen? How is that possible?"

"I mean that some one has wiped this cutlery free of prints. Odd, eh?" Ellery lit a cigaret absently. "Examine it, however. This is Euphemia Tarkle's bedtray, her food, her dishes, her cutlery. She is known to eat in bed, and alone. But if only Euphemia handled the cutlery, who wiped off the prints? She? Why should she? Some one else? But surely there would be no sense in some one else's wiping off *Euphemia's* prints. Her fingerprints have a right to be there. Then, while Euphemia's prints were probably on these implements, some one else's prints were also on them, which accounts for their having been wiped off. Some one else, therefore, handled Euphemia's cutlery. Why? I begin,'' said Ellery in the grimmest of voices, "to see daylight. Miss Curleigh, would you like to serve as handmaiden to Justice?'' Miss Curleigh, overwhelmed, could only nod. Ellery began to wrap the cold food leftovers from the invalid's tray. "Take this truck down to Dr. Samuel Prouty—here's his address—and ask him to analyze it for me. Wait there, get his report, and meet me back here. Try to get in here without being observed.''

"The *food?*''

"The food.''

"Then you think it's been—''

"The time for thinking,'' said Mr. Ellery Queen evenly, "is almost over.''

When Miss Curleigh had gone, he took a final look around, even to the extent of examining some empty cupboards which had a look of newness about them, set his lips firmly, locked the front door behind him—pocketing the master-key which Mrs. Potter had given him—took the elevator to the ground floor, and rang the bell of the Potter apartment.

A short thickset man with heavy, coarse features opened the door; his hat was pushed back on his head. Ellery saw the agitated figure of Mrs. Potter hovering in the background.

"That's the policeman!'' shrilled Mrs. Potter. "Harry, don't get mixed up in—''

"Oh, so you're the dick,'' growled the thickset man, ignoring the fat woman. "I'm the super here—Harry Potter. I just got home from the plant and my wife tells me there's somethin' wrong up in the Tarkle flat. What's up, for God's sake?''

"Now, now, there's no cause for panic, Potter," murmured Ellery. "Glad you're home, though; I'm in dire need of information which you can probably provide. Has either of you found anywhere on the premises recently—*any dead cats*?"

Potter's jaw dropped, and his wife gurgled with surprise. "Now that's damn' funny. We sure have. Mrs. Potter says one of 'em's dead up in 5-C now—I never thought *those* two old dames might be the ones—"

"Where did you find them, and how many?" snapped Ellery.

"Why, down in the incinerator. Basement."

Ellery smacked his thigh. "Of course! What a stupid idiot I am. I see it all now. The incinerator, eh? There were six, Potter, weren't there?"

Mrs. Potter gasped: "How'd you know that, for mercy's sake?"

"Incinerator," muttered Ellery, sucking his lower lip. "The bones, I suppose—the skulls?"

"That's right," exclaimed Potter; he seemed distressed. "I found 'em myself. Empty out the incinerator every mornin' for ash-removal. Six cats' skulls and a mess o' little bones. I raised hell around here with the tenants lookin' for the damn' fool who threw 'em down the chute but they all played dumb. Didn't all come down the same time. It's been goin' now maybe four-five weeks. One a week, almost. The damn' fools. I'd like to get my paws on—"

"You're certain you found six?"

"Sure."

"And nothing else of a suspicious nature?"

"No, *sir*."

"Thanks. I don't believe there will be any more trouble. Just forget the whole business." And Ellery pressed a bill into the man's hand and strolled out of the lobby.

He did not stroll far. He strolled, in fact, only to the sidewalk steps leading down into the basement and cellar. Five minutes later he quietly let himself into Apartment 5-C again.

When Miss Curleigh stopped before the door to Apartment 5-C in late afternoon, she found it locked. She could hear Ellery's voice murmuring inside and a moment later the click of a telephone receiver. Reassured, she pressed the bell-button; he appeared instantly, pulled her inside, noiselessly shut the door again, and led her to the bedroom, where she slumped into a rosewood chair, an expression of bitter disappointment on her pleasant little face.

"Back from the wars, I see," he grinned. "Well, sister, what luck?"

"You'll be dreadfully put out," said Miss Curleigh with a scowl. "I'm sorry I haven't been more helpful—"

"What did good Dr. Prouty say?"

"Nothing encouraging. I like your Dr. Prouty, even if he *is* the Medical Examiner or something and wears a horrible little peaked hat in the presence of a lady; but I can't say I'm keen about his reports. He says there's not a thing wrong with that food you sent by me! It's a little putrefied from standing, but otherwise it's pure enough."

"Now isn't that too bad?" said Ellery cheerfully. "Come, come, Diana, perk up. It's the best news you could have brought me."

"Best n—" began Miss Curleigh with a gasp.

"It substitutes fact for theory very nicely. Fits, lassie, like a *brassière* on Mae West. We have," and he pulled over a chair and sat down facing her, "arrived. By the way, did any one see you enter this apartment?"

"I slipped in by the basement and took the elevator from there. No one saw me, I'm sure. But I don't underst—"

"Commendable efficiency. I believe we have some time for expatiation. I've had an hour or so here alone for thought, and it's been a satisfactory if morbid business." Ellery lit a cigaret and crossed his legs lazily. "Miss Curleigh, you have sense, plus the advantage of an innate feminine shrewdness, I'm sure. Tell me: Why should a wealthy old lady who is almost completely paralyzed stealthily purchase six cats within a period of five weeks?"

Miss Curleigh shrugged. "I told you I couldn't make it out. It's a deep, dark mystery to me." Her eyes were fixed on his lips.

"Pshaw, it can't be as completely baffling as all that. Very well, I'll give you a rough idea. For example, so many cats purchased by an eccentric in so short a period suggests—vivisection. But neither of the Tarkle ladies is anything like a scientist. So that's out. You see?"

"Oh, yes," said Miss Curleigh breathlessly. "I see now what you mean. Euphemia couldn't have wanted them for companionship, either, because she hates cats!"

"Precisely. Let's wander. For extermination of mice? No, this is from Mrs. Potter's report a pest-free building. For mating? Scarcely; Sarah-Ann's cat was a male, and Euphemia also bought only males. Besides, they were nondescript tabbies, and people don't play Cupid to nameless animals."

"She might have bought them for gifts," said Miss Curleigh with a frown. "That's possible."

"Possible, but I think not," said Ellery dryly. "Not when you know the facts. The superintendent found the skeletal remains of six cats in the ashes of the incinerator downstairs, and the other one lies, a very dead pussy, in the bathtub yonder." Miss Curleigh stared at him, speechless. "We seem to have covered the more plausible theories. Can you think of some wilder ones?"

Miss Curleigh paled. "Not—not for their *fur*?"

"Brava," said Ellery with a laugh. "There's a wild one among wild ones. No, not for their fur; I haven't found any fur in the apartment. And besides, no matter who killed Master Tom in the tub, he remains bloody but unskinned. I think, too, that we can discard the even wilder food theory; to civilized people killing cats for food smacks of cannibalism. To frighten Sister Sarah-Ann? Hardly; Sarah is used to cats and loves them. To scratch Sarah-Ann to death? That suggests poisoned claws. But in that case there would be as much danger to Euphemia as to Sarah-Ann; and why *six* cats? As—er—guides in eternal dark? But Euphemia is not blind, and besides she never leaves her bed. Can you think of any others?"

"But those things are *ridiculous*!"

"Don't call my logical meanderings names. Ridiculous, perhaps, but you can't ignore even apparent nonsense in an elimination."

"Well, I've got one that isn't nonsense," said Miss Curleigh suddenly. "Pure hatred. Euphemia loathed cats. So, since she's cracked, I suppose, she's bought them just for the pleasure of exterminating them."

"All black tomcats with green eyes and identical dimensions?" Ellery shook his head. "Her mania could scarcely have been so exclusive. Besides, she loathed cats even before Sarah-Ann bought her distinctive tom from you. No, there's only one left that I can think of, Miss Curleigh." He sprang from the chair and began to pace the floor. "It's not only the sole remaining possibility, but it's confirmed by several things . . . *Protection.*"

"Protection!" Miss Curleigh's devastating eyes widened. "Why, Mr. Queen. How could that be? People buy dogs for protection, not cats."

"I don't mean that kind of protection," said Ellery impatiently. "I'm referring to a compound of desire to remain alive and an incidental hatred for felines that makes them the ideal instrument toward that end. This is a truly horrifying business, Marie. From every angle. Euphemia Tarkle was afraid. Of what? Of being murdered for her money. That's borne out amply by the letter she wrote to Morton, her nephew; and it's bolstered by her reputed miserliness, her distrust of banks, and her dislike for her own sister. How would a cat be protection against intended murder?''

"Poison!" cried Miss Curleigh.

"Exactly. *As a food-taster.* There's a reversion to mediævalism for you! Are there confirming data? A-plenty. Euphemia had taken to eating alone of late; that suggests some secret activity. Then she re-ordered cats five times within a short period. Why? Obviously, because each time her cat, purchased from you, had acted in his official capacity, tasted her food, and gone the way of all enslaved flesh. The cats were poisoned, poisoned by food intended for Euphemia. So she had to re-order. Final confirmation: the six feline skeletons in the incinerator."

"But she can't walk," protested Miss Curleigh. "So how could she dispose of the bodies?"

"I fancy Mrs. Potter innocently disposed of them for her. You'll recall that Mrs. Potter said she was often called here to take garbage to the incinerator for Euphemia when Sarah-Ann was out. The 'garbage,' wrapped up, I suppose, was a cat's dead body."

"But why all the black, green-eyed tomcats of the same size?"

"Self-evident. Why? Obviously, again, *to fool Sarah-Ann.* Because Sarah-Ann had a black tomcat of a certain size with green eyes, Euphemia purchased from you identical animals. Her only reason for this could have been, then, to fool Sarah-Ann into believing that the black tom she saw about the apartment at any given time was her own, the original one. That suggests, of course, that Euphemia used Sarah-Ann's cat to foil the

first attempt, and Sarah-Ann's cat was the first poison-
victim. When he died, Euphemia bought another from
you—without her sister's knowledge.

"How Euphemia suspected she was slated to be poisoned, of course, at the very time in which the poisoner
got busy, we'll never know. It was probably the merest
coincidence, something psychic—you never know about
slightly mad old ladies."

"But if she was trying to fool Sarah-Ann about the
cats," whispered Miss Curleigh, aghast, "then she suspected—"

"Precisely. She suspected her sister of trying to poison her."

Miss Curleigh bit her lip. "Would you mind giving
me a—a cigaret? I'm—" Ellery silently complied. "It's
the most terrible thing I've ever heard of. Two old
women, sisters, practically alone in the world, one dependent on the other for attention, the other for subsis-
tence, living at cross-purposes—the invalid helpless to
defend herself against attacks. . . ." She shuddered.
"What's *happened* to those poor creatures, Mr.
Queen?"

"Well, let's see. Euphemia is missing. We know that
there were at least six attempts to poison her, all unsuccessful. It's logical to assume that there was a seventh attempt, then, and that—since Euphemia is gone
under mysterious circumstances—*the seventh attempt
was successful.*"

"But how can you *know* she's—she's dead?"

"Where is she?" asked Ellery dryly. "The only other
possibility is that she fled. But she's helpless, can't
walk, can't stir from bed without assistance. Who can
assist her? Only Sarah-Ann, the very one she suspects
of trying to poison her. The letter to her nephew shows
that she wouldn't turn to Sarah-Ann. So flight is out
and, since she's missing, she must be dead. Now, follow. Euphemia knew she was the target of poisoning

attacks via her food, and took precautions against them; then how did the poisoner finally penetrate her defenses—the seventh cat? Well, we may assume that Euphemia made the seventh cat taste the food we found on the tray. We know that food was not poisoned, from Dr. Prouty's report. The cat, then, didn't die of poisoning from the food itself—confirmed by the fact that he was beaten to death. But if the cat didn't die of poisoned *food,* neither did Euphemia. Yet all the indications are that she must have died of poisoning. Then there's only one answer: she died of poisoning not in eating but *in the process of* eating.''

"I don't understand," said Miss Curleigh intently.

"The cutlery!" cried Ellery. "I showed you earlier this afternoon that some one other than Euphemia had handled her knife, spoon, and fork. Doesn't this suggest that the poisoner had *poisoned the cutlery* on his seventh attempt? If, for example, the fork had been coated with a colorless odorless poison which dried, Euphemia would have been fooled. The cat, flung bits of food by hand—for no one feeds an animal with cutlery—would live; Euphemia, eating the food with the poisoned cutlery, would die. Psychologically, too, it rings true. It stood to reason that the poisoner, after six unsuccessful attempts one way, should in desperation try a seventh with a variation. The variation worked and Euphemia, my dear, is dead.''

"But her body— Where—"

Ellery's face changed as he whirled noiselessly toward the door. He stood in an attitude of tense attention for an instant and then, without a word, laid violent hands upon the petrified figure of Miss Curleigh and thrust her rudely into one of the bedroom closets, shutting the door behind her. Miss Curleigh, half-smothered by a soft sea of musty-smelling feminine garments, held her breath. She had heard that faint scratching of metal upon metal at the front door. It must be—if Mr.

Queen acted so quickly—the poisoner. Why had he come back? she thought wildly. The key he was using— easy—a duplicate. Earlier when they had surprised him and he had barricaded the door, he must have entered the apartment by the roof and fire-escape window because he couldn't use the key . . . some one may have been standing in the hall. . . .

She choked back a scream, her thoughts snapping off as if a switch had been turned. A hoarse, harsh voice— the sounds of a struggle—a crash . . . they were fighting!

Miss Curleigh saw red. She flung open the door of the closet and plunged out. Ellery was on the floor in a tangle of threshing arms and legs. A hand came up with a knife . . . Miss Curleigh sprang and kicked in an instantaneous reflex action. Something snapped sharply, and she fell back, sickened, as the knife dropped from a broken hand.

"Miss Curleigh—the door!" panted Ellery, pressing his knee viciously downward. Through a dim roaring in her ears Miss Curleigh heard pounding on the door, and tottered toward it. The last thing she remembered before she fainted was a weird boiling of blue-clad bodies as police poured past her to fall upon the struggling figures.

"It's all right now," said a faraway voice, and Miss Curleigh opened her eyes to find Mr. Ellery Queen, cool and immaculate, stooping over her. She moved her head dazedly. The fireplace, the crossed swords on the wall . . . "Don't be alarmed, Marie," grinned Ellery; "this isn't an abduction. You have achieved Valhalla. It's all over, and you're reclining on the divan in my apartment."

"Oh," said Miss Curleigh, and she swung her feet unsteadily to the floor. "I—I must look a sight. What happened?"

"We caught the bogey very satisfactorily. Now you rest, young lady, while I rustle a dish of tea—"

"Nonsense!" said Miss Curleigh with asperity. "I want to know how you performed that miracle. Come on, now, don't be irritating!"

"Yours to command. Just what do you want to know?"

"Did you *know* that awful creature was coming back?"

Ellery shrugged. "It was a likely possibility. Euphemia had been poisoned, patently, for her hidden money. She must have been murdered at the very latest yesterday—you recall yesterday's milk-bottle—perhaps the night before last. Had the murderer found the money after killing her? Then who was the prowler whom we surprised this afternoon and who made his escape out the window after barricading the door? It must have been the murderer. But if he came back *after* the crime, then he had not found the money when he committed the crime. Perhaps he had so much to do immediately after the commission of the crime that he had no time to search. At any rate, on his return we surprised him— probably just after he had made a mess of the bed. It was quite possible that he had still not found the money. If he had not, I knew he would come back—after all, he had committed the crime for it. So I took the chance that he would return when he thought the coast was clear, and he did. I 'phoned for police assistance while you were out seeing Dr. Prouty."

"Did you *know* who it was?"

"Oh, yes. It was demonstrable. The first qualification of the poisoner was availability; that is, in order to make those repeated poisoning attempts, the poisoner had to be near Euphemia or near her food at least since the attempts began, which was presumably five weeks ago. The obvious suspect was her sister. Sarah-Ann had motive—hatred and possibly cupidity; and certainly opportunity, since she prepared the food herself. But Sarah-Ann I eliminated on the soundest basis in the world.

"For who had brutally beaten to death the seventh black tomcat? Palpably, either the victim or the murderer in a general sense. But it couldn't have been Euphemia, since the cat was killed in the bathroom and Euphemia lay paralyzed in the bedroom, unable to walk. Then it must have been the murderer who killed the cat. But if Sarah-Ann were the murderer, would she have clubbed to death a cat—she, who loved cats? Utterly inconceivable. Therefore Sarah-Ann was not the murderer."

"Then what—"

"I know. What happened to Sarah-Ann?" Ellery grimaced. "Sarah-Ann, it is to be feared, went the way of the cat and her sister. It must have been the poisoner's plan to kill Euphemia and have it appear that Sarah-Ann had killed her—the obvious suspect. Sarah-Ann, then, should be on the scene. But she isn't. Well, her disappearance tends to show—I think the confession will bear me out—that she was accidentally a witness to the murder and was killed by the poisoner on the spot to eliminate a witness to the crime. He wouldn't have killed her under any other circumstances."

"Did you find the money?"

"Yes. Lying quite loosely," shrugged Ellery, "between the pages of a Bible Euphemia always kept in her bed. The Poe touch, no doubt."

"And," quavered Miss Curleigh, "the bodies. . . ."

"Surely," drawled Ellery, "the incinerator? It would have been the most logical means of disposal. Fire is virtually all-consuming. What bones there were could have been disposed of more easily than . . . Well, there's no point in being literal. You know what I mean."

"But that means— Who was that fiend on the floor? I

never saw him before. It couldn't have been Mr. Morton's f-father . . . ?"

"No, indeed. Fiend, Miss Curleigh?" Ellery raised his eyebrows. "There's only a thin wall between sanity and—"

"You called me," said Miss Curleigh, "Marie before."

Ellery said hastily: "No one but Sarah-Ann and Euphemia lived in the apartment, yet the poisoner had access to the invalid's food for over a month—apparently without suspicion. Who could have had such access? Only one person: the man who had been decorating the apartment in late afternoons and evenings—around dinner-time—for over a month; the man who worked in a chemical plant and therefore, better than any one, had knowledge of and access to poisons; the man who tended the incinerator and therefore could dispose of the bones of his human victims without danger to himself. In a word," said Ellery, "the superintendent of the building, Harry Potter."

A Little Intelligence

RANDALL GARRETT

Sister Mary Magdalene felt apprehensive. She glanced worriedly at the priest facing her and said, "But—I don't understand. Why quarter the aliens *here*?"

Her gesture took in her office, the monastery, the convent, the school, the Cathedral of the Blessed Sacrament. "Because," said Father Destry patronizingly, "there is nothing here for them to learn."

The nun eyed Father Destry uneasily. The single votive candle flickering before the statue of the Virgin in the wall niche beside him cast odd shadows over his craggy, unhandsome face. She said, "You mean that the beings of Capella IX are so well versed in the teachings of the Church that they couldn't even learn anything here?'' She added with innocent sarcasm, ''My, how wonderful for them!''

''Not quite, Sister. The Earth Government isn't worried about the chances of the Pogatha learning anything about the Church. But the Pogatha would be hard put to learn anything about Terrestrial science in a Cathedral.''

''The walls are full of gadgets,'' she said, keeping her voice flat. ''Vestment color controls, sound suppressor fields for the confessional, illumination—''

''I know, I know,'' the priest interrupted testily. ''I'm talking specifically about military information. And I don't expect them to tear down our walls to learn the secrets of the vestment color controls.''

Sister Mary Magdalene shrugged. She had been deliberately baiting Father Destry, and she realized she was taking out on him her resentment against the government for having dumped a delegation of alien beings into her otherwise peaceful life.

''I see,'' she said. ''While the—Pogatha?—Pogatha delegation is here, they're to be kept within the cathedral grounds. The Earth government is assuming they'll be safe here.''

''Not only that, but the Pogatha themselves will feel safer here. They know Terrestrial feelings still run high since the war, and they know there could be no violence here. The Government wanted to keep them in a big hotel somewhere—a place that would be as secure as any. But the Pogatha would have none of it.''

''And one last question, Father. Why does it fall to the Sisters of the Holy Nativity to put them up? Why can't the Holy Cross Fathers take care of them? I mean—really, I understand that they're alien beings, but they *are* humanoid—''

''Quite so. They are females.''

The nun's eyebrows rose. ''They are?''

Father Destry blushed faintly. ''I won't go into the

biology of Capella IX, partly because I don't completely understand it myself. But they do have a matri-
archal society. They are oviparous mammals, but the
rearing of children is always left to the males, the physically weaker sex. The fighters and diplomats are definitely female.''

"In that case"—the nun shrugged in defeat—"if
those are the bishop's wishes, I'll see that they're carried out. I'll make the necessary arrangements.'' She
glanced at her wristwatch and said curtly, "It's almost
time for Vespers, Father.''

The priest rose. "The Government is preparing a
brochure on the—ah—physical needs of the Pogatha.
I'll have it sent to you as soon as it arrives.''

"*Care and Feeding of Aliens,* eh? Very well, father.
I'll do my best.''

"I'm sure you will, Sister." He looked down at his
hands as though suddenly unsure of himself. "I know
this may be a hard job, Sister, but"—he looked up,
smiling suddenly—"you'll make it. The prayers of everyone here will be with you.''

"Thank you, Father.''

The priest turned and walked out. Sister Mary Magdalene, unhappily conscious that though she respected
Father Destry's learning and piety she could feel no
warmth toward him as a person, watched him depart.
As he reached the door a lithe coal-black shape padded
over to him and rubbed itself lingeringly against the
priest's legs.

Father Destry smiled at the cat, but it was a hollow,
artificial smile. The priest did not enjoy the affections
of Sister Mary Magdalene's pet. He closed the office
door.

The cat leaped to the top of the nun's desk.

"Miaou,'' it said calmly.

"Exactly, Felicity,'' said Sister Mary Magdalene.

* * *

Sister Mary Magdalene spent the next two days reading the digests of the war news. She had not, she was
forced to admit, kept up with the war as much as she
might have. Granted, a nun was supposed to have re-
nounced the devil, the flesh and the world, but it was
sometimes a good idea to check up and see what all
three were up to.

When the Government brochure came, she studied
it carefully, trying to get a complete picture of the
alien race that Earth was fighting. If she was going to
have to coddle them, she was going to have to know
them.

The beginning of the war was shrouded in mystery.
Earth forces had landed on Capella IX 30 years before
and had found a civilization two centuries behind that
of Earth, technologically speaking. During the next 20
years, the Pogatha had managed to beg, borrow and
steal enough technology from the Earth colonies to almost catch up. And then someone had blundered.

There had been an "incident"—and a shooting war
had begun. The Pogatha feeling, late in arising, was
that Earthmen had no right settling on Capella IX; they
were aliens who must be driven off. The colonists refused to abandon 20 years' effort without a fight.

It was a queer war. The colonists, badly outnum-
bered, had the advantage of technological superiority.
On the other hand, they were hindered by the necessity
of maintaining a supply line 42 light-years long, which
the Pogatha could and did disrupt. The colonists were
still dependent on Earth for war material and certain
supplies.

The war had waggled back and forth for nearly ten
years without any definite advantage to either side.
Thermonuclear weapons had not been used, since they
would leave only a shattered planet of no use to anyone.

Both sides were weary; both sides wanted to quit, if

it could be done without either side losing too much
face. Human beings had an advantage in that Earth itself was still whole, but the Pogatha had an almost equal
advantage in the length of the colonists' supply lines.
Earth would win eventually; that seemed obvious. But
at what cost? In the end, Earth would be forced to smash
the entire Pogatha civilization. And they did not want
to do that.

There was an element of pride in the Pogatha view-
point. They asked themselves: would not suicide be
better than ignominious slaughter at the hands of the
alien Earthmen? Unless a peace with honor could be
negotiated, the Pogatha would fight to the last Pogath,
and would quite likely use thermonuclear bombs in a
final blaze of self-destructive glory.

The four Pogatha who were coming to the little convent of the Cathedral Chapter of the Sisters of the Holy
Nativity were negotiators that had to be handled with
the utmost care. Sister Mary Magdalene was no military expert, and she was not an interstellar diplomat,
but she knew that the final disposition of a world might
rest with her. It was a heavy cross to bear for a woman
who had spent 20 years of her life as a nun.

Sister Mary Magdalene turned her school duties over
to Sister Angela. There was mild regret involved in this;
one of Sister Mary Magdalene's joys had been teaching
the dramatics class in the parochial high school. They
had been preparing a performance of *Murder in the
Cathedral* for the following month. Well, Sister Angela
could handle it well enough.

The supplies necessary for the well-being of the Pogatha were sent by the government, and they consisted
mostly of captured goods. A cookbook translated by
government experts came with the food, along with a
note: *"These foods are not for human consumption.
Since they are canned, there is no need to season them.*

Under no circumstances try to mix them with Terrestrial foods. Where water is called for, use only distilled water, never tap water. For other liquids, use only those provided.''

There was also a book of etiquette and table settings for four. The Pogatha would eat alone. There would be no diplomatic banquets here. Sister Mary Magdalene found out why when she went, accompanied by Felicity, to talk to the sisters who prepared the meals for the convent.

Sister Elizabeth was a plumpish, smiling woman who loved cooking and good food and who ruled her domain with an almost queenly air. Looking like a contented plump *hausfrau* in her kitchen uniform, she smiled as Sister Mary Magdalene came in.

"Good morning, Sister."

"Have you opened any of the Pogatha food cans yet?" the sister-in-charge wanted to know.

"I didn't know whether I should," Sister Elizabeth said. Seeing Felicity prowling on the worktable in search of scraps of food, she goodnaturedly waved at the cat and said, "Stay away from there, Felicity! That's lunch!"

The cat glowered at her and leaped to the floor.

Sister Mary Magdalene said, "I'd like to have a look at the stuff they're going to eat. Suppose you pick a can at random and we'll open it up."

Sister Elizabeth nodded and went into the storeroom. She returned carrying an ordinary-looking can. Its label was covered with queer script, and it bore a picture of a repulsive-looking little animal. Above the label was pasted a smaller label which read, in Roman characters, VAGHA.

Sister Mary Magdalene flipped open the translated Pogatha cookbook and ran her finger along the "V" section of the index. Finding her reference, she turned the pages and read. After a moment she announced,

"It's supposed to be something like rabbit stew. Go ahead and open it."

Sister Elizabeth put it in the opener and pressed the starter. The blade bit in. The top of the can lifted.

"*Whoof!*" said Sister Mary Magdalene.

"*Ugh!*" said Sister Elizabeth.

Even Felicity, who had been so interested that she had jumped up to the table to watch the proceedings, wrinkled her bewhiskered nose in disgust and backed away.

"It's spoiled," Sister Elizabeth said sadly.

But the odor was not quite that of decay. True, there was a background of Limburger cheese overlaid with musk, but this was punctuated pungently with something that smelled like a cross between butyl mercaptan and ammonia.

"No," said Sister Mary Magdalene unhappily. "It says in the book that the foods have distinctive odors."

"With the accent on the *stinc*. Do you mean I have to prepare stuff like that in my kitchen?"

"I'm afraid so," said Sister Mary Magdalene.

"But everything else will smell like that! It'll absolutely ruin everything!"

"You'll just have to keep our own food covered. And remember that ours smells just as bad to them."

Sister Elizabeth nodded, tightlipped, the joviality gone from her face. Now she, too, had her cross to bear.

The appearance of the Pogatha, when they finally arrived, did not shock Sister Mary Magdalene; she had been prepared for the sight of ugly caricatures of human beings by the photographs in the brochure. Nor was she bothered by the faint aroma, not after the much stronger smell of the can of stew. But to have one of them address her in nearly perfect English almost floored her.

Somehow she had simply not prepared herself for intelligent speech from alien lips.

Father Destry had brought them in from the spaceport, along with the two Earthmen who were their honor escort. She had been watching the courtyard through the window of her office, and had thought she was quite prepared for them when Father Destry escorted them into the office.

"Sister Mary Magdalene, permit me to introduce our guests. This is Vor Nollig, chief diplomat, and her assistants: Vor Betla, Vor Gontakel and Vor Vun."

And Vor Nollig said, "I am honored, Sister."

The voice was deep, like that of a man's, and there was certainly nothing effeminate about these creatures. The nun, in her surprise, could only choke out a hasty: "Thank you." Then she stood back, trying to keep a pleasant smile on her face while the others spoke their pieces.

They were not tall—no taller than Sister Mary Magdalene's own five five—but they were massively built. Their clothing was full and bright-colored. And, in spite of their alienness, the nun could tell them apart with no difficulty. Vor Nollig and Vor Betla had skins of a vivid cobalt-blue color. Vor Gontakel was green, while Vor Vun was yellow.

The Government brochure, Sister Mary Magdalene recalled, had remarked that the Pogatha had races that differed from each other as did the races of Earth. The blue color was a pigment, while the yellow color was the color of their blood—thus giving the Pogatha a range of yellow-green-blue shades according to the varying amount of pigment in the skin.

In an odd parallel to Earth history, the Blues had long been the dominant race, holding the others in subjection. It had been less than a century ago that the Yellows had been released from slavery, and the Greens were still poverty-stricken underdogs. Only the coming of the Earthmen had brought the three races together in a common cause.

Father Destry was introducing the two Earthmen.

". . . Secretary Masterson and Secretary Bass. They will be staying at the Holy Cross Monastery during the negotiations."

Sister Mary Magdalene had recovered her composure by now. Looking around with a sweeping gesture that took in Father Destry, the four aliens, the stocky Masterson and the elongated Bass, she said, "Won't you all sit down?"

"You are most gracious," said Vor Nollig brusquely, "but our trip has been a long one, and we are most anxious to—ah—the word—freshen up, is it?"

The nun nodded. "I'll show you to your rooms."

"You are most kind."

"I think you'll find everything prepared. If you don't, just ask for whatever you'll need."

She left the men in her office and escorted the four Pogatha outside, across to the part of the convent where they would be staying. When the aliens were installed in their rooms, Sister Mary Magdalene returned to her office and was surprised to find Father Destry and the two U.N. Secretaries still there. She had supposed that the priest would have taken the U.N. men over to the monastery.

"About the Pogatha," said Secretary Masterson with a nervous quirk of his fleshy lips. "Be rather careful with them, will you, Sister? They're rather—uh—prejudiced, you see."

"So am I. Against them, that is."

"No, no. I don't mean prejudiced against you or any other human. Naturally we don't expect much genuine warmth between peoples who are fighting. But I'm referring to the strong racial antipathy among themselves."

"Between the Blues, Yellows and the Greens," Secretary Bass put in. "They try to be polite to each other, but there's no socializing. It's a different kind of prejudice entirely, Sister."

"Yes," Masterson said. "Any one of them might be willing to sit down to talk to you, but not while one of another color was around."

"I see," said the sister. "I'll keep that in mind. Is there anything else I should remember?"

Secretary Masterson smiled understandingly. "It's hard to say. Handling an alien race isn't easy—but remember, they don't expect us to do everything right. They just want us to show that we're not purposely trying to offend them."

"I'll do my best," said Sister Mary Magdalene.

An hour later, Sister Mary Magdalene decided that she, in her capacity as a hostess here at the convent, had best go around to see how her guests were doing. Her robes swished softly as she went down the hallway. Behind her, Felicity padded silently along.

Sister Mary Magdalene paused outside Vor Nollig's door and rapped. After a moment it opened a little. The alien was dimly visible just inside the doorway.

"Yes, Sister?" said Vor Nollig.

Sister Mary Magdalene forced herself to smile ingratiatingly. "I hope everything's satisfactory."

"Oh, yes. Yes indeed." The door opened another few inches, far enough to let the nun see that Vor Betla stood behind Vor Nollig.

"Please you yes come in?" asked Vor Betla diffidently. There was something in the alien's tone that indicated that the invitation had been offered in an attempt at politeness, and that the Pogatha woman was not anxious to have it actually accepted.

Sister Mary Magdalene was still trying to decide what she should say when suddenly Vor Betla looked down and in a startled voice said, "What is?"

The nun's glance went to the floor. Felicity was standing there, her gleaming green eyes observing the Pogath woman intently. Sister Mary Magdalene scooped the cat up affectionately and held it against her. "This is Felicity. My cat."

"Gat?" said Vor Betla, puzzled.

"Cat," Vor Nollig corrected her. A babble of incomprehensible syllables followed. Finally Vor Nollig turned to the nun and said softly, "Pardon my breach of etiquette, but Vor Betla doesn't understand your language too well. She had never heard of a cat, and I was explaining that they are dumb animals kept as pets. We do not keep such animals on Pogathan."

"I see," said Sister Mary Magdalene, trying to keep the chill out of her voice. She was not pleased by the slighting reference to the cat. "If everything is fine, I'll look after my other guests. If you need anything, just ask."

"Of course, Sister," said Vor Nollig, closing the door.

The nun repressed what would have been an irrational and sinful current of anger. She swept on down the hall to the next apartment and knocked. "Poor Felicity," she murmured soothingly to the cat resting on her other arm. "Don't let their insults upset you. After all, they aren't humans, you know."

The door opened.

"I beg pardon?" said the green-skinned Vor Gontakel.

"Oh," Sister Mary Magdalene said, feeling awkward. "Sorry. I was talking to Felicity."

"Ah," said the green Pogatha.

"We came to see if everything was comfortable in your room. Didn't we, Felicity?"

"Meerorow," Felicity said.

"Oh, yes," said Vor Gontakel. "All is quite as should be. Quite."

"Meerowou," Felicity said. "Mrourr."

Vor Gontakel said, "This means what?"

Sister Mary Magdalene smiled. "Felicity says she hopes you'll call us if anything is not to your liking."

Vor Gontakel smiled broadly, showing her golden teeth. "I am quite comfortable, thank you, Sister. And thank you, Felicity."

The door closed. Sister Mary Magdalene felt more cheerful. Vor Gontakel had at least been pleasant.

One more trip to make. The last, thank Heaven. The nun rapped on the final door.

Vor Vun slowly opened her door, peered out, stepped back in alarmed distaste. "A cat!" she exclaimed.

"I'm sorry if I frightened you," Sister Mary Magdalene said quickly.

"Frightened? No. I just do not like cats. When I was a prisoner aboard one of your spaceships, they had a cat." The alien woman held out a saffron-skinned arm. Three furrows of scar tissue stood out darkly. "I was scratched. Infection set in, and none of the Earthmen's medicine could be used. It is a good thing that there was an exchange of prisoners, or I might have died."

The alien paused, as if realizing that her speech was not precisely diplomatic. "I am sorry," she said, forcing a smile. "But—you understand?"

"Certainly," the nun said. For the third time in ten minutes she went through the necessary ritual of asking after her guest's comfort, and for the third time she was assured that all was well.

Sister Mary Magdalene returned to her office. "Come on, Felicity," she whispered soothingly. "Can't have you worrying our star boarders."

Father Destry was waiting for Sister Mary Magdalene when she came back from Mass the following morning. He was looking at her with a puzzled air.

"Where is everyone?"

Ignoring his question for the moment, Sister Mary Magdalene jabbed furiously at the air conditioner button. "Isn't this thing working?" she asked fretfully of no one in particular. "It seems as though I can still smell it." Then she realized that the priest had addressed her, and that he was still waiting with imperious patience for an answer.

"Father Pierce kindly invited us to use the monastery chapel this morning," she said, feeling a twinge of embarrassment at her own unintentional rudeness. "Our own is too close to the kitchen."

Father Destry's face showed his lack of comprehension. "You went over to the monastery? Kitchen?"

Sister Mary Magdalene sighed patiently. "Father Destry, I'm morally certain that it would have been impossible for anyone to have retained a properly reverent attitude at Mass if it was held in a chapel that smelled to high Heaven of long dead fish!"

Her voice had risen in pitch during the last few words, and she cut off the crescendo with a sudden clamping together of her lips before her indignation distressed the priest. "The Pogatha rose early for breakfast. They wouldn't let Sister Elizabeth cook it. Vor Vun—that's the yellow one—did the honors, and each one ate in his—her—own room. That meant that those meals were carried from the kitchen to the rooms. You should have been here. We just barely made it through Lauds."

Father Destry was obviously trying to control a smile, which inwardly pleased Sister Mary Magdalene. It was encouraging to know that even Father Destry could be amused by something.

"I imagine the air conditioners have taken care of it by now," he said carefully. "I didn't notice a thing when I came through the courtyard." He glanced at the big clock on the wall. "The first meeting between the official representatives of Pogatha and Earth begins in an hour. I want—"

There was a rap at the door.

"Yes?"

Sister Martha, one of the younger nuns, entered. There was a vaguely apprehensive look on her young face. "The Pogatha are here to see you, Sister."

She stood aside while the four aliens trooped in, led by the imposing Blue, Vor Nollig. Sister Mary Magdalene greeted them with as much heartiness as she could muster, considering the episode of breakfast.

Vor Nollig said, "If it is at all possible, we would like to stroll around the grounds, look at your buildings. Perhaps you could take us on a tour?"

Hostess or not, the last thing Sister Mary Magdalene wanted to do now was shepherd the four aliens around the Cathedral grounds. She glanced meaningfully at Father Destry, who scowled faintly, then brightened and nodded.

"It would be a pleasure," the priest said. "I'll be glad to show you the Cathedral grounds."

And bless you for it, the nun thought as the little group left. After they had gone, she rubbed a finger speculatively across the tip of her nose. Was she wrong or did there seem to be something peculiar in the actions of the aliens? They had seemed to be in a tremendous hurry to leave, and the expressions on their faces were strained. Or were they? It was hard to correlate any Pogatha expressions with their human equivalents. And, of course, Sister Mary Magdalene was no expert on extraterrestrial psychology.

Abruptly she ceased worrying about the behavior of the Pogatha. With her finger still on her nose, she caught the aroma of the morning's coffee drifting from the kitchen, where it was being prepared. She smiled. Then she indulged in the first deep, joyous laugh she had had in two weeks.

* * *

That evening, after the Pogatha had returned to their quarters, Sister Mary Magdalene's private meditations were interrupted by a phone call from Secretary Masterson, the heavyset U.N. man. His fleshy face had a tense, worried look on it.

"Sister, I know this might be overstepping my authority, but I have the fate of a war to deal with."

"Just what's the trouble, Mr. Masterson?"

"At the meeting today, the Pogatha seemed—I don't quite know how to put it—*offended,* I suppose. They were touchy and unreasonable, and they quarrelled among themselves during the conference—all in a strictly diplomatic way, of course. I'm afraid we got rather touchy ourselves."

"How sad," the nun said. "We all have such high hopes for the success of these negotiations."

"Was there some incident that might have irritated them, Sister? I don't mean to imply any carelessness, but was there anything that might have upset them?"

"The only thing I can think of is the smell of the morning coffee," said the nun. "They came to me asking to be taken on a tour of the Cathedral grounds, and they seemed in an awful hurry to get out of the building. When they were gone I smelled the coffee being prepared. It must have nauseated them as much as their foods bother us."

Masterson's face cleared a little. "That might be it. They *are* touchy people, and maybe they thought the coffee odor that they found so revolting had been generated for their benefit." He paused for a long moment before he said, "Well, that sort of thing is too much for you, and it's obviously too much for them. I'll speak to Bishop Courtland tonight. We'll have to make better arrangements. Meanwhile, do you think you could do something about supper tonight? Get them out of there somehow, and—"

"That might be a little difficult," said Sister Mary Magdalene. "I think it would be better if we ate out."

"Very well. And I'll talk to the bishop."

She waited a moment for the screen to clear after Secretary Masterson broke contact, then dialed the number of the Holy Cross Monastery on the far side of the Cathedral. The face of a monk appeared on the screen, the cowl of his white robe lying in graceful folds around his throat.

Sister Mary Magdalene said, "Father Pierce, you were gracious enough to ask us to your chapel this morning because of the alien aroma here. I wonder if you'd be good enough to ask us to dinner tonight? Our alien friends don't seem to like our odors any more than we like theirs, and so we can't cook here."

Father Pierce laughed cheerfully. "We'll have to use the public dining hall, of course. But I think we can manage it."

"It'll have to be in two shifts," the nun said. "We can't leave this place deserted, much as we'd like to while they're eating."

"Don't worry, Sister. We'll arrange something. But what about tomorrow and the next day?"

Sister Mary Magdalene smiled. "We'll worry about that if we have to, but I think the Pogatha are on their way out of here. Secretary Masterson is going to make different arrangements with the bishop."

"You don't think they'll be transferred to *us*?"

"Hardly, Father Pierce. They'll have to leave the Cathedral entirely."

It was a pleasant, if ungracious, thought. But Sister Mary Magdalene had taken no vows to put herself and her nuns into great inconvenience for the sake of unpleasant alien creatures. She would be glad to see them go.

Morning came. Sister Mary Magdalene sat in Choir, listening to the words of the Divine Office and wondering why the Church had been chosen as a meeting place for the two so alien races. It had not been a successful meeting thus far; but, she pondered, was there some deeper reason for the coming-together than mere political negotiation?

The soft, sweet voices of the women, singing alternately from opposite sides of the chapel in the *Domine, Dominus noster*, were like the ringing of crystal chimes rather than the deeper, bell-like ringing that resounded from the throats of the monks on the opposite sides of the great cathedral.

And, like crystal, their voices seemed to shatter under the impact of the hoarse, ugly, bellowing scream that suddenly filled the air.

A moment later, the singing resumed, uncertainly but gamely, as monks and nuns compelled themselves to continue the service regardless. Sister Mary Magdalene felt the unaccustomed tingle of fear within her. What had happened? Trouble with the aliens? Or merely an excitable visitor taken aback by a surprise encounter with one of the Pogatha?

It might be almost anything. Tension grew within the nun. She had to know.

She rose from her seat and slipped away down the aisle. Behind her, the singing continued with renewed vigor. But that ungodly scream still echoed in her ears.

God in Heaven, thought Sister Mary Magdalene an hour later. *What are You doing to Your servants and hand-maidens now? Whoever heard of a convent full of cops?*

She hadn't realized that she had spoken the last sentence half aloud until she saw Father Destry's astonished and reproachful expression. She reddened at once.

"Please, Sister!" the priest murmured. "They're not

'cops'—they're World Bureau of Criminal Investigation officers!''

Sister Mary Magdalene nodded contritely and glanced through the open door of her office at the trio of big, bulky men who were conferring in low tones in the corridor. The label, she thought glumly, made no difference. WBCI or not, they were still *cops*.

The nun felt dazed. Too much had happened in the past hour. Sister Mary Magdalene felt as though everything were twisted and broken around her, as the body of Vor Nollig had been twisted and broken.

Vor Nollig, the Blue; Vor Nollig, the female Pogath; Vor Nollig, the Chief Diplomat of Pogathan—dead, with a common carving knife plunged into her abdomen and her alien blood all over the floor of the room in which she had slept the night before.

She still slept there. She would sleep eternally. The WBCI men had not yet removed the body.

Vor Betla, the other Blue, had found her, and it had been the outraged scream of Vor Betla that had broken the peace of the convent. Sister Mary Magdalene wondered bleakly if that peace would ever be whole again.

First the scream, then the violence of the raging fight as the other two Pogatha had tried to subdue Vor Betla, who seemed to be intent on destroying the convent with her bare hands. And now, the quiet warmth of Sister Mary Magdalene's inviolate little world had suddenly and jarringly been defiled by the entrance of a dozen men, one right after another. But they had come too late. The blood had already been shed.

"You look ill, Sister," said Father Destry, suddenly solicitous. "Wouldn't you like to lie down for a while!"

Sister Mary Magdalene shook her head violently. "No! No, I'll be all right. It's just the—the shock."

"The bishop gave me strict orders to make sure that none of this disturbs you."

"I know what he said, and I appreciate it. But I'm

afraid we have already been disturbed.'' There was a touch of acid in her voice.

Bishop Courtland, his fine old face looking haggard and unhappy, had come and gone again. Sister Mary Magdalene wished he had not gone, but there was no help for it; the bishop had to deal with the stratoplane load of high officials who had rocketed in as soon as the news had reached the Capital.

One of the WBCI men removed his hat in a gesture of respect and stepped into the nuns' office. She noticed out of the corner of her eye that the other WBCI men, belatedly remembering where they were, were taking their hats off, too.

''I'm Major Brock, Sister. Captain Lehmann told me that you're the sister-in-charge here.''

Sister Mary Magdalene nodded wordlessly. Captain Lehmann had been in charge of the group that had come rushing in at Father Destry's call; they had been hidden outside the cathedral grounds, ostensibly to protect the alien visitors.

''I know this is—unpleasant,'' Major Brock said. He was a big man who was obviously finding it difficult to keep his voice at the soft level he believed was appropriate in here. ''It's more than a matter of one life at stake, Sister. We have to find out who did this.''

Sister Mary Magdalene nodded, thinking, *The sooner you find out, the sooner all of you will leave here.* ''I'll do all I can to help,'' she told him.

''We'd like to question the sisters,'' he said apologetically. ''We'd like to know if any of them saw or heard anything unusual during the night.''

The nun frowned. ''What time was the alien killed, Major?''

''We don't know. If she were human, we'd be able to pinpoint it within a matter of seconds. But we don't know how fast the blood—'' He stopped suddenly on the ''d'' of "blood," as though he had realized that such gory subjects might not be proper conversation here.

Sister Mary Magdalene was amused at the WBCI man's exaggerated tact. "How fast the blood coagulates," she completed, a bit surprised at her own calmness. "Nor, I suppose, how soon *rigor mortis* sets in, nor how long it takes the body to cool."

"That's about it. We'll just have to check with everybody to see if anyone saw anything that might help us."

"Would you tell me one thing?" Sister Mary Magdalene said, glancing hesitantly at the silent, glowering figure of Father Destry. "Can you tell me who the suspects are? And please don't say 'everybody'—I mean the immediate suspects."

"Frankly," said Major Brock, "we think it might be one of the aliens. But I'm afraid that might just be prejudice. There are other possibilities."

"You don't suspect one of us!"

"Not now. But I can't overlook the possibility. If any of the sisters has a brother or a father in the Space Service—"

"I concede the possibility," said Sister Mary Magdalene reluctantly. "And I suppose the same thing might hold true for anyone else."

"It might, but conditions here pretty well confine the suspects to the sisters and the aliens. After all, you've been pretty closely guarded, and you're pretty secure here." The WBCI man smiled. "Except from invasion by cops." He won Sister Mary Magdalene's undying love with that last sentence.

Father Destry swallowed hard to maintain his composure and said, "I suppose I'll have to remain if the sisters are to be questioned. The bishop—"

"I understand, Father. I'll try not to take too long."

Sister Mary Magdalene sighed and checked the schedule of Masses in the Cathedral of the Blessed Sacrament. There would be little chance of her hearing Mass in the chapel here, with all this going on.

The nightmarish morning dragged slowly along. Sister Mary Magdalene phoned the Mother Superior of the order in Wisconsin to assure her that everything was under control; it was true, if not wholly accurate. Then it was the nun's task to interview each of her sisters, one by one, to learn her story of the night before.

They knew nothing. None of them was lying, Sister Mary Magdalene knew, and none of them was capable of murder.

Not until the Major came to Sister Angela did anything new come up. Sister Angela was asked if she had noticed anything unusual.

"Yes," she said flatly. "There was someone in the courtyard last night. I saw him from my window."

"Him?" Sister Mary Magdalene repeated in astonishment, sitting bolt upright in her chair. *"Him?"*

Sister Angela nodded nervously. "It—it looked like a monk."

"How do you know it was a monk?" asked the Major.

"Well, he was wearing a robe—with the cowl down. The moon was pretty bright. I could see him clearly."

"Did you recognize him?"

"It wasn't *that* bright, Major. But I'm sure it was—well, a man dressed in a monk's habit."

Major Brock frowned and chewed at the ends of his mustache. "We'll have to investigate this more fully."

Sister Mary Magdalene rose. A quick glance at the clock told her that it was her last chance to make it to Mass. For an instant, a niggling inward voice told her that missing Mass just this once would be excusable under the circumstances, but she fought it down.

"Would you excuse me?" she said to Brock. "I must attend Mass at this hour."

"Of course, Sister," Brock did not seem pleased at the prospect of having to carry on without her, but, as always, he maintained careful respect for the churchly activities going on about him.

Sister Mary Magdalene went out, headed for the cathedral. Outside, everything looked so normal that she could hardly believe anything had really happened. It was not until she reached the cathedral itself that depression again struck her.

The vestment radiations were off.

The vestments of the clergy were fluorescent; under the radiation from the projectors in the walls, the chasubles, tunics and dalmatics, the stoles, maniples and altar frontal, all glowed with color. The color depended on the wave-length of the radiation used. There was the somber violet of the penitential seasons of Lent and Advent, the restful green of Epiphany and the long weeks after Trinity, the joyous white of Christmas and Easter, and the blazing red of Pentecost. But without the radiations, the vestments were black—the somber black of the Requiem, the Mass of the Dead.

For a moment Sister Mary Magdalene's thoughts were as black as the hangings on the altar. And then she realized that, again, there was Reason behind whatever was going on here. There was no doubt in her own mind that the Pogatha were intelligent, reasoning beings, although the question had never been settled on a theological level by the Church. She would pray for the repose of the soul of Vor Nollig.

Forty-five minutes later, she was walking back toward the convent, her own soul strangely at rest. For just a short time, there toward the end, she had felt oddly apprehensive about having had Vor Nollig in mind while the celebrant intoned the *Agnus Dei*: "O Lamb of God that takest away the sins of the world, grant them rest eternal.'' But then the words of the Last Gospel had come to reassure her: ''All things were made by Him, and without Him was not anything made.'' Surely it could not be wrong to pray for the happiness of one of God's creatures, no matter how strangely made.

She was to think that thought again within the next five minutes.

Sister Elizabeth, round and chubby and looking almost comically penguinlike, was standing at the gate, tears rolling down her plump cheeks.

''Why, Sister Elizabeth—what's the trouble?''

''Oh, Sister, Sister!'' She burst into real sobs and buried her head miserably in Sister Mary Magdalene's shoulder. ''She's dead—*murdered!*''

For a wild moment, Sister Mary Magdalene thought that Sister Elizabeth was referring to the dead Pogatha, Vor Nollig, but then she knew it was not so, and her numbed mind refused to speculate any further. She could only shake Sister Elizabeth and say, ''Who? Who is dead? Who?''

''Her—her little head's all burned off!'' sobbed the tearful nun. She was becoming hysterical now, shaking convulsively. Sister Mary Magdalene gripped Sister Elizabeth's shoulders firmly.

''*Who?*''

Sister Elizabeth looked up. When she spoke it was in a shocked whisper. ''Felicity, Sister. Your cat! She's dead!''

Sister Mary Magdalene remained quite still, letting the first tide of grief wash over her. A moment later she was calm again. The cat had been her beloved companion for years, but Sister Mary Magdalene felt no grief now. Merely pity for the unfortunate one who could have done such a brutal deed, and sorrow over the loss of a dear friend. A moment later the anger began, and Sister Mary Magdalene prayed for the strength to unravel the mystery of the sudden outbreak of violence in these peaceful precincts.

When she returned to her office a few moments later, the three living aliens were standing grouped together near one wall of the room. Secretary Masterson and Secretary Bass were not too far away. Major Brock was seated in the guest chair, with Father Destry standing behind him. Brock was speaking.

". . . and that's about it. Someone—we don't know who—came in here last night. One of the Sisters saw him heading toward the back gate of the courtyard, and another has told us that the back gate was unlocked this morning—and it shouldn't have been, because she's positive she locked it the night before." Brock looked up at Sister Mary Magdalene and his expression changed as he saw the frozen mask of her face. The nun was filled with hot anger, burning and righteous, but under complete and icy control.

"What is it, Sister?"

"Would you come with me, Major Brock? I have something to show you. And Father Destry, if you would. I would prefer that the rest of you remain here." She spoke crisply. This was, after all, her domain.

She led the two men, priest and policeman, to the courtyard and around to the rear of the convent. Then they went out to the broad park beyond. Fifteen yards from the gate lay the charred, pitiful remains of the cat.

Major Brock knelt to look at it. "A dead cat," he said in a blank voice.

"Felicity," said Father Destry. "I'm sorry, Sister." The nun knew the sorrow was for her; Father Destry had never felt much warmth for the little animal.

Major Brock rose and said, softly, "I'm afraid I don't quite see what this has to do with—"

"Look at her head," said the nun in a hot-cold voice. "Burned! That's the work of a Brymer beamgun. Close range; not more than ten feet, possibly less."

Brock knelt again, picking up the body and studying it closely for a silent moment. When he looked up, the cat still in his hands, there was new respect in his eyes. "You're right, Sister. There's the typical hardening of the tissues around the burn. This wasn't done with a torch."

Father Destry blinked confusedly. "Do you think the killing of Sister Mary Magdalene's pet has something to do with the—uh—murder of Vor Nollig?"

"I don't know," Brock said slowly. "Sister? What do you think?"

"I think it does. But I'm not sure how. I think you'll find a connection."

"This brings something new into the picture, at least," said the Major. "Now we can look for a Brymer beamgun."

Vor Betla, the second Blue, who had never been able to speak English well, had given it up completely. She was snarling and snapping at Vor Vun, who was translating as best she could. It appeared that all three of the aliens seemed to feel that they might be the next to get a carving knife in their insides.

Vor Vun said, "We feel that you are not doing as well as you might, Major Brock. We don't blame the government of Earth directly for this insult, but obviously the precautions that were taken to protect us were insufficient."

The Major shook his head. "The entire grounds around the Cathedral were patrolled and guarded by every detection instrument known to Earth. No one could have gotten in."

Vor Gontakel put the palms of her green hands together, almost as if she were praying. "It makes a sense. You would not want us to get out, of course, so you would have much of safeguards around."

"We grant that," agreed Vor Vun. "But someone nonetheless killed Vor Nollig, and her loss is great."

Vor Betla snarled and yapped.

Vor Vun translated: "You must turn the killer over to us. If you do not, there can be no further talk of peace."

"How do we know it wasn't one of you three?" asked Secretary Masterson suddenly.

Vor Betla barked something. Vor Vun said, "We would have no reason for it."

Major Brock sighed. "I know. That's what bothered me all along. Where's the motive?"

Sister Mary Magdalene, watching silently, eyed the three aliens. Which one of them would have killed Vor Nollig? Which one might have killed Felicity?

Vor Vun? She hated cats; had she also hated Vor Nollig? Or had it been Vor Gontakel, the despised Green? But why would she kill Felicity? Had Vor Betla done it so she could be head of the delegation? That made even less sense.

Motive. What was the motive?

Had someone else done it? One of the secretaries, perhaps? Was there a political motive behind the crime?

And then—she had to force herself to think of it— there was the possibility that one of the monks, or, worse yet, one of her own sisters had done it.

If an Earthman had done it, it was either a political motive or one of hatred; there could be nothing personal in it. Vor Nollig, if she had been killed by an Earthman, had been killed for some deep, unknown or unknowable political machination, probably by order of the government itself, or else she had been killed because some Earthman just hated the enemy to such an extent that—

Sister Mary Magdalene did not want to think of blind hatred such as that.

On the other hand, if one of the three remaining Pogatha had done it, the motive could be any one of several. It could be personal, or political, or it might even have a basis in racial prejudice.

The nun thought it over for several minutes without reaching any conclusions. Motive would have to be abandoned as a way of finding the killer. For once, motive could not enter into the solution at all.

Method, then. What was the method?

Major Brock was saying: "Even the best of modern aids to crime detection can't reconstruct the past for us. But we do know part of the killer's action. He—"

There was a rap on the door, and Captain Lehmann thrust his head inside. "Excuse me if I'm interrupting. See you a minute, Major?"

Brock frowned, rose, and went outside, closing the door behind him. Father Destry leaned over and whispered to the nun, "They may suspect me."

"Nonsense, Father!"

Father Destry pursed his lips suddenly and said nothing more. Major Brock put his head in the door. "Sister, would you come here a minute?"

She stepped into the hall to confront two very grim WBCI men. Captain Lehmann was holding a Brymer beamgun in one hand and a bundle of black cloth in the crook of his arm. A faint but decidedly foul stench was perceptible.

"This is the gun," Lehmann said, "that killed your cat. At least, as far as we know. An energy beam has no traceable ballistics characteristics. We found it wrapped in this—" He gestured toward the black bundle. "And shoved under one of the pews in the chapel."

With a sudden movement he flipped out the cloth so it was recognizable. Sister Mary Magdalene had no difficulties in recognizing it. It was the habit of a nun.

"The lab men have already gone over it," Major Brock said. "We can prove who the owner is by perspiration comparison, but there also happens to be an identification strip in it. The odor is the blood of Vor Nollig. It spurted out when she was stabbed through the heart."

Brock opened the habit so the ID tag became visible. It said, *Sister Elizabeth, S.H.N.*

"We'll have to talk to her," said the Major.

"Of course," said Sister Mary Magdalene calmly. "I imagine you'll find it was stolen from her room. Tell me, why should Father Destry think you suspect him?"

The sudden, casual change of subject apparently puzzled Major Brock. He paused a moment before answering. "We don't, really. That is—" Again he paused. "He had a brother. A colonist on Pogathan. The Pogatha caught him. He died—not pleasantly, I'm afraid." He looked at the floor. "We have a similar bit of information on Sister Elizabeth. An uncle."

"You haven't mentioned my nephew yet," said Sister Magdalene.

The Major looked surprised. "No. We hadn't."

"It's of no importance, anyway. Let's go check with Sister Elizabeth. I can tell you now that she knows nothing about it. She probably doesn't even know her spare habit is missing yet, because it was stolen from the laundry. The laundry room is right across from the aliens' quarters."

"Wait," Brock said. "You'd rather we didn't talk to her, don't you?"

"It would only upset her."

"How do you know she didn't do it?"

"For the same reason you don't think she did, Major. This thing is beginning to make sense. I'm beginning to understand the mind that did this awful thing."

He looked at her curiously. "You have a strange mind

yourself, Sister. I didn't realize that nuns knew so much about crime.''

"Major," she said evenly, "when I took my vows, I chose the name 'Mary Magdalene.' I didn't pick it out of the hat."

The Major nodded silently, and his gaze shifted to the closed door of the nun's office. "The thing is that the whole pattern *is* beginning to make sense. But I can't quite see it."

"It was a badly fumbled job, really," said Sister Mary Magdalene. "If an Earthman had done it, you'd have spotted him immediately."

Again the Major nodded. "I agree. That much of the picture is clear. It *was* one of those three. But unless we know which one, and know beyond any smidgen of doubt, we don't dare make any accusations."

The nun turned to Captain Lehmann. "Did your lab men find out where that gun was discharged?"

"Why, yes. We found faint burn marks on the floor near the door to Vor Nollig's room."

"In the corridor outside, about four to five feet away?"

"That's right."

"Now—and this is important—where were they in relation to the door? I mean, if a person were facing the door, looking at someone inside the room, would the burn marks be behind him or in front?"

"Well—let's see—the door opens in, so they'd have to stand at an angle—mmm. Behind."

"I thought so!" Sister Mary Magdalene exclaimed in triumph.

Major Brock frowned. "It almost makes sense, but I don't quite—"

"That's because I have a vital clue that you don't have, Major."

"Which is?"

She told him.

* * *

"We know what was done," said Major Brock levelly. "We know *how* it was done." He looked the three aliens over. "One of you will tell us *why* it was done."

"If you are going to accuse one of us," said Vor Gontakel, rubbing her green hands carefully, "I'm afraid we will have to resist arrest. Is it not called a 'frame'?"

"Is insult!" snapped Vor Betla. "Is stupid! Is lie!"

The Major leaned back in his chair and looked at the two Terran diplomats, Bass and Masterson. "What makes this so tough," he said, "is that we don't know the motive. If the plot was hatched by all three of them, we're going to have a hell of a time—excuse me, Sister—proving it, or at least a rough time doing anything about it."

Masterson considered. "Do you think you could prove it to the satisfaction of an Earth court?"

"Maybe." Brock paused. "I *think* so. I'm a cop, not a prosecuting attorney."

Masterson and Bass conferred a moment. "All right—go ahead," Masterson said finally. "If it's a personal motive, then the other two will be sensible enough to see that the killer has greatly endangered the peace negotiations, besides murdering their leader. And I don't think it's a political motive on the part of all three."

"Though if it is," Bass interjected, "nothing we say will matter anyhow."

"Okay," Brock said. "Here's what happened. Sometime early this morning, around two—if Sister Angela's testimony is accurate—the killer went into the laundry room and picked up one of the nun's habits. Then the killer went to the kitchen, got a carving knife, came back and knocked on the door of Vor Nollig's room. Vor Nollig woke and came to the door. She opened the door a crack and saw what appeared to be a nun in the dim corridor. Not suspecting anything, Vor Nollig opened the door wider and stepped into full view. The killer stabbed her in the heart with the knife.''

"Earthman,'' said Vor Betla positively.

"No. Where's your heart, Vor Betla?''

The Pogath patted the base of her throat.

"Ours is here,'' Brock said. :'An Earthman would have instinctively stabbed much lower, you see.''

Sister Mary Magdalene repressed a smile. The Major was bluffing there. Plenty of human beings had been stabbed in the throat by other human beings.

Brock said, "But now comes the puzzling part. You do not like cats, Vor Vun. What would you do if one came near you? Are you afraid of them?''

Vor Vun sniffed. "Afraid? No. They are harmless. They can be frightened easily. I would not pick one up, or allow it too close, but I am not afraid.''

"How about you, Vor Betla?''

"Do? Don't know. Know nothing of cats, but that they harmless dumb animals. Maybe kick if came too close.''

"Vor Gontakel?''

"I too know nothing of cats. I only saw one once.''

"One of you,'' said the Major judiciously, "is telling an untruth. Let's go on with the story.''

Sister Mary Magdalene watched their faces, trying to read emotion in those alien visages as the Major spoke.

"The killer did a strange thing. She turned around and saw Felicity, the cat. Possibly it had meowed from behind her and attracted her attention. And what does the killer do? She draws a Brymer beamgun and kills the cat! Why?''

The Pogatha looked at each other and then back at the Major. Their faces, thought Sister Mary Magdalene, were utterly unreadable.

"Then the killer picked up the cat, walked outdoors through the rear gate and threw it into the meadow. It was the killer that Sister Angela saw last night, but the killer had pushed the cowl back, so she didn't recognize the fact that it was a nun's habit, not a monk's. When the killer had disposed of the cat, she removed the habit, wrapped the beamgun in it and went into the chapel and put it under one of the pews.''

''Very plausible,'' said Vor Vun. ''But not proof that one of *us* did it.''

''Not so far. But let's keep plugging. Why did the killer wear the nun's habit?''

''Because was nun!'' said Vor Betla. She pointed an accusing blue finger at Sister Mary Magdalene.

''No,'' Brock said. ''Because she wanted Vor Nollig to let her get close enough to stab her. You see, we've eliminated you, Vor Betla. You shared the room; you would have been allowed in without question. But Vor Nollig would never have allowed a Green or a Yellow into her room, would she?''

''No,'' admitted the Blue, looking troubledly at Vor Vun and Vor Gontakel.

''Another point in your favor is the fact that the killer looked like a monk to Sister Angela. There are no dark-skinned monks at this cathedral, and Sister Angela would have commented on it if the skin had looked as dark as yours does. But colors are almost impossible to see in moonlight. A yellow or light green would have looked pretty much like human skin, and the features at a distance would be hard to recognize as belonging to a Pogath.''

''You are playing on prejudices,'' said Vor Vun angrily. ''This is an inexpensive trick!''

''A *cheap* trick,'' corrected Major Brock. ''Except that it isn't. However, we must now prove that it was a Pogath. We've smelled each others' food, haven't we? Now, a burnt cat would smell no differently than, say, a broiled steak—except maybe a little more so. Why would the killer take the trouble to remove the cat from the building? Why not leave it where it was? If she expected to get away with one killing, she could have expected to get away with two. She took the cat out simply because she couldn't stand the overpowering odor! There was no other possible reason to expose herself that way to the possible spying eyes of Sister Angela or any other nun who happened to be looking out the window. It was clever of the killer to think of dropping the wimple back and disposing of the white part of the headdress so that she would appear to be a monk. I imagine it also took a lot of breathholding to stand to carry that burnt cat that far.''

The Pogatha were definitely eyeing each other now, but the final wedge remained to be driven.

"Vor Gontakel!" the Major said sharply. ''What would you say if I told you that another cat at the far end of the corridor saw you stab Vor Nollig and burn down Felicity?''

Vor Gontakel looked perfectly unruffled and unperturbed. No Earthman's bluff was going to get by *her*! ''I would say the cat was lying,'' she said.

"The other two Pogatha got a confession out of her,'' said Major Brock that evening. ''They'll take her back to Pogathan to stand trial.''

Father Destry folded his hands and smiled. "Sister, you seem to have all the makings of a first-class detective. How did you figure out that it was Vor Gontakel? I mean, what started you on that train of thought?''

"Sister Elizabeth,'' the nun said. ''She told me that Felicity had been murdered. And she *had* been— murdered, I mean, not just 'killed.' Vor Gontakel saw me talking to the cat, and Felicity meowed back. How was she to know that the cat wasn't intelligent? She knew nothing about Terrestrial life. The other two did. Felicity was murdered because Vor Gontakel thought she was a witness. It was the only possible motive for Felicity's murder.''

''What about the motive for Vor Nollig's murder?'' Father Destry said to the Major.

''Political. There's a group of Greens, it seems, that has the idea the war should go on. Most of the war is being fought by Blues, and if they're wiped out the so-called minority groups could take over. I doubt if it would work that way, but that's what this bunch thinks. Vor Gontakel simply wanted to kill a Blue and have it blamed on the Earthmen in order to stop the peace talks. But there's one thing I think we left untied here, Sister. Have you stopped to wonder why she used a knife on Vor Nollig instead of the beamgun she was carrying?''

Sister Mary Magdalene nodded. ''She didn't want every sister in the place coming out to catch her before she had a chance to cover up. She knew that burnt Pogatha would smell as bad to us as burnt cat did to her. But she didn't have a chance to use a knife on Felicity; the cat would have run away.''

Major Brock nodded in appreciation. ''A very neat summation, Sister. I bow to your fine deductive abilities. And now, I imagine, we can get our staff off the cathedral premises and leave you people to your devotions.''

''It's unfortunate we had to meet under such unhappy circumstances, Major,'' the nun said.

''But you were marvelously helpful, Sister.''

The Major smiled at the nun, shook Father Destry's hand tentatively, as if uncertain that such a gesture was appropriate, and left. Sister Mary Magdalene sighed gently in relief.

Police and aliens and all were leaving. The cathedral was returning to its normal quietude. In the distance the big bell was tolling, and it was time for prayer. She was no longer a detective; she was simply

Sister Mary Magdalene of the Sisters of the Holy Nativity.

It would be good to have peace here again. But, she admitted wryly to herself, the excitement had been a not altogether unwelcome change from normal routine. The thought brought up old memories of a life long buried and sealed away with vows. Sister Mary Magdalene frowned gently, dispelling the thoughts, and quietly began to pray.

The Invisible Cat

BETTY REN WRIGHT

Most towns have a Miss Cassells who serves, self-appointed, as its guardian of morals. Our Miss Cassells was fortyish, and apparently always had been, was given to letter-writing, white collars, and pointed shoes, and was a great patron of repentant sinners. Her notes signed "An Anxious Friend" and "One Who Cares" are part of the town legend, and her murder—no matter what story you believe—was as neatly appropriate as the third-act curtain of a college student's first play.

The town misses the old girl. In her day she was credited with breaking up eleven marriages (including Katherine's and mine), being the direct cause of three suicides, and driving two ministers to request posts in other cities. She wasn't good, but she was interesting, and in a dull town like our town she was therefore important.

It was on the Fourth of July, seven years ago, that we lost her—a day hot enough to be remembered for that reason alone. The temperature had stayed in the upper nineties for a week, and on the morning of the Fourth you could feel the town bracing itself for the long haul ahead. In our town there are certain things that are always done on the holiday, and it takes a lot more than the weather to change the schedule. In this case, the heat just got things started earlier; by five thirty A.M., the kids were roaming the streets and firecrackers were popping like corn in a hot pan. Over on the south end the racket is always the worst, and it was there that the Travvers boys—scrounging in the dump for tin cans— found the first body.

Eddie Travvers called the police station. And right after his call, Miss Cassells phoned in to say that a man in a baggy white suit had jumped out at her neighbor, Caroline Smith, when Caroline opened the back door to let in the cat. Miss Cassells' voice was as chilly as ever, but in the background Caroline could be heard, all stops open.

You see, the state mental hospital is only a quarter mile from our city square and folks are likely to think of that first when there is trouble. Dick Repa, who is one-third of our police department, called the hospital; they made a quick check, and sure enough one of the most violent patients was missing. The superintendent of the hospital was frantic and promised to send some men immediately to help with the search. But the terror had begun. It was a situation our town worries about, the way other places worry about earthquakes or floods.

The body the Travvers kids had found was that of Joe Diggs, a harmless old sponger who lived off a disability pension and anything the townspeople wanted to give him. There was no question but what the lunatic had done it; old Joe had been strangled with a sock of the kind issued by the hospital and carrying an identifying mark. Our switchboard operator, Mae Purtell, got busy and within half an hour every kid in town was back home and houses were locked up tight. Skittery old maids began hailing the police station faster than Mae could handle the calls, and a volunteer posse followed up each SOS, poking through attics and cellars that hadn't seen a man in twenty years. By eight thirty that morning, a tourist—driving through on his way north to one of the resorts—would have thought a plague had hit us. Except for the posse, there wasn't a soul in the streets, and every house had a withdrawn look, as though begging the lunatic not to notice it.

They couldn't find him. They combed garages, barns, and woodsheds, timidly at first, then with more courage as they were joined by state police. The morning passed, and the temperature rose. Miss Cassells finished a furious letter to the hospital superintendent (found on her desk later, by neighbors) and started one to the governor. The troopers distributed tear gas bombs.

By noon, folks were saying the crazy man must have left town, and some of the reckless ones were opening their second story windows a crack for a breath of air. Emmeline Loring, known far and wide for foolhardiness, even went out to feed the chickens she kept behind her garage. Tommy Parks and Ellis Townes found her there, the back of her head completely crushed in, and her fist closed tight over something. When the state troopers came they pried open her fingers, and a little stream of chicken corn poured out.

Right then and there, a certain percentage of the volunteer help disappeared. You could see why. Murder in the abstract—at the city dump, and done upon a nobody while Mr. Ordinary Man was asleep in his bed—was rather exciting. But murder at noon on the Fourth of

July, when the parade ought to be breaking up at the
city square and the kids getting their ice cream, murder
done to a friendly opinionated old lady who was re-
duced now to complete indifference, that was something else. At a time like that the bravest man is likely
to start saving himself for his wife and children.

Of those who stayed, two took poor Emmeline down
to the police station in a car while the rest continued
searching on foot. More troopers arrived and threw a
cordon around the town so that no one could come in
or leave. We were like a lot of mice locked up with an
invisible cat, wondering where the thing was and
whether it was still hungry.

At four o'clock nothing had changed except the temperature, which had passed the all-time record. It was
too hot to move away from the radio and its frequent
bulletins, so few people saw Miss Cassells as she
walked through town to the church. It would have been
a sight to remember: dark blue cotton dress and broad
white collar, white gloves, long white pointed shoes.
With the temperature pushing 105°, and a homicidal
maniac loose in the streets, Miss Cassells was all
dressed up and going about her business.

It developed later that at least six of the posse met
her on her way. Most of us were searching on the out-
skirts of town, but a few men were patrolling the square,
and they all recalled their surprise and horror at seeing
a woman alone on the street. After they identified her
the feeling changed; it seemed pretty unlikely that even
a lunatic would attack Miss Cassells, and besides—well,
if you'd even received one of the old witch's letters you'd
know why the feeling changed. She had a real gift for
sending vicious half-truths, where they would do the
most harm.

Even so, all six men made it their job to warn her,
and got condescending smiles for their trouble. She *always* practiced the organ at four thirty, and that was

that. Gene Pierce followed her to the church and waited while she unlocked the door and let herself in. He said afterward that he would have gone in, too, and stayed, if it had been anyone else. Instead, he waited across the street in the shade for a while, then walked across the square with Binny Draper.

Miss Cassells told the state troopers the rest of the story that night—how she went straight to the organ in the choir loft without bothering to turn on the overhead lights. Under the particular circumstances of that afternoon, she was probably the only person in town who would have considered the lights a bother. But that was what she said. Many Sunday mornings, sitting alone in my pew, I've pictured her climbing one of the two staircases to the loft, her white collar disembodied in the darkness until she switched on the console lamp—for the last time.

She played a Bach Invention first, to loosen up her fingers, then started working on the offertory music for the following Sunday. While she played, she glanced once in a while into the little mirror fastened at the side of the organ. It's there so the organist can tell when the choir, or the bride, is ready to come down the aisle, but Miss Cassells always used it to check up on who had come to church and who hadn't. I suppose that even when the church was empty, it was hard to break the habit. She had been playing about fifteen minutes, glancing into the mirror occasionally, when she saw a man standing at the altar rail down in the church. He was wearing rumpled white pajamas.

They figured afterward that he must have gone to the church right after killing Emmeline Loring, and crawled in through an unlocked basement window. He stayed there all afternoon, maybe even slept in the church kitchen, until the sound of the organ got him moving again.

At first Miss Cassells, being herself, kept right on

playing. The man's face was turned up toward the music; he had a placid, rather pathetic look, like a child disturbed in the middle of a dream, and she may have thought that if she kept on he would wander away. Then his arms moved and she saw that he had come prepared to play the critic. There was a knife in his hand.

What followed may have lasted only a few minutes, or much longer; Miss Cassells wasn't sure. She slid off the console bench and started toward the stairs on the left. When she reached them, he was waiting at the bottom. She turned back, and he turned, too. It was like a queer, pointless game that could go on forever. He did not look at her—his head had dropped when the music ended—but he seemed able to anticipate her every step. There was something terrifying in the way he moved; it was as if nothing could distract him.

"I thought of the men on whose conscience my death would lie," she told the troopers that night. "Those negligent doctors at the asylum. I hope they will be made to understand what it was like. I hope they'll have to pay. And the ones to blame for that hallway. They should suffer for it."

The hallway to which she referred so kindly is a narrow little passage leading up from the basement to the center of the loft. It hasn't been used by the choir for at least ten years, and at the last redecorating, paneling was laid across the door, with hidden hinges so that the hall behind the panel could still be used for storage. They had been playing their follow-the-leader game for quite a while when Miss Cassells thought of that hallway, and the memory must have seemed like a reprieve straight from heaven. If she could go through the panel without his looking up, she thought, he might not be able to find the opening for several minutes—long enough for her to go down the hallway, through the basement, and up again to the front door.

For the last time she started across the loft. This time

she walked behind the choir benches instead of in front of them, and slid her hand lightly over the panels until she found the right one. It opened, and the man did not look up. She stepped inside.

There was no light. In the old days Miss Cassells had used the hallway a hundred times, and under any other circumstances she would have realized at once that it was unnaturally dark. But this time she believed the hall was heaven's answer to a deserving prayer, and she didn't begin to doubt the answer until her outstretched hands struck something hard in front of her. Then the darkness had to be explained, and, as clearly as if she had helped them, she remembered the day the choir members crated up all the old hymnals and little-used music and carried the boxes through the panel. From floor to ceiling the crates were piled, and they made a blind alley of the little hall.

"I began to pray," Miss Cassells told the troopers that night. "I prayed God to remember the life I had led and to reward me with a quick and easy death. And to punish those who were responsible. It was sinful ignorance to leave a hallway completely blocked that way."

She was nearly unconscious when the panel opened and the lunatic in his rumpled white suit stood in the light. "I fell down," she recalled. "I fell on my knees and tried to pray. But I couldn't look away from the knife. He was staring at it, too, and then he looked over his shoulder at something and the knife fell on the floor. It was right in front of me. He walked away, and I heard him go down the stairs and out through the chancel door. Then a man called hello from the rear of the church and I heard someone coming down the aisle. Everything got horribly dark, and that's all I remember."

They caught the lunatic as he was strolling across the square, and five minutes after that Ed Burns and Tom

Nichols found Miss Cassells. She had been stabbed twice, and had bled a great deal, but they roused her at the hospital, and for a couple of hours it looked as if she was going to pull through. That was when the state troopers got her story.

"Now you find him," she said. "The devil who stabbed me. I've told you everything just as it happened. Now you find the devil who would stab an unconscious woman."

They tried. Some of us, who were known to have had dealings with her in the past, had to put up with quite a bit of questioning. But the knife had no-fingerprints on it at all, and as for opportunity, every man in town had had a chance to slip away from home, or from the posse, if he wanted to. She was always in the church from four thirty to five thirty; with any kind of luck, the madman would have got the blame. And as for motive, there was plenty to go around. Miss Cassells summed it up well with her last words. "One spends one's life trying to help others, but the world is never grateful."

That was how we lost her. Or at least, that was how she said we lost her. There are a few cynics and parlor psychoanalysts in our town who believe it really was the maniac who stabbed Miss Cassells, and that the second man in her story was born of a guilty conscience, of just plain meanness.

I don't take part in the discussions; I find the speculation rather amusing. In any case, half this town is going to look with suspicion at the other half for as long as we all shall live, and Miss Cassells couldn't have wished herself a more appropriate memorial than that.

The Outside Ledge

L. T. MEADE and ROBERT EUSTACE

A CABLEGRAM MYSTERY

I had not heard from my old friend Miss Cusack for some time, and was beginning to wonder whether anything was the matter with her, when on a certain Tuesday in the November of the year 1892 she called to see me.

"Dr. Lonsdale," she said, "I cannot stand defeat, and I am defeated now."

"Indeed," I replied, "this is interesting. You so seldom are defeated. What is it all about?"

"I have come here to tell you. You have heard, of course, of Oscar Hamilton, the great financier? He is the victim of a series of frauds that have been going on

during the last two months and are still being perpe-
trated. So persistent and so unaccountable are they that
the cleverest agents in London have been employed to
detect them, but without result. His chief dealings are,
as you know, in South African Gold Mines, and his
income is, I believe, nearer fifty than thirty thousand a
year. From time to time he receives private advices as
to the gold crushings, and operates accordingly. You
will say, of course, that he gambles, and that such gam-
bling is not very scrupulous, but I assure you the matter is not at all looked at in that light on the Stock
Exchange.

"Now, there is a dealer in the same market, a Mr.
Gildford, who, by some means absolutely unknown,
obtains the same advice in detail, and of course either
forestalls Mr. Hamilton, or, on the other hand, dis-
counts the profits he would make, by buying or selling
exactly the same shares. The information, I am given
to understand, is usually cabled to Oscar Hamilton in
cipher by his confidential agent in South Africa, whose
bona fides is unquestionable, since it is he who profits
by Mr. Hamilton's gains.

"This important information arrives as a rule in the
early morning about nine o'clock, and is put straight
into my friend's hands in his office in Lennox Court.
The details are discussed by him and his partner, Mr.
Le Marchant, and he immediately afterwards goes to
his broker to do whatever business is decided on. Now,
this special broker's name is Edward Gregory, and time
after time, not invariably, but very often, Mr. Gregory
has gone into the house and found Mr. Gildford doing
the identical deals that he was about to do."

"That is strange," I answered.

"It is; but you must listen further. To give you an
idea of how every channel possible has been watched,
I will tell you what has been done. In the first place it
is practically certain that the information found its way

from Mr. Hamilton's office to Mr. Gildford's, because no one knows the cipher except Mr. Hamilton and his partner, Mr. Le Marchant.''

"Wireless telegraphy," I suggested.

Miss Cusack smiled, but shook her head.

"Listen," she said. "Mr. Gildford, the dealer, is a man who also has an office in Lennox Court, four doors from the office of Mr. Hamilton, also close to the Stock Exchange. He has one small room on the third floor back, and has no clerks. Now Mr. Gregory, Mr. Hamilton's broker, has his office in Draper's Gardens. Yesterday morning an important cable was expected, and extraordinary precautions were adopted. Two detectives were placed in the house of Mr. Gildford, of course unknown to him—one actually took up his position on the landing outside his door, so that no one could enter by the door without being seen. Another was at the telephone exchange to watch if any message went through that way. Thus you will see that telegrams and telephones were equally cut off.

"A detective was also in Mr. Hamilton's office when the cable arrived, the object of his presence being known to the clerks, who were not allowed to use the telephone or to leave the office. The cable was opened in the presence of the younger partner, Mr. Le Marchant, and also in the presence of the detective, by Mr. Hamilton himself. No one left the office, and no communication with the outside world took place. Thus, both at Mr. Gildford's office and at Mr. Hamilton's, had the information passed by any visible channel it must have been detected either leaving the former office or arriving at the latter.''

"And what happened?" I inquired, beginning to be much interested in this strange story.

"You will soon know what happened. I call it witchery. In about ten minutes' time Mr. Hamilton left his office to visit his broker, Mr. Gregory, at the Stock

Exchange, everyone else, including his partner, Mr. Le Marchant, remaining in the office. On his arrival at the Stock Exchange he told Mr. Gregory what he wanted done. The latter went to carry out his wishes, but came back after a few moments to say that the market was spoiled, Mr. Gildford having just arrived and dealt heavily in the very same shares and in the same manner. What do you make of it, Dr. Lonsdale?''

''There is only one conclusion for me to arrive at,'' I answered; ''the information does not pass between the offices, but by some previously arranged channel.''

''I should have agreed with you but for one circumstance, which I am now going to confide to you. Do you remember a pretty girl, a certain Evelyn Dudley, whom you once met at my house? She is the only daughter of Colonel Dudley of the Coldstream Guards, and at her father's death will be worth about seven thousand a year.''

''Well, and what has she to do with the present state of things?''

''Only this: she is engaged to Mr. Le Marchant, and the wedding will take place next week. They are both going to dine with me to-night. I want you to join the party in order that you may meet them and let me know frankly afterwards what you think of him.''

''But what has that to do with the frauds?'' I asked.

''Everything, and this is why.'' She lowered her voice, and said in an emphatic whisper, ''I have strong reasons for suspecting Mr. Le Marchant, Mr. Hamilton's young partner, of being in the plot.''

''Good heavens!'' I cried, ''you cannot mean that. The frauds are to his own loss.''

''Not at all. He has only at present a small share in the business. Yesterday from a very private source I learned that he was in great financial difficulties, and in the hands of some money-lenders; in short, I imagine—mind, I don't accuse him yet—that he is staving off his crash until he can marry Evelyn Dudley, when he hopes to right himself. If the crash came first, Colonel Dudley would not allow the marriage. But when it is a *fait accompli* he will be, as it were, forced to do something to prevent his son-in-law going under. Now I think you know about as much of the situation as I do myself. Evelyn is a dear friend of mine, and if I can prevent it I don't want her to marry a scoundrel. We dine at eight—it is now past seven, so if you will dress quickly I can drive you back in my brougham. Evelyn is to spend the night with me, and is already at my house. She will entertain you till I am ready. If nothing happens to prevent it, the wedding is to take place next Monday. You see, therefore, there is no time to lose in clearing up the mystery.''

"There certainly is not," I replied, rising. "Well, if you will kindly wait here I will not keep you many minutes."

I went up to my room, dressed quickly, and returned in a very short time. We entered the brougham which was standing at the door, and at once drove off to Miss Cusack's house. She ushered me into the drawing-room, where a tall, dark-eyed girl was standing by the fire.

"Evelyn," said Miss Cusack, "you have often heard me talk of my great friend Dr. Lonsdale. I have just persuaded him to dine with us to-night. Dr. Lonsdale, may I introduce you to Miss Evelyn Dudley?"

I took the hand which Evelyn Dudley stretched out to me. She had an attractive, bright face, and during Miss Cusack's absence we each engaged the other in brisk conversation. I spoke about Miss Cusack, and the girl was warm in her admiration.

"She is my best friend," she said. "I lost my mother two years ago, and at that time I do not know what I should have done but for Florence Cusack. She took me to her house and kept me with her for some time, and taught me what the sin of rebellion meant. I loved my mother so passionately. I did not think when she was taken from me that I should ever know a happy hour again.''

"And now, if report tells true, you are going to be very happy," I continued, "for Miss Cusack has confided some of your story to me. You are soon to be married?''

"Yes," she answered, and she looked thoughtful. After a moment she spoke again.

"You are right: I hope to be very happy in the future—happier than I have ever been before. I love Henry Le Marchant better than anyone else on earth.''

I felt a certain pity for her as she spoke. After all, Miss Cusack's intuitions were wonderful, and she did not like Henry Le Marchant—nay, more, she suspected him of underhand dealings. Surely she must be wrong. I hoped when I saw this young man that I should be able to divert my friend's suspicions into another channel.

"I hope you will be happy," I said; "you have my best wishes.''

"Thank you," she replied. She sat down near the fire as she spoke, and unfurled her fan.

"Ah! there is a ring," she said, the next moment. "He is coming. You know perhaps that he is dining here to-night. I shall be so pleased to introduce you.''

At the same instant Miss Cusack entered the room.

"Our guest has arrived," she said, looking from Miss Dudley to me, and she had scarcely uttered the words before Henry Le Marchant was announced.

He was a tall, young-looking man, with a black, short moustache and very dark eyes. His manner was easy and self-possessed, and he looked with frank interest at me when his hostess introduced him.

The next moment dinner was announced. As the meal proceeded and I was considering in what words I could convey to Miss Cusack my impression that she was altogether on a wrong tack, something occurred which I thought very little of at the time, but yet was destined to lead to most important results presently.

The servant had just left the room when a slight whiff of some peculiar and rather disagreeable odour caught my nostrils. I was glancing across the table to see if it was due to any particular fruit, when I noticed that Miss Cusack had also caught the smell.

"What a curious sort of perfume!" she said, frowning slightly. "Evelyn, have you been buying any special new scent today?"

"Certainly not," replied Miss Dudley; "I hate scent, and never use it."

At the same moment Le Marchant, who had taken his handkerchief from his pocket, quickly replaced it, and a wave of blood suffused his swarthy cheeks, leaving them the next instant ashy pale. His embarrassment was so obvious that none of us could help noticing it.

"Surely that is the smell of valerian," I said, as the memory of what it was came to me.

"Yes, it is," he replied, recovering his composure and forcing a smile. "I must apologize to you all. I have been rather nervous lately, and have been ordered a few drops of valerian in water. I cannot think how it got on my handkerchief. My doctor prescribed it for me yesterday."

Miss Cusack made a common-place reply, and the conversation went on as before.

Perhaps my attitude of mind was preternaturally suspicious, but it occurred to me that Le Marchant's explanation was a very lame one. Valerian is not often ordered for a man of his evidently robust health, and I wondered if he were speaking the truth.

Having a case of some importance to attend, I took my departure shortly afterward.

During the three following days I heard nothing further from Miss Cusack, and made up my mind that her conjectures were all wrong and that the wedding would of course take place.

But on Saturday these hopes were destined to be rudely dispersed. I was awakened at an early hour by my servant, who entered with a note. I saw at once that it was in Miss Cusack's handwriting, and tore it open with some apprehension. The contents were certainly startling. It ran as follows—

"I want your help. Serious developments. Meet me on Royal Exchange steps at nine this morning. Do not fail."

After breakfast I sent for a cab, and drove at once to the city, alighting close to the Bank of England. The streets were thronged with the usual incoming flux of clerks hurrying to their different offices. I made my way across to the Royal Exchange, and the first person I saw was Miss Cusack standing just at the entrance. She turned to me eagerly.

"This is good of you, doctor; I shall not forget this kindness in a hurry. Come quickly, will you?"

We entered the throng, and moved rapidly down Bartholomew Lane into Throgmorton Street; then, turning round sharp to the left, found ourselves in Lennox Court.

I followed my guide with the greatest curiosity, wondering what could be her plans. The next moment we entered a house, and, threading our way up some bare, uncarpeted stairs, reached the top landing. Here Miss Cusack opened a door with a key which she had with her, pushed me into a small room, entered herself, and locked the door behind us both. I glanced around in some alarm.

The little room was quite bare, and here and there round the walls were the marks of where office furniture had once stood. The window looked out on to the backs of the houses in Lennox Court.

"Now we must act quickly," she said. "At 9:30 an

important cable will reach Mr. Hamilton's office. This room in which we now find ourselves is next door to Mr. Gildford's office in the next house, and is between that and Mr. Hamilton's office two doors further down. I have rented this room—a quarter's rent for one morning's work. Well, if I am successful, the price will be cheap. It was great luck to get it at all.''

"But what are you going to do?" I queried, as she proceeded to open the window and peep cautiously out.

"You will see directly," she answered; "keep back, and don't make a noise."

She leant out and drew the ends of her boa along the little ledge that ran outside just below the window. She then drew it in rapidly.

"Ah, ha! do you remember that, Dr. Lonsdale?" she cried softly, raising the boa to my face.

I started back and regarded her in amazement.

"Valerian!" I exclaimed. "Miss Cusack, what is this strange mystery?"

"Hush! not another word yet," she said. Her eyes sparkled with excitement. She rapidly produced a pair of very thick doeskin gloves, put them on, and stood by the window in an attitude of the utmost alertness. I stood still in the middle of the room, wondering whether I was in a dream, or whether Miss Cusack had taken leave of her senses.

The moments passed by, and still she stood rigid and tense as if expecting something. I watched her in wonderment, not attempting to say a word.

We must have remained in this extraordinary situation fully a quarter of an hour, when I saw her bend forward, her hand shot out of the window, and with an inconceivably rapid thrust she drew it back. She was now grasping by the back of the neck a large tabby cat; its four legs were drawn up with claws extended, and it was wriggling in evident dislike at being captured.

"A cat!" I cried, in the most utter and absolute bewilderment.

"Yes, a cat; a sweet pretty cat, too; aren't you, pussy?" She knelt down and began to stroke the creature, who changed its mind and rubbed itself against her in evident pleasure. The next moment it darted towards her fur boa and began sniffing at it greedily. As it did so Miss Cusack deftly stripped off a leather collar round its neck. A cry of delight broke from her lips as, unfastening a clasp that held an inner flap to the outer leather covering, she drew out a slip of paper.

"In Henry Le Marchant's handwriting," she cried. "What a scoundrel! We have him now."

"Henry Le Marchant's handwriting!" I exclaimed, bending over the slip as she held it in her hand.

"Yes," she answered; "see!"

I read with bated breath the brief communication which the tiny piece of paper contained. It was beyond doubt a replica of the telegram which must have arrived at Hamilton's office a few moments ago. Miss Cusack also read the words. She flung the piece of paper to the ground. I picked it up.

"We must keep this, it is evidence," I said.

"Yes," she answered, "but this has upset me. I have heard of some curious methods of communication, but never such a one as this before. It was the wildest chance, but thank God it has succeeded. We shall save Evelyn from marrying a man with whom her life would have been intolerable."

"But what could have led you to this extraordinary result?" I said.

"A chain of reasoning starting on the evening we dined together," she replied. "What puzzled me was this. What had Henry Le Marchant to do with valerian on his handkerchief? It was that fact which set me thinking. His explanation of using it as a nerve sedative was so obviously a lie on the face of it, and his embarrassment was so evident, that I did not trouble myself with this way out of the mystery for a single moment. I went through every conceivable hypothesis with regard to valerian, but it was not till I looked up its properties in a medical book that the first clue came to me. Valerian is, as you of course know, doctor, a plant which has a sort of intoxicating, almost maddening effect on cats. so much so that they will search out and follow the smell to the exclusion of any other desire. They are an independent race of creatures, and not easily trained like a dog. Then the amazing possibility suggested itself to me that the method employed by Mr. Le Marchant to communicate with Mr. Gildford, which has nonplussed every detective in London, was the very simple one of employing a cat.

"Come to the window and I will explain. You see that narrow ledge along which our friend pussy strolled so leisurely a moment ago. It runs, as you perceive, straight from Mr. Hamilton's office to that of Mr. Gildford. All Mr. Gildford had to do was to sprinkle some valerian along the ledge close to his own window. The peculiar smell would be detected by a cat quite as far off as the house where Mr. Hamilton's office is. I thought this all out, and, being pretty sure that my surmises were correct, I called yesterday on Henry Le Marchant at the office with the express purpose of seeing if there was a cat there.

"I went with a message from Evelyn. Nestling on his knee as he sat at his table writing in his private room was this very animal. Even then, of course, there was no certainty about my suspicions, but in view of the event which hung upon them—namely, his marriage to Evelyn—I was determined to spare no pains or trouble to put them to the test. I have done so, and, thank God, in time. But come, my course now is clear. I have a painful duty before me, and there is not a moment to lose."

As Miss Cusack spoke she took up her fur boa, flicked it slowly backwards and forwards to remove the taint of the valerian, and put it round her neck.

Five minutes later we were both communicating her extraordinary story to the ears of one of the sharpest detectives in London. Before that night Henry Le Marchant and James Gildford were both condemned to suffer the severest punishment that the law prescribes in such cases.

But why follow their careers any further? Evelyn's heart very nearly broke, but did not quite, and I am glad to be able to add that she has married a man in every respect worthy of her.

The Theft of the Mafia Cat

EDWARD D. HOCH

Nick Velvet had always harbored a soft spot for Paul Matalena, ever since they'd been kids together on the same block in the Italian section of Greenwich Village. He still vividly remembered the Saturday afternoon when a gang fight had broken out on Bleecker Street, and Paul had yanked him out of the path of a speeding police car with about one inch to spare. He liked to think that Paul had saved his life that day, and so, being something of a sentimentalist, Nick responded quickly to his old friend's call for help.

He met Paul in the most unlikely of places—the Shakespeare garden in Central Park, where someone many years ago had planned a floral gathering which was to include every species of flower mentioned in the works of the Bard. If the plan had never come to full blossom, it still produced a colorful setting, a backdrop for literary discussion.

" 'There's rosemary, that's for remembrance,' " Paul quoted as they strolled among the flowers and shrubs. " 'And there is pansies, that's for thoughts.' "

Nick, who could hardly be called a Shakespeare scholar, had come prepared. " 'A rose by any other name would smell as sweet,' " he countered.

"You've gotten educated since we were kids, Nick."

"I'm still pretty much the same. What can I do for you, Paul?"

"They tell me you're in business for yourself these days. Stealing things."

"Certain things. Those of no great value. You might call it a hobby."

"Hell, Nick, they say you're the best in the business. I been hearing about you for years now. At first I couldn't believe it was the same guy."

Nick shrugged. "Everyone has to earn a living somehow."

"But how did you ever get started in it?"

The beginning was something Nick rarely thought about, and it was something he'd never told another person. Now, strolling among the flowers with his boyhood friend, he said, "It was a woman, of course. She talked me into helping her with a robbery. We were going to break into the Institute for Medieval Studies over in New Jersey and steal some art treasures. I got a truck and helped her remove a stained-glass window so we could get into the building. While I was inside she drove off with the window. That was all she'd been after in the first place. It was worth something like $50,000 to collectors."

Paul Matalena gave a low whistle. "And you never got any of it?"

Nick smiled at the memory. "Not a cent. The girl was later arrested, and the window recovered, so perhaps it's just as well. But that got me thinking about the kind of objects people steal. I discovered there are things of little or no value that can be worth a great deal to certain people at certain times. By avoiding the usual cash and jewelry and paintings I'm able to concentrate on the odd, the unusual, the valueless.''

"They say you get $20,000 a job, and $30,000 for an especially dangerous one."

Nick nodded. "My price has been the same for years. No inflation here."

"Would you do a job for me, Nick?"

"I'd have to charge you the usual rate, Paul."

"I understand. I wasn't asking for anything free."

"Some say you're a big man in the Mafia these days. Is that true?"

Matalena shot him a sideways glance. "Sure, it's true. I'm right up with the top boys. But we don't usually talk about it."

"Why not? I'm an Italian-American just like you, Paul, and I think it's wrong to act as if organized crime doesn't exist. What we should do is admit it, and then go on to stress the accomplishments of other Italian-Americans—men like Fiorello LaGuardia, John Volpe, and John Pastore in government, Joe DiMaggio in sports, and Gian Carlo Menotti in the arts."

"I stay out of policy matters, Nick. I've got me a nice laundry business that covers restaurants and private hospitals. Brings me in a nice fat income, all legit. In the beginning I had to lean on some of the customers, but when they found out I was Mafia they signed up fast. And no trouble with competition."

"You must be doing well if you can afford my price. What do you want stolen?"

"A cat."

"No problem. I once stole a tiger from a zoo."

"This cat might be tougher. It's Mike Pirrone's pet."

Nick whistled softly. Pirrone was a big man in the

Syndicate—one of the biggest still under 50. He lived in a country mansion on the shore of a small New Jersey lake. Not many people visited Mike Pirrone. Not many people wanted to.

"The cat is on the grounds of his home?"

Matalena nodded. "You can't miss it. A big striped tabby named Sparkle. Pirrone is always being photographed with it. This is from a magazine."

He showed Nick a picture of Mike Pirrone standing with an older, white-haired man identified as his lawyer. The Mafia don was holding the big tabby in his arms, almost like a child. Nick grunted and put the picture in his pocket. "First time I ever saw Pirrone smiling."

"He loves that cat. He takes it with him everywhere."

"And you want to kidnap it and hold it for ransom?"

Matalena chuckled. "Nick, Nick, these wild ideas of yours! You haven't changed since schooldays."

"All right. It's not my concern, as long as your money's good."

"This much on account," Matalena said, slipping an envelope to Nick. "I need results by the weekend."

They strolled a bit longer among the flowers, talking of old times, then parted. Nick caught a taxi and headed downtown.

Mike Pirrone's mansion was a sprawling ranch located on a hill overlooking Stag Lake in northern New Jersey. It was a bit north of Stag Pond, in an area of the state that boasted towns with names like Sparta and Athens and Greece. It was fishing country, and the man at the gas station told Nick, "Good yellow perch in these lakes."

"Might try a little," Nick admitted. "Got my fishing gear in back. How's Stag Lake?"

"Mostly private. If you come ashore at the wrong spot it could mean trouble."

Nick thanked him and drove on, turning off the main road to follow a rutted lane that ran along the edge of the Pirrone estate. The entire place was surrounded by a wall topped by three strands of electrified wire. As he passed the locked gates and peered inside, he saw the large sprawling house on its hill about two hundred feet back. The lake lay at the end of the road, and a chain-link fence ran from the end of the wall into the water. Mike Pirrone was taking no chances on uninvited guests.

Nick was studying the layout when a girl's voice spoke from very close behind him. "Thinking of doing some fishing?"

He turned and saw a willowy blonde in white shorts and a colorful print blouse standing by the back of his car. He hadn't heard her approach and he wondered how long she'd been watching him. "I might try for some yellow perch. I hear they're biting."

"It's mostly private property around here," she said. Her face was hard and tanned, with features that might have been Scandinavian and certainly weren't Italian.

"I noticed the wall. Who lives there—Howard Hughes?"

"A man named Mike Pirrone. You probably never heard of him."

"What business is he in?"

"Management."

"It must be profitable."

"It is."

"You know him?"

She smiled at Nick and said, "I'm his wife."

After his unexpected encounter with Mrs. Pirrone, Nick knew there was no chance for a direct approach to the house. He rented a boat in mid-afternoon and set off down the lake, trolling gently along the shoreline. No one was more surprised than Nick when he hooked a large fish almost at once. It could have been a yellow perch, but he wasn't sure. Fishing was not his sport.

The boat drifted down to a point opposite the Pirrone estate, and Nick checked the shoreline for guards. No one was visible, but through his binoculars he could see a group of wire cages near the main house. Since the cat Sparkle could be expected to sleep indoors, the cages seemed to indicate dogs—probably watchdogs that prowled the grounds after dark.

Working quickly, Nick filled his jacket pockets with fishhooks, lengths of nylon leader, and a folded and perforated plastic bag. A few other items were already carefully hidden on his person, but the binoculars and fishing pole would have to be abandoned. He used a small hand drill to bore a tiny hole in the bottom of the boat, then watched while the water began to seep in. He half stood up in the boat, giving an image of alarm to anyone who might have been watching, then threw the drill overboard and quickly headed the boat toward the shore. In five minutes he was beached on the Pirrone estate; the boat was half full of water.

For a few minutes he stood by it as if pondering his next move. Then he looked up toward the house on the hill and started off for it, carrying his fish. Almost at once he heard the barking of dogs and suddenly two large German shepherds were racing toward him across the expanse of lawn. Nick broke into a run, heading for the nearest tree, but as the dogs seemed about to overtake him they stopped dead in their tracks.

Nick leaned against the tree, panting, and watched a white-haired man walking across the lawn toward him. It was the man in the picture—Pirrone's lawyer—and he held a shiny silver dog whistle in one hand.

"They're well trained," Nick said by way of greeting.

"That they are. You could be a dead man now, if I hadn't blown this whistle."

"My boat," Nick said, gesturing helplessly toward the water. "It sprang a leak. I wonder if I could use your phone?"

The man was well dressed, in the sporty style of the town and country gentleman. He eyed Nick up and down, then nodded. "There's a phone in the gardener's shed."

Nick had hoped to make it into the house, but he had no choice. As the lawyer led the way, Nick held up his fish and said, "They're really biting today."

The man grunted and said nothing more. He led Nick to a small shack where tools and fertilizer were stored and pointed to the telephone on the wall. Nick put down his fish and dialed information, seeking the number of a taxi company. He'd just got the operator when the fish by his foot gave a sudden lurch. He looked down to see a large striped tabby cat pulling at it with a furry paw.

"Sparkle," Nick whispered. "Here, Sparkle."

The cat lifted its head in response to the name. It seemed to be awaiting some further conversation. Nick bent to stroke it under the chin and saw the legs of a man in striped slacks and golf shoes. His eyes traveled upward to a broad firm chest and the familiar beetle-browed face above. It was Mike Pirrone, and he wasn't smiling. In his hand he held a snubnosed revolver pointed at Nick's face.

"To what do I owe this pleasure, Mr. Velvet?"

The house was fit for a don, or possibly a king, with a huge beamed living room that looked out over the lake. The furniture was expensive and tasteful, and Pirrone's blond wife fitted the setting perfectly. She was much younger than her husband, but seeing them together one quickly forgot the difference in ages. Pirrone was approaching 50 gracefully, with a hint of youth that occasionally broke through the dignified menace of his stony face.

"He's the fisherman I told you about," Mrs. Pirrone said as they entered. Her eyes darted from Nick to her husband.

"Yes," Pirrone said softly. "It seems he was washed up on our shore, and I recognized him. His name is Nick Velvet."

"The famous thief?"

"None other."

Nick smiled. He still held the fish at the end of a line in one hand. "You have me at a disadvantage. I don't believe we've ever met."

"We met. A long time ago at a political dinner. I never forget a face, Velvet. It costs money to forget faces. Sometimes it costs lives. I'm Mike Pirrone, as you certainly know. This is my wife, Frieda, and my lawyer, Harry Beaman."

The white-haired man nodded in acknowledgment and Nick said deliberately, "I thought he was your dog trainer."

Mike Pirrone laughed softly and Beaman flushed. "He does have a way with the dogs," Pirrone said. "He's trained them well. But they only guard the place. I'm a cat fancier myself." As if to illustrate he bent and cupped his arms. Sparkle took a running leap and landed in them. "This cat goes everywhere I go."

"Beautiful animal," Nick murmured.

Pirrone continued to stroke the cat for a few moments, then put it down. "All right, Velvet," he said briskly. "What do you want here?"

"Merely to use the phone. My boat sprang a leak."

"You're no fisherman," Pirrone said, pronouncing the words like a final judgment.

"Here's my fish," Nick countered, holding it up; but the don was unimpressed.

"You scouted my place and you managed to get inside. What for?"

"Even a thief needs a vacation now and then."

"You don't take vacations, Velvet. I investigated you quite closely a few years back, when I almost hired you for a job. I know your habits and I know where you live. Who hired you, and why?"

"I didn't even know this was your place till I met your wife this morning."

"I heard you call my cat by name, out in the shed."

Nick hesitated. Mike Pirrone was no fool. "Everybody knows Sparkle. You're always photographed with him."

"Her. Sparkle is a her."

Harry Beaman cleared his throat. "What do you plan to do with him, Mike? If you try to hold him against his will it could be a serious legal matter. So far you've been within your rights to treat him as a trespasser, but that could change."

Pirrone threw up his hands. "Lawyers! Things were simple in the old days—right, Velvet?"

"I wouldn't know."

A maid appeared with cocktails and Pirrone waved his hand. "You're a guest here, Velvet. You arrived in time for the cocktail hour." He took a glass himself and went off to an adjoining study to make some phone calls. Nick wondered what Pirrone had in mind for him.

Frieda Pirrone rose from the sofa and came to sit by him. "You should have told me you wanted to meet my husband. I could have arranged it much more easily. Are you really a thief?"

"I steal women's hearts, among other things."

Her eyes met his for just an instant. "It would take a brave man—or an idiot—to steal anything from Mike Pirrone."

"I'm neither of those." He watched Sparkle move slowly across the carpet, stalking some imaginary prey.

"Just what sort of thief are you?"

"Sometimes I'm a cat burglar."

"Really? You mean one of those who climbs across rooftops?"

Before he could answer, Pirrone returned and handed his lawyer a sheaf of papers. "Business can be a bore at times, Velvet. I'm being a poor host."

"Perfectly all right. Your drinks are very good."

The dark-browed don nodded. "My chauffeur will be driving Harry to the train shortly. You're free to leave with them."

"Thank you."

"But one word of advice. If anything turns up missing from this house—now or later—I'll know just where to look. I'll send somebody for you, Velvet, and it'll be just like the old days. Understand?"

"I understand."

"Good! Whoever paid you, tell them the deal is off."

Nick nodded. He needed to be careful now. There would be no other chance to enter the Pirrone domain. Whatever the risk, he had to take Sparkle out of the house with him. He glanced at his watch. It was just after five. "Could I use your bathroom?"

Mike Pirrone nodded. "Go ahead. The maid will show you." Then, as Nick started to follow her, the don called out, "Taking your fish with you? Now I've seen everything!"

The maid waved him into a large tiled bathroom and departed. Nick checked his watch again. He had perhaps three minutes before they would grow suspicious. Quickly he crossed to the door and opened it. As he'd hoped, Sparkle had followed the trail of the fish and was hovering in the hall. With a bit of coaxing Nick had her in hand. He only hoped Pirrone wouldn't come looking for her right away.

Close up, Sparkle was a handsome feline, uniquely spotted and with a curious expression all her own. Perhaps that was why Pirrone liked her—because she was one of a kind. Nick held her firmly and injected a quick-acting sleeping drug. Sparkle gave one massive yawn and curled up on the floor. Then, working fast, he wrapped the disposable syringe in a tissue and put it in his pocket. He lifted Sparkle's limp body and slipped it into the perforated plastic bag.

Carrying the cat in one hand, Nick opened the bathroom door again and glanced down the hall toward the living room. No one was in sight. He crossed the hall quickly, entering a spare bedroom which he hoped was the room he sought. From the road he'd observed the telephone line running up the hill to the house and he thought it reached the wall just outside this room. Opening the window he saw that he'd been correct. The phone wire was just above his head, about a foot beyond the window.

He removed two fishhooks from his pocket and attached one to each end of a length of nylon leader. Reaching up he looped the fishing leader over the telephone wire and left it dangling there while he lifted the plastic-bagged cat. The fishhooks snagged two of the perforations in the bag and held it dangling beneath the telephone wire.

Nick tested it for weight, drew a deep prayerful breath, then gave the bag a shove. It began to slide slowly down the phone line, across the wide side yard, and finally over the wall to the telephone pole by the road. Near the pole the bag came to a stop, but by carefully tugging on his end of the wire Nick was able to propel it over the last few feet.

He sighed and closed the window. The whole operation had taken him four minutes—one minute more than he'd planned. He went back to the living room, still carrying his fish, and saw at once that Pirrone and Frieda and the lawyer were waiting for him. A large man in a chauffeur's uniform stood by the door.

Mike Pirrone smiled slightly and brought out the snubnosed revolver once more. "I hope you'll excuse the precaution, Velvet, but we don't want you leaving with anything that doesn't belong to you. Search him, Felix."

Nick raised his arms and the chauffeur ran quick firm hands over his body. After a few seconds he yanked one hand away; it was bleeding. "Damn! What's he got in there?"

"Fishhooks," Nick answered with the trace of a smile. "I should have warned you."

Felix cursed and finished the search. "He's clean, Mr. Pirrone."

"All right." The don put away his gun. "You can go now, Velvet."

"Thanks," Nick said, and started to follow the chauffeur and Beaman to the car.

He was halfway down the front walk when he heard Pirrone ask his wife, "Where's Sparkle?"

Nick kept walking steadily, glancing across the wall at the distant telephone pole and its hanging plastic bag. "I think she went outside," Frieda answered.

Suddenly Pirrone called, "Velvet! Hold it!"

Nick froze. The chauffeur, Felix, had turned toward the don, waiting for instructions. "What is it?" he asked as Pirrone came down the walk.

"That fish—let me have it. You could have hidden something small inside it. And if you didn't it'll make a nice supper for Sparkle."

Nick handed it over with feigned reluctance, then climbed into the car with Beaman. On the drive into town the white-haired lawyer tried to smooth things over. "You have to understand Mike. He's a real gentleman, with a heart of gold, but he lives in constant fear of rivals trying to take over what he's spent his life building."

"I assumed he had something to fear when I saw the gun," Nick said, nodding.

Beaman went on, "Frieda doesn't like it. She doesn't like anything connected with his old life, but Mike has to be careful."

"Of course."

Beaman dropped him at the marina and went on to the station. Shortly after dark Nick drove back to the Pirrone estate, climbed the telephone pole outside the wall, and removed the perforated plastic bag from the overhead wire. The cat was still sleeping peacefully. From inside the wall Nick could hear one of the servants calling for Sparkle.

Paul Matalena was overjoyed. "Nick, I never thought you could do it!" He stroked the cat on his lap and listened to it purr. "How in hell did you manage it?"

"I have my methods, Paul."

"Here's the rest of your money. And my thanks."

"You realize that Sparkle is a unique cat. She's been photographed with Pirrone a hundred times, and could hardly be mistaken for anyone else's pet. When people see it they'll know it's Pirrone's."

"That's exactly the idea, Nick."

"If you're planning to hold Sparkle for ransom you're playing with dynamite."

"It's nothing like that. In fact, I only want the cat for a meeting tomorrow afternoon. Then you can have her back. If Pirrone recovers his pet within a day, the whole thing shouldn't upset him too much."

"You mean you only want Sparkle for one day?"

"That's right, Nick." Matalena went to the phone and started making calls. The hour was late, but that didn't seem to bother him. Sparkle watched for a time, then ran over to Nick and rubbed against his leg. Suddenly, listening to Paul's words on the telephone, Nick knew why his old schoolmate was willing to pay

$20,000 to have Sparkle for one day. He looked at Paul Matalena and chuckled.

"What's so funny, Nick?"

"Paul, you always were something of a phony, even back in school."

"What?"

Nick got to his feet and headed for the door. "Good luck to you."

The following evening, as Nick sat on his front porch drinking a beer, Gloria called to him. "Telephone for you, Nicky."

He went in, setting down his beer on the table near the phone. She grabbed it up at once and wiped away the damp ring. Grinning, he said, "You're acting more like a wife every day."

The voice on the phone was soft and feminine. "Nick Velvet?"

"Yes."

"This is Frieda Pirrone. My husband is on his way to kill you. He thinks that somehow you stole Sparkle."

"Thanks for the warning."

"I don't want him to go back to killing, back to the way it used to be."

"Neither do I," Nick said. He hung up and turned to Gloria.

"Trouble, Nicky?"

"Just a little business problem." He bit his lip and pondered. "Look, Gloria, I've got a man coming over to see me. Why don't you go to a movie or something?"

"That was no man on the phone, Nicky."

"Come on," he grinned. "Ask no questions and I'll buy you that little foreign sports car you've been wanting."

"Will you, Nicky? You really mean it?"

"Sure I mean it."

When she'd gone he turned out all the lights in the house and sat down to wait. Just before ten o'clock a big black limousine pulled up and parked across the street. Nick had always considered his home to be forbidden territory, away from the dangers of his career; but this time it was different. Two men left the car and crossed the street to his house. One was the chauffeur, Felix. The other was a burly hood Nick didn't recognize. Mike Pirrone would be waiting in the car.

As they reached the porch Nick opened the door. Felix's hand dived into his pocket and the hood grabbed Nick, who didn't resist when they forced him back into the house. "I want to see Pirrone," Nick said.

"You'll see him." While the hood pinioned Nick, Felix went to the door and signaled across the street. Mike Pirrone left the car and came slowly up the walk, studying the house and the tree-lined street.

"Nice little place you have here, Velvet."

"Good to see you again so soon."

"Did you think you wouldn't?" He stepped close to Nick. "Did you think I'd let you get away with Sparkle?"

"No. Not really."

"Where is she?"

"Right here—I'll get her."

"No tricks." Pirrone had drawn his gun again, and this time he looked as if he meant to use it.

"No tricks," Nick agreed. He stepped into the kitchen with Felix at his side and called, "Sparkle!"

The big striped tabby came running at the sound of her name, rubbed briefly against Nick's leg, then bounded into Pirrone's waiting arms. He put away the gun and stroked her fur while he carefully examined her.

"All right," he said quietly. "Sparkle is all right, so I'll let you live. But Felix and Vic here are going to teach you a little lesson about stealing from me."

"Wait!" Nick said, holding up his hand. "Can't we talk this over?"

"There's no need for talk. You were warned, Velvet."

"At least let me tell you a story first. It's about the man who hired me to steal Sparkle."

"Tell me. We'll want to pay him a visit, too."

Nick started to talk fast. "You might almost call this a detective story in reverse. Instead of discovering a guilty person, I found one who's innocent."

"What are you talking about, Velvet?" Pirrone's patience was wearing thin.

"The man who hired me, who shall be nameless, runs a highly profitable business in New York City. He was able to establish the business, and maintain it profitably for years, mainly by convincing both his customers and his competitors that he is an important member of the Mafia."

Mike Pirrone frowned. "You mean he isn't one?"

"Exactly," Nick said. "He is not a member of the Mafia, never has been. He's a simple hard-working guy who took advantage of his Italian name and the fact that many people are willing to believe that any Italian in business must be in the Mob. By fostering the idea that he had important Syndicate connections, he got a lot of business from people who were afraid to go elsewhere.

"But recently some of his customers began to have doubts. The word started circulating that he wasn't a big Mafia man at all. Faced with the loss of his best customers he decided to call a meeting to keep them in line. Ideally, he would have liked someone like Mike Pirrone with him at the meeting. But since he didn't even know Mike Pirrone he settled for the next best thing—Mike Pirrone's cat."

"What?" Pirrone's mouth hung open. "You mean he had the cat stolen so he could con people into thinking he was a friend of mine?"

Nick Velvet smiled. "That's right. It was worth my fee of $20,000 to keep his customers in line. He showed up at the meeting today with Sparkle in his arms. Naturally, in an audience like that, all of them knew the cat by sight—and they knew that Mike Pirrone couldn't be far away. It convinced them."

"Didn't he think I'd hear about something like that?"

"Possibly. But by that time you'd have Sparkle back safe and sound, and you'd probably be reluctant to admit the theft to anyone."

"Tell me this guy's name."

"So you can beat him up or kill him? Where's your sense of humor? You have Sparkle back and the man has his customers back. No one's been harmed, and there's a certain humor in the situation. At a time when the Mafia is taking great pains to deny its existence, here is someone cashing in on the false story that he belongs to the Mafia. In fact, it was his open talking about it that made me suspicious in the first place. The real dons don't brag about it."

Felix shifted position. "What should I do, Mr. Pirrone?"

Pirrone studied Nick for a moment, then smiled slightly. "Let him go, Felix. You've got one hell of a nerve, Velvet—you and the guy who hired you." He started out of the house, but then paused by the door. "How did you do it? How did you get Sparkle out of my house?"

"Sorry. That's a trade secret. But I'll give you a tip about something else."

"What sort of tip?"

"Your watchdogs have been well trained by Harry Beaman."

Pirrone shrugged. "He likes them, I guess."

"He called them off me, and he could call them off his friends, too, if they happened to come visiting you late some night."

"I trust Harry," Pirrone said quickly, but his eyes were thoughtful.

"Think it over. You might live a few years longer."

Pirrone took a step forward and shook Nick's hand. "You've got a brain, Velvet. I could use someone like you in the organization."

Nick smiled and shook his head. "Organizations aren't for me. But remember me if you ever need anything stolen. Something odd or unusual"—Nick grinned—"or valueless."

Mr. Strang and the Cat Lady

WILLIAM BRITTAIN

It was a Wednesday in late fall. The fifth period was almost over, and Mr. Strang stood at the window of his classroom. The crumbs of the sandwich that had been his lunch lay unnoticed on his jacket lapels and rumpled necktie. He was speculating on how many more days it would be before the maple trees in front of Aldershot High School would be completely bare of leaves when he felt a tugging at the far reaches of his consciousness. Something odd had happened. Or rather, something had *not* happened, and that was equally odd. But it was several minutes before he realized what it was.

Miss Pinderek had not passed the school on her daily walk to the grocery store.

Until 17 years before, Agnes Pinderek had been a history teacher at Aldershot High. Then, at the age of 72, she had retired, with a minimum of fuss and fanfare, to her little cottage just around the corner. Few of the present staff even knew Miss Pinderek existed. But Mr. Strang knew, remembering the advice and encouragement she had showered on him long ago when he was only a young teacher just out of normal school. Mr. Strang ran gnarled fingers through his sparse crop of gray hair, realizing that by now Agnes Pinderek must be almost 90.

And yet every day at 12:15, in spite of her age, Agnes Pinderek walked by the school on her way to the grocery store three blocks away. And every day at one o'clock she returned, head erect and spine ramrod-straight, clutching a small paper bag as if daring someone to try and take it from her. Rain, snow, sleet, and hail did not deter her. Through them all she marched at her appointed times. In retirement she was the same as she had been in the classroom—proud, punctual, self-sufficient.

But on this day Miss Pinderek had not appeared.

Mr. Strang decided to pay her a visit as soon as school was over. He knew this would not please her. While she sometimes returned to school to see old friends, she was adamant about refusing to allow visitors to her home. "I'm an old lady, Leonard," she had told Mr. Strang on one occasion when he'd requested the privilege of making a call. "I've worked hard for my privacy, and now I intend to have it. Besides, I've spent so long in school that you might not recognize me away from it. I'd love to chat with you in your classroom after school, but my home is not open to visitors."

And that had been that.

Still, Miss Pinderek might be ill. Perhaps too ill to summon help. And he might not need to even enter the house. If he shouted through the door at her and received an answer, that would be enough to reassure him.

For the rest of the day Mr. Strang's classes came and went. Chemistry, general science, biology. And through them all the old teacher couldn't get Miss Pinderek out of his mind. Finally the school day ended. Mr. Strang placed a sign on his door canceling the meeting of the Science Club, took his keyring to the main office, and left the building just as the last of the buses was pulling out of the driveway.

Miss Pinderek's tiny front yard was overrun with ivy which not only choked out the weeds but climbed the clapboard sides of the house, partially obscuring the fact that the structure was badly in need of paint.

Mr. Strang pressed the doorbell. He heard no chime or buzz from inside the house. Finally he rapped loudly on the front door, his knuckles avoiding the panes of glass, three of which were cracked, while the fourth was missing, the opening blocked by a piece of cardboard.

No answer. He knocked again. Then he rattled the doorknob. The door creaked open a scant twelve inches and then struck against something.

The teacher pushed his way through the opening. He found himself standing between two towering piles of boxes, one of which had kept the door from opening fully. Beyond the boxes piles of ancient magazines and newspapers filled the entryway, leaving only a narrow passage along which the teacher walked.

"Agnes! Agnes Pinderek!" he called. The piles of debris muffled the sound of his voice. There was no answer except for a faint rustling which told of mice scampering for safety. Finally he reached the living room.

It was there he found the body of Agnes Pinderek.

Even as he absorbed the shock of finding the dead woman, Mr. Strang's brain was considering what must have happened. She had died painfully, horribly. The threadbare rug was pulled and twisted where her body had thrashed about on the floor, and an old brass lamp had been toppled, breaking its white glass bowl. Several of the piles of books about the room had been dragged down, and a copy of Charles Dickens' *Bleak House* was lying beneath the body. The old lady's long fingernails had pierced the palms of her hands, silent testimony to the agony she had suffered.

Someone had to be notified. Mr. Strang looked around for a telephone and found none. He walked toward the rear of the house, shivering uncontrollably. What kind of illness or injury could have caused such suffering?

He found the box of rat poison on the shelf in the kitchen. It was almost empty. In the sink were two white china cups and a teaspoon, all washed clean.

Pale and queasy, Mr. Strang left the house and hurried to the telephone booth on the corner in front of the school. From there he called the Aldershot police and asked to speak to Detective Sergeant Paul Roberts.

As if by magic a crowd collected in front of Miss Pinderek's house shortly after the arrival of the first police car. A pair of uniformed patrolmen, beefy and poker-faced, was stationed at the front door, and others were keeping the onlookers behind hastily erected barricades. Official-looking men carrying brief cases, cameras, and bags of investigative equipment moved back and forth between the house and the line of cars parked at the curb. Miss Pinderek's body, covered with a sheet, was brought out on a stretcher to be taken to the morgue for examination.

Paul Roberts came out of the house and beckoned to the teacher. Mr. Strang followed the bulky detective through the crowd until they reached a car at the curb. As Mr. Strang opened the door and got in on the passenger's side, he couldn't help thinking how much Agnes Pinderek would have disapproved of all this fuss being made over her. Proudly independent for nearly

90 years, she was receiving in death the attention she had spurned while alive.

Roberts sprawled onto the seat beside him and braced a clipboard against the steering wheel. "Do you have any idea who did it?" asked the teacher.

"I dunno. She didn't seem to have any enemies, according to the neighbors. She lived a pretty lonely existence, as far as we can make out."

Mr. Strang removed his black-rimmed glasses and rubbed at his eyes. "Paul," he said, "are you sure it's murder? After all, Agnes—Miss Pinderek—was an old lady. Couldn't she have just died of natural causes?"

Roberts shook his head. "The police surgeon said it was poison. Arsenic—all the classic symptoms. Apparently she died some time yesterday afternoon."

"The rat poison?"

Roberts shifted the holstered pistol at his hip to a more comfortable position. "That's how we figure it," he said. "A couple of spoonfuls of that stuff would contain enough arsenic to kill a horse. We tried to lift prints from the box, but the cardboard was so wrinkled and greasy we couldn't get anything worthwhile. The cups and the spoon in the sink were clean too."

"Two cups," said Mr. Strang. "So there probably was a visitor. But up to now Agnes has never allowed a visitor in her house. Not even her best friends."

"Yeah," said Roberts musingly. "Well, she had one yesterday, all right."

"Any idea who it could have been?"

"We've got a pretty good—" Suddenly Roberts clamped his mouth shut and looked at the teacher, shaking his head. "Always want to play detective, don't you—?" he grinned. "Suppose I ask the questions and you give the answers."

"All right, Paul. Fire away."

"Okay. Since Miss Pinderek didn't allow visitors, how come you picked today to come calling?"

The teacher told Roberts about Miss Pinderek's daily trips to the grocery store.

"But today she didn't go, eh?"

Mr. Strang nodded. "For the first time I know of in years. I came over thinking something might be wrong. But I never suspected—"

"Yeah." Roberts slapped the clipboard onto the seat next to him. He turned the key in the ignition, and the starter whirred. "Let's take a ride. It's not much of a lead, but I'd better follow it up."

"Follow what up, Paul?"

"The grocery store. That would be the supermarket on Ripley Street. It's the only one in walking distance from here. I'd like to know what Miss Pinderek usually bought there every day."

In the parking lot Mr. Strang waited in the car while Roberts entered the supermarket. He was gone less than fifteen minutes. Returning, he opened the door, sat down, and shrugged dejectedly. "Catfood," he rumbled, frowning into the rearview mirror. "Damn!"

"What's the matter?"

"The clerks remember her, all right," Roberts replied. "One or two of the older ones used to have her for a teacher. Every day she'd come into the store at about twelve-thirty. She'd pick up a few vegetables, maybe, or a loaf of old bread on sale. But there's one thing she bought every day. A can of Tabby-Yum catfood—tuna flavor."

"Well, that's innocent enough," said the teacher. "I doubt anyone would murder Miss Pinderek just because she kept a cat."

"Okay. But tell me this. What happened to the cat?"

"I beg your pardon?"

"About thirty men have gone through Miss Pinderek's house with a fine-tooth comb. There was no sign of any cat."

"Perhaps it ran away."

Roberts shook his head. "No way, Mr. Strang. I know cats. We've got two of 'em at home. They tend to hang around wherever they've been used to getting chow."

"Maybe it's at a neighbor's house."

Roberts rubbed his chin thoughtfully. "Could be. But you'd think we'd have found a food dish or a litter box—something to show a cat lived there."

"Paul, are you saying the murderer took the cat?"

"That would explain why it's missing, at least. If the killer was after the cat and if Miss Pinderek caught him—"

"What then?" Mr. Strang shook his head. "I doubt she'd have offered him a cup of coffee or tea."

"Yeah, that's true. But how's this? Miss Pinderek's visitor is let in. She offers him something—tea, probably. The visitor spikes Miss Pinderek's tea with the rat poison. She drinks it. She dies. Then the killer takes away the cat and all its equipment. How does that grab you?"

"Frankly, Paul," said Mr. Strang, "it leaves me with a good many questions unanswered. Why, for example, did Agnes allow this one person in when she'd kept all visitors out for years? And why did the killer choose a slow-acting poison like arsenic? And why was the cat taken away at all?"

"This is a weird one, all right," said Roberts with a shake of his head. "The whole thing's crazy. No motive. The killer steals a cat. If we're dealing with a maniac, he's going to be devilishly hard to locate."

"But you do have another lead, don't you, Paul?" Mr. Strang regarded the detective with an owlish stare.

"Like I said, that's police business," said Roberts, starting the car. "You stick to schoolteaching. C'mon, I'll take you home."

It was two days later, on Friday evening, that Roberts called on Mr. Strang at the teacher's room in Mrs.

Mackey's boardinghouse. Mr. Strang offered the detective a chair, which was accepted, and a brandy, which was refused.

"I gotta have your help on the Pinderek case," said the detective reluctantly.

"Why, I wouldn't think of meddling in police business," said Mr. Strang, a smile playing across his lips. "I'm a schoolteacher, remember?"

"Okay, so I shot my mouth off," said Roberts. "But you've got to help me on this one. Seems like everybody in Aldershot knew of Miss Pinderek. They've been demanding action on her murder. The chief's been catching all kinds of flak, and he's dropped the whole thing in my lap. I've got twenty-four hours to come up with an answer."

"But how can I help?" Mr. Strang asked.

"Do you know a kid in the high school named Gary Eklund?"

Mr. Strang stared intently at Roberts. "What's Gary got to do with this?"

"I just want to talk to him, that's all. But if I drop around at his house by myself, the whole family's going to start getting excited—a detective questioning their son and all that. But I understand Gary's in one of your classes."

Mr. Strang nodded.

"Well, that's the answer then," said Roberts. "You come with me. You're his teacher. He'll be more open with you."

Mr. Strang shook his head. "Gary lives with his mother, Paul. The father's been dead less than a year. I'm not about to use my position as Gary's teacher to make him say things he wouldn't talk to a detective about. You'll have to do your own dirty work."

"Okay." Roberts stood up and jammed his hat onto his head. "I thought it would be easier this way, that's all. I guess I'll just have to pull the kid in for question-ing."

He was almost to the door when Mr. Strang stopped him. "Paul, wait. You must have some evidence against Gary. Tell me what it is. If what you've got is legiti-mate—if you're not just going on a fishing expedition—I'll help you. I'm afraid of how Gary's mother would react to his being arrested."

Roberts moved back into the room and sat down again. "Evidence," he said. "Yeah, we got evidence. Apparently Gary Eklund was the visitor Miss Pinderek had on the day she died."

From a coat pocket he took out a notebook. Opening it, he removed a small piece of paper. "This," he said, "is a receipt form for the school edition of the *Morning Record* newspaper. According to what we've found out, young Eklund handles the delivery of those papers in Aldershot High School. Is that right?"

"Yes. I take it myself. Seven cents a day, thirty-five cents per week. A special school rate. Gary earns a few dollars by distributing the papers to the classroom."

"But he's not supposed to deliver anywhere except in school," said Roberts. "Correct?"

"Yes, but—"

"Then how come this receipt was found in Miss Pin-derek's house? It was under the rug next to the body. It's dated the day of the murder—last Tuesday. It's got Miss Pinderek's name on it, Mr. Strang. It's made out for thirty-five cents. And the words *Cancel Subscription* are written across the front of it. Last but not least, Gary Eklund's signature is at the bottom."

"Then Gary was in that house the day Agnes was murdered," said the teacher.

"That's right. And there's another thing. Have you taken a look at Gary's left hand in the last couple of days?"

"No, I—"

"According to his friends, Mr. Strang, there are scratches across the back of it. Scratches that look like they were made by a cat's claws."

The teacher sat down limply. "But Gary's only a boy."

"I know that, Mr. Strang. That's why I want you to be the one to ask him about the receipt and the scratches. Hell, maybe it was an accident. I dunno. I'm not out to frame the kid. I just want to find out what really happened in Miss Pinderek's house last Tuesday."

"When do you want to see Gary, Paul?"

"Right away."

"I'll get my coat."

It was nearly eight o'clock when Roberts and Mr. Strang arrived at the Eklund house, a small shingled bungalow at the far end of town. Mr. Strang rapped at the door, while Roberts hung back in the shadows.

The door was opened by a frail woman with graying hair, wearing a faded housedress. "Why Mr. Strang," she smiled, swinging the door wide. "What a pleasure to see you. Won't you come in?"

Mr. Strang entered the house, followed by Roberts. "We'd like to talk to Gary for a few minutes, if you don't mind, Mrs. Eklund. This man is a detective with the Aldershot—"

There was a sudden scurrying at the rear of the house and the sound of a door opening and closing. Immediately Roberts reopened the front door and raced out into the darkness.

For a moment there was only the slap of footsteps circling the house. Then a scuffling sound, followed by a shrill yell. Finally Roberts' loud voice echoed through the evening stillness.

"Get up, Gary, and come inside. I don't want to hurt you."

Roberts entered, almost carrying a youth wearing blue jeans, a flannel shirt, and once-white sneakers.

"Gary! Mr. Strang!" gasped Mrs. Eklund, her eyes wide and the palms of her hands pressed against her face. "What's happening? I don't understand."

"Sit down, Mrs. Eklund," said the teacher softly. "There really isn't any easy way to say this. You see, Detective Roberts believes Gary knows something about Agnes Pinderek's death last Tuesday."

"But—but that's impossible, Mr. Strang. Gary wouldn't—"

"Tell me something, Gary," said Roberts, staring down at the boy. "Did you visit Miss Pinderek at any time last Tuesday?"

"I don't have to talk to you." Gary turned uncertainly to the teacher. "Do I, Mr. Strang?"

After a glance at Roberts, Mr. Strang shook his head. He knelt beside the boy's chair.

"Gary," he said softly, "I'm on your side. I don't think you did anything wrong."

Slowly Gary raised his eyes toward his mother's worried face. "But I did," he whimpered. "I did do something wrong."

There was a gasp from Mrs. Eklund. But Mr. Strang went on as if he hadn't heard. "What was it, Gary? What did you do that was wrong?"

"It was on Tuesday. I sneaked out of school during my study hall the last period. You see, Miss Pinderek asked me to come to her house. And old Mrs. Lewis never takes attendance in study hall anyway. So I thought nobody would know."

"Why did Miss Pinderek want to see you?" asked Mr. Strang. Behind him, Gary's mother had gripped Roberts' sleeve, and her thin body was trembling.

"She takes the paper, Mr. Strang. Oh, I know I'm only supposed to deliver to people in school. But one day last year I saw her in the hall and she said she'd like to take the paper if it was at all possible. She seemed real nice, and it was no trouble at all to go over there before homeroom, so I did it. I guess when they find out about this, they'll take my job away."

"So you've been delivering the paper to Miss Pinderek every day, is that it? That's the 'something wrong' you were talking about? And she asked you to stop by on Tuesday so she could pay you?"

"Yes, sir. She owed me for the week. It was then she said she wanted to cancel the subscription. I made out a receipt just so I'd have a carbon copy for the circulation manager."

"Did you go *into* the house, Gary?"

The boy nodded. "It was the first time she ever let me inside. It was kind of spooky in there, but she made me a cup of tea. I don't like tea, but she was so nice I drank it so I wouldn't hurt her feelings."

"Did you see a box of rat poison?" asked the teacher.

Gary stared at him blankly. "I don't know anything about rat poison, Mr. Strang. After we'd had our tea, Miss Pinderek paid me, and I left."

"Is that all, Gary?"

"That's all. Honest. The next day I was leaving school when I saw all the police cars by Miss Pinderek's house. When I got home I heard on the radio that she'd been—been—"

Roberts tapped Mr. Strang on the shoulder. "That story's all fine and dandy," he said. "But he still hasn't said anything about how the cat put those scratches on the back of his hand."

Gary considered his left hand as if seeing the scratches for the first time. "What's he talking about?" he asked Mr. Strang.

"The cat," Roberts said. "What did you do with the cat?"

"Cat? What cat, Mr. Strang?"

"Gary," said the teacher, rising stiffly to his feet.

"Mr. Roberts wants to know how you got those scratches on your hand. Was it Miss Pinderek's cat that did it?"

"It wasn't any cat," said Gary. "It was a girl. We were down at the Malt Shop after school on Wednesday. In a booth. I was kind of—you know. Playing around a little. She got mad. So she dug her fingernails into my hand. I pulled it away, and that's how I got scratched."

"Holy Moses on a bicycle!" Paul Roberts shook his head in disgust. "Where did you dream up that fairy tale? If a girl did that, what's her name?"

Tight-lipped, Gary stared at the floor, shaking his head.

"I dunno," said Roberts. "There's no way to get a straight answer out of the kid. And we haven't gotten a single bit of information about the cat. Or the rat poison. Or—"

The teacher sank into a chair, staring at the opposite wall. "Rat poison," he murmured. "Rat poison. That's got to be it."

"Got to be what, Mr. Strang?" asked the detective.

The teacher rose and faced the little group before him. From a jacket pocket he took his glasses and began polishing them on his necktie. "Paul," he said, "it's pretty obvious that you think Gary is lying."

"Sure he's lying. How do you explain his taking off as soon as he found out I was a detective? And what about that business of the girl? He won't give her name. Why? Because there wasn't any girl. It was a cat, I tell you. Look, I'll grant I haven't figured out his motive yet. But of all the crazy yarns—"

"Paul, I want you to do something for me. It won't be easy for you, but try your best."

"Sure, Mr. Strang. Anything to get to the bottom of this. What is it?"

"I want you to assume for a short while that Gary is

telling the absolute truth, that he has left out nothing of importance.''

Roberts stared at the teacher in amazement. "Oh, come on!" he barked in an outraged tone.

"Now if Gary told the truth," Mr. Strang went on calmly, "then he paid Miss Pinderek a visit but left her alive and well. A day later, however, he finds out she's been murdered. As perhaps the only visitor Miss Pinderek has had in years, he realizes he'll be the Number One suspect. And then this evening a detective comes to his home. Wouldn't that explain his sudden flight out the back door? Gary tried to escape not because he was guilty but because he was afraid you thought he was.''

"Well, yeah, maybe. But what about that business of the girl scratching him? That's a lot of—"

Mr. Strang held up a warning finger. "We're assuming Gary's telling the truth, remember? Paul, when you were young, did you ever get fresh with a girl?''

The answer came grudgingly. "Yeah. Couple of times. One of 'em took a good sock at me.''

"Would you have been willing to discuss those times with adults if they'd asked you?''

"Not on your life. I mean—''

"So much for Gary's silence concerning the girl," the teacher went on. "Yes, Gary's afraid. He's afraid he'll lose his paper route because he was doing an old lady a favor by making a delivery outside of school. He's afraid he'll be disciplined for cutting school during a study hall. He's afraid you suspect him of a murder he never committed. But still, I'm convinced he's telling the truth. He went to see Miss Pinderek on Tuesday afternoon. He collected what was owed, gave her a receipt, then left. That's all.''

"And what about the cat?" Roberts asked.

"Ah, yes, the elusive cat. I'm glad you brought that up, Paul, because that's what convinced me Gary was *not* lying.''

"Where is it, then?" the detective demanded.

"The cat, which you thought made the scratches on Gary's hand, and which the killer supposedly did away with, can't be found for the simple reason that it never existed. The fleeing feline is a figment of the imagination, Paul. A phantom."

"But there had to be a cat!" Roberts exclaimed.

"Why, Paul? Why?" Mr. Strang continued relentlessly. "There was no sign of one. No bedding, no food dish—nothing. And once we eliminate the non-existent cat from our thinking, Agnes Pinderek's death is much easier to explain."

"Now, hang on, Mr. Strang." Roberts held up a hand like a student during a class discussion, then furiously jerked it down again. "We know Agnes Pinderek bought a can of Tabby-Yum every day. So how can you say she never owned a cat?"

"Because of the rat poison. Paul, why would a woman who kept a cat—a cat big and healthy enough to consume a can of catfood every day—need rat poison? And yet the box of poison was old and stained and nearly empty. Now, not even the most determined poisoner would need an entire box of rat poison. Clearly the poison was there because Miss Pinderek was plagued with rats. But whoever heard of rat poison being necessary in a home where there's a healthy cat? Therefore, Miss Pinderek did not own a cat."

There was a long silence. From deep in Roberts' throat came a noise like a clogged drain. "Why, I— I—" he stammered.

But Mr. Strang pressed on. "Furthermore, when I first entered Miss Pinderek's house I distinctly heard mice playing among those boxes. Surely mice wouldn't run about so freely if there was a cat in the house."

"No cat," said Roberts slowly. "Okay, Gary seems to have been telling the truth. But if Miss Pinderek was all right when he left the house, what did happen? As far as we know, she had no other visitors. Who could have killed her?''

"The only person possible. Agnes herself.''

"Suicide?'' Roberts whispered the word. "But why?''

"Paul, I knew Miss Pinderek for several years before her retirement. She was a fiercely independent woman. She told me many times of her dread of one day being forced to accept charity.''

Mr. Strang removed a handkerchief from his pocket and blew his nose loudly. "Seventeen years ago Agnes Pinderek retired. She'd made a few investments and felt that with the income from those plus what she got from the retirement fund, she'd be able to get along.

"Now, whether the investments went bad or rising prices were more than her fixed income could take, I don't know. But look at her house. It's run-down in a way she'd never have allowed if she'd had the money for its upkeep. I'd also imagine you'll find it's mortgaged to the hilt. She took to saving everything and anything that might one day be turned into cash. She bought stale bread, and even got the newspaper at school rates to save a few cents a week.

"Paul, the woman was a pauper. But still she wished to maintain her independence. Therefore she allowed herself no visitors who might see how badly off she was and take pity on her. Pity was the one emotion she couldn't tolerate when it was directed at her.

"And then one day she realized she could go on no longer. It became impossible for her to support herself. Accept charity? Never—not Agnes Pinderek. But there was another way. A solution that a proud woman of ninety might have found quite acceptable. Certainly from her point of view much more honorable than the indignity she would have suffered from accepting public assistance.

"But first her affairs had to be put in order. And that

involved paying all her debts—including what she owed Gary. She invited him inside. We can only speculate on why she did this after having kept visitors away for so many years. But he was, after all, the last human she'd ever see. And she remembered to cancel the newspaper. At her death she would leave no loose ends behind.

"Once Gary had left the house, Agnes made a second cup of tea in the same cup she'd first used and mixed in the arsenic. Being tasteless, it was easily swallowed. Then she washed the cups and spoon, not to conceal evidence, but simply from force of habit. The cramps and stomach pains didn't come until later."

Mr. Strang rubbed one hand across his eyes, which were glistening wetly.

"You've drawn a helluva lot of conclusions from a box of rat poison and a missing cat," said Roberts. "How can you be so sure that—"

A tear ran down Mr. Strang's cheek.

"It really had to happen the way you said, didn't it?" Roberts murmured softly. "I'll run a check on Miss Pinderek's finances to make sure, but—well, how else could it have been?"

With one hand he rubbed at the back of his neck. "But I still don't understand about the catfood."

"Tabby-Yum costs about one-third the price of a can of tunafish," said Mr. Strang. "For the past few years it was about the only thing keeping Miss Pinderek alive."

The Cyprian Cat

DOROTHY L. SAYERS

It's extraordinarily decent of you to come along and
see me like this, Harringay. Believe me, I do appreciate
it. It isn't every busy K.C. who'd do as much for such
a hopeless sort of client. I only wish I could spin you
a more workable kind of story, but honestly, I can only
tell you exactly what I told Peabody. Of course, I can
see he doesn't believe a word of it, and I don't blame
him. He thinks I ought to be able to make up a more
plausible tale than that—and I suppose I could, but
where's the use? One's almost bound to fall down somewhere if one tries to swear to a lie. What I'm going to
tell you is the absolute truth. I fired one shot and one
shot only, and that was at the cat. It's funny that one
should be hanged for shooting at a cat.

Merridew and I were always the best of friends;

school and college and all that sort of thing. We didn't see very much of each other after the war, because we were living at opposite ends of the country; but we met in town from time to time and wrote occasionally and each of us knew that the other was there in the background, so to speak. Two years ago, he wrote and told me he was getting married. He was just turned forty and the girl was fifteen years younger, and he was tremendously in love. It gave me a bit of a jolt—you know how it is when your friends marry. You feel they will never be quite the same again; and I'd got used to the idea that Merridew and I were cut out to be old bachelors. But of course I congratulated him and sent him a wedding present, and I did sincerely hope he'd be happy. He was obviously over head and ears; almost dangerously so, I thought, considering all things. Though except for the difference of age it seemed suitable enough. He told me he had met her at—of all places—a rectory garden-party down in Norfolk, and that she had actually never been out of her native village. I mean, literally—not so much as a trip to the nearest town. I'm not trying to convey that she wasn't pukka, or anything like that. Her father was some queer sort of recluse—a mediævalist, or something—desperately poor. He died shortly after their marriage.

I didn't see anything of them for the first year or so. Merridew is a civil engineer, you know, and he took his wife away after the honeymoon to Liverpool, where he was doing something in connection with the harbour. It must have been a big change for her from the wilds of Norfolk. I was in Birmingham, with my nose kept pretty close to the grindstone, so we only exchanged occasional letters. His were what I can only call deliriously happy, especially at first. Later on, he seemed a little worried about his wife's health. She was restless; town life didn't suit her; he'd be glad when he could finish up his Liverpool job and get her away into the country. There wasn't any doubt about their happiness, you understand—she'd got him body and soul as they say, and as far as I could make out it was mutual. I want to make that perfectly clear.

Well, to cut a long story short, Merridew wrote to me at the beginning of last month and said he was just off to a new job—a waterworks extension scheme down in Somerset; and he asked if I could possibly cut loose and join them there for a few weeks. He wanted to have a yarn with me, and Felice was longing to make my acquaintance. They had got rooms at the village inn. It was rather a remote spot, but there was fishing and scenery and so forth, and I should be able to keep Felice company while he was working up at the dam. I was about fed up with Birmingham, what with the heat and one thing and another, and it looked pretty good to me, and I was due for a holiday anyhow, so I fixed up to go. I had a bit of business to do in town, which I calculated would take me about a week, so I said I'd go down to Little Hexham on June 20th.

As it happened, my business in London finished itself off unexpectedly soon, and on the sixteenth I found myself absolutely free and stuck in a hotel with road-drills working just under the windows and a tar-spraying machine to make things livelier. You remember what a hot month it was—flaming June and no mistake about it. I didn't see any point in waiting, so I sent off a wire to Merridew, packed my bag and took the train for Somerset the same evening. I couldn't get a compartment to myself, but I found a first-class smoker with only three seats occupied, and stowed myself thankfully into the fourth corner. There was a military-looking old boy, an elderly female with a lot of bags and baskets, and a girl. I thought I should have a nice, peaceful journey.

So I should have, if it hadn't been for the unfortunate way I'm built. It was quite all right at first—as a matter of fact, I think I was half asleep, and I only woke up properly at seven o'clock when the waiter came to say that dinner was on. The other people weren't taking it, and when I came back from the restaurant car I found that the old boy had gone, and there were only the two women left. I settled down in my corner again, and gradually, as we went along, I found a horrible feeling creeping over me that there was a cat in the compartment somewhere. I'm one of those wretched people who can't stand cats. I don't mean just that I prefer dogs—I mean that the presence of a cat in the same room with me makes me feel like nothing on earth. I can't describe it, but I believe quite a lot of people are affected that way. Something to do with electricity, or so they tell me. I've read that very often the dislike is mutual, but it isn't so with me. The brutes seem to find me abominably fascinating—make a bee-line for my legs every time. It's a funny sort of complaint, and it doesn't make me at all popular with dear old ladies.

Anyway, I began to feel more and more awful and I realized that the old girl at the other end of the seat must have a cat in one of her innumerable baskets. I thought of asking her to put it out in the corridor, or calling the guard and having it removed, but I knew how silly it would sound and made up my mind to try and stick it. I couldn't say the animal was misbehaving itself or anything, and she looked like a pleasant old lady; it wasn't her fault that I was a freak. I tried to distract my mind by looking at the girl.

She was worth looking at, too—very slim, and dark with one of those dead-white skins that make you think of magnolia blossom. She had the most astonishing eyes, too—I've never seen eyes quite like them; a very pale brown, almost amber, set wide apart and a little slanting, and they seemed to have a kind of luminosity of their own, if you get what I mean. I don't know if this sounds—I don't want you to think I was bowled

over, or anything. As a matter of fact she held no sort
of attraction for me, though I could imagine a different
type of man going potty about her. She was just unusual, that was all. But however much I tried to think
of other things I couldn't get rid of the uncomfortable
feeling, and eventually I gave it up and went out into
the corridor. I just mention this because it will help you
to understand the rest of the story. If you can only realize how perfectly awful I feel when there's a cat
about—even when it's shut up in a basket—you'll understand better how I came to buy the revolver.

Well, we got to Hexham Junction, which was the
nearest station to Little Hexham, and there was old
Merridew waiting on the platform. The girl was getting
out too—but not the old lady with the cat, thank
goodness—and I was just handing her traps out after
her when he came galloping up and hailed us.

"Hullo!" he said, "why that's splendid! Have you
introduced yourselves?" So I tumbled to it then that the
girl was Mrs. Merridew, who'd been up to Town on a
shopping expedition, and I explained to her about my
change of plans and she said how jolly it was that I
could come—the usual things. I noticed what an attractive low voice she had and how graceful her movements
were, and I understood—though, mind you, I didn't
share—Merridew's infatuation.

We got into his car—Mrs. Merridew sat in the back
and I got up beside Merridew, and was very glad to feel
the air and to get rid of the oppressive electric feeling
I'd had in the train. He told me the place suited them
wonderfully, and had given Felice an absolutely new
lease of life, so to speak. He said he was very fit, too,
but I thought myself that he looked rather fagged and
nervy.

You'd have liked that inn, Harringay. The real, old
fashioned stuff, as quaint as you make 'em, and everything genuine—none of your Tottenham Court Road an-

tiques. We'd all had our grub, and Mrs. Merridew said she was tired; so she went up to bed early and Merridew and I had a drink and went for a stroll round the village. It's a tiny hamlet quite at the other end of nowhere; lights out at ten, little thatched houses with pinched-up attic windows like furry ears—the place purred in its sleep. Merridew's working gang didn't sleep there, of course—they'd run up huts for them at the dams, a mile beyond the village.

The landlord was just locking up the barn when we came in—a block of a man with an absolutely expressionless face. His wife was a thin, sandy-haired woman who looked as though she was too down-trodden to open her mouth. But I found out afterwards that was a mistake, for one evening when he'd taken one or two over the eight and showed signs of wanting to make a night of it, his wife sent him off upstairs with a gesture and a look that took the heart out of him. That first night she was sitting in the porch, and hardly glanced at us as we passed her. I always thought her an uncomfortable kind of woman, but she certainly kept her house most exquisitely neat and clean.

They'd given me a noble bedroom, close under the eaves with a long, low casement window overlooking the garden. The sheets smelt of lavender, and I was between them and asleep almost before you could count ten. I was tired, you see. But later in the night I woke up. I was too hot, so took off some of the blankets and then strolled across to the window to get a breath of air. The garden was bathed in moonshine and on the lawn I could see something twisting and turning oddly. I stared a bit before I made it out to be two cats. They didn't worry me at that distance, and I watched them for a bit before I turned in again. They were rolling over one another and jumping away again and chasing their own shadows on the grass, intent on their own mysterious business—taking themselves seriously, the way cats always do. It looked like a kind of ritual dance. Then something seemed to startle them, and they scampered away.

I went back to bed, but I couldn't get to sleep again. My nerves seemed to be all on edge. I lay watching the window and listening to a kind of soft rustling noise that seemed to going on in the big wisteria that ran along my side of the house. And then something landed with a soft thud on the sill—a great Cyprian cat.

What did you say? Well, one of those striped grey and black cats. Tabby, that's right. In my part of the country they call them Cyprus cats, or Cyprian cats. I'd never seen such a monster. It stood with its head cocked sideways, staring into the room and rubbing its ears very softly against the upright bar of the casement.

Of course, I couldn't do with that. I shooed the brute away, and it made off without a sound. Heat or no heat, I shut and fastened the window. Far out in the shrubbery I thought I heard a faint miauling; then silence. After that, I went straight off to sleep again and lay like a log till the girl came in to call me.

The next day, Merridew ran us up in his car to see the place where they were making the dam, and that was the first time I realised that Felice's nerviness had not been altogether cured. He showed us where they had diverted part of the river into a swift little stream that was to be used for working the dynamo of an electrical plant. There were a couple of planks laid across the stream, and he wanted to take us over to show us the engine. It wasn't extraordinarily wide or dangerous, but Mrs. Merridew peremptorily refused to cross it, and got quite hysterical when he tried to insist. Eventually he and I went over and inspected the machinery by ourselves. When we got back she had recovered her temper and apologized for being so silly. Merridew abased himself, of course, and I began to feel a little *de trop*. She told me afterwards that she had once fallen into the river as a child, and been nearly drowned, and it had left her with a what d'ye call it—a complex about running water. And but for this one trifling episode I never heard a single sharp word pass between them all the time I was there; nor, for a whole week, did I notice anything else to suggest a flaw in Mrs. Merridew's radiant health. Indeed, as the days wore on to midsummer and the heat grew more intense, her whole body seemed to glow with vitality. It was as though she was lit up from within.

Merridew was out all day and working very hard. I thought he was overdoing it and asked him if he was sleeping badly. He told me that, on the contrary, he fell asleep every night the moment his head touched the pillow, and—what was most unusual with him—had no dreams of any kind. I myself felt well enough, but the hot weather made me languid and disinclined for exertion. Mrs. Merridew took me out for long drives in the car. I would sit for hours, lulled into a half-slumber by the rush of warm air and the purring of the engine, and gazing at my driver, upright at the wheel, her eyes fixed unwaveringly upon the spinning road. We explored the whole of the country to the south and east of Little Hexham, and once or twice went as far north as Bath. Once I suggested that we should turn eastward over the bridge and run down into what looked like rather beautiful wooded country. But Mrs. Merridew didn't care for the idea; she said it was a bad road and that the scenery on that side was disappointing.

Altogether, I spent a pleasant week at Little Hexham, and if it had not been for the cats I should have been perfectly comfortable. Every night the garden seemed to be haunted by them—the Cyprian cat that I had seen the first night of my stay, and a little ginger one and a horrible stinking black Tom were especially tiresome, and one night there was a terrified white kitten that

mewed for an hour on end under my window. I flung
boots and books at my visitors till I was heartily weary,
but they seemed determined to make the inn garden
their rendezvous. The nuisance grew worse from night
to night; on one occasion I counted fifteen of them,
sitting on their hinder-ends in a circle, while the Cyprian cat danced her shadow-dance among them, working in and out like a weaver's shuttle. I had to keep my
window shut, for the Cyprian cat evidently made a habit
of climbing up by the wisteria. The door too; for once
when I had gone down to fetch something from the
sitting-room, I found her on my bed, kneading the cov-
erlet with her paws—pr'rp, pr'rp, pr'rp—with her eyes
closed in sensuous ecstasy. I beat her off, and she spat
at me as she fled into the dark passage.

I asked the landlady about her, but she replied rather
curtly that they kept no cat at the inn, and it is true that
I never saw any of the beasts in the daytime; but one
evening about dusk I caught the landlord in one of the
outhouses. He had the ginger cat on his shoulder, and
was feeding her with something that looked like strips
of liver. I remonstrated with him for encouraging the
cats about the place and asked whether I could have a
different room, explaining that the nightly caterwauling
disturbed me. He half opened his slits of eyes and murmured that he would ask his wife about it; but nothing
was done, and in fact I believe there was no other bedroom in the house.

And all this time the weather got hotter and heavier,
working up for thunder, with the sky like brass and the
earth like iron, and the air quivering over it so that it
hurt your eyes to look at it.

All right, Harringay—I am trying to keep to the point.
And I'm not concealing anything from you. I say that
my relations with Mrs. Merridew were perfectly ordinary. Of course I saw a good deal of her, because as I
explained Merridew was out all day. We went up to the

dam with him in the morning and brought the car back, and naturally we had to amuse one another as best we could till the evening. She seemed quite pleased to be in my company, and I couldn't dislike her. I can't tell you what we talked about—nothing in particular. She was not a talkative woman. She would sit or lie for hours in the sunshine, hardly speaking—only stretching out her body to the light and heat. Sometimes she would spend a whole afternoon playing with a twig or a pebble, while I sat by and smoked. Restful! No. No—I shouldn't call her a restful personality, exactly. Not to me, at any rate. In the evening she would liven up and talk a little more, but she generally went up to bed early, and left Merridew and me to yarn together in the garden.

Oh! about the revolver. Yes. I bought that in Bath, when I had been at Little Hexham exactly a week. We drove over in the morning, and while Mrs. Merridew got some things for her husband, I prowled round the secondhand shops. I had intended to get an air-gun or a pea-shooter or something of that kind, when I saw this. You've seen it, of course. It's very tiny—what people in books describe as "little more than a toy", but quite deadly enough. The old boy who sold it to me didn't seem to know much about firearms. He'd taken it in pawn some time back, he told me, and there were ten rounds of ammunition in it. He made no bones about a licence or anything—glad enough to make a sale, no doubt, without putting difficulties in a customer's way. I told him I knew how to handle it, and mentioned by way of a joke that I meant to take a pot-shot or two at the cats. That seemed to wake him up a bit. He was a dried-up little fellow, with a scrawny grey beard and a stringy neck. He asked me where I was staying. I told him at Little Hexham.

"You better be careful, sir," he said. "They think a heap of their cats down there, and it's reckoned unlucky to kill them.'' And then he added something I couldn't quite catch, about a silver bullet. He was a doddering old fellow, and he seemed to have some sort of scruple about letting me take the parcel away, but I assured him that I was perfectly capable of looking after it and my-self. I left him standing in the door of his shop, pulling at his beard and staring after me.

That night the thunder came. The sky had turned to lead before evening, but the dull heat was more op-pressive than the sunshine. Both the Merridews seemed to be in a state of nerves—he sulky and swearing at the weather and the flies, and she wrought up to a queer kind of vivid excitement. Thunder affects some people that way. I wasn't much better, and to make things worse I got the feeling that the house was full of cats. I couldn't see them but I knew they were there, lurking behind the cupboards and flitting noiselessly about the corridors. I could scarcely sit in the parlour and I was thankful to escape to my room. Cats or no cats I had to open the window, and I sat there with my pyjama jacket unbuttoned, trying to get a breath of air. But the place was like the inside of a copper furnace. And pitch-dark. I could scarcely see from my window where the bushes ended and the lawn began. But I could hear and feel the cats. There were little scrapings in the wisteria and scufflings among the leaves, and about eleven o'clock one of them started the concert with a loud and hideous wail. Then another and another joined in—I'll swear there were fifty of them. And presently I got that foul sensation of nausea, and the flesh crawled on my bones, and I knew that one of them was slinking close to me in the darkness. I looked round quickly, and there she stood, the great Cyprian; right against my shoulder, her eyes glowing like green lamps. I yelled and struck out at her, and she snarled as she leaped out and down. I heard her thump the gravel, and the yowling burst out all over the garden with renewed vehemence. And then all in a moment there was utter silence, and in the far distance there came a flickering blue flash and then another. In the first of them I saw the far garden wall, topped along all its length with cats, like a nursery frieze. When the second flash came the wall was empty.

At two o'clock the rain came. For three hours before that I had sat there, watching the lightning as it spat across the sky and exulting in the crash of the thunder. The storm seemed to carry off all the electrical disturbance in my body; I could have shouted with excitement and relief. Then the first heavy drops fell; then a steady downpour; then a deluge. It struck the iron-backed garden with a noise like steel rods falling. The smell of the ground came up intoxicatingly, and the wind rose and flung the rain in against my face. At the other end of the passage I heard a window thrown to and fastened, but I leaned out into the tumult and let the water drench my head and shoulders. The thunder still rumbled intermittently, but with less noise and farther off, and in an occasional flash I saw the white grille of falling water drawn between me and the garden.

It was after one of these thunder-peals that I became aware of a knocking at my door. I opened it, and there was Merridew. He had a candle in his hand, and his face was terrified.

"Felice!" he said, abruptly. "She's ill. I can't wake her. For God's sake, come and give me a hand."

I hurried down the passage after him. There were two beds in his room—a great four-poster, hung with crimson damask, and a small camp bedstead drawn up near the window. The small bed was empty, the bedclothes tossed aside; evidently he had just risen from it. In the four-poster lay Mrs. Merridew, naked, with only a sheet upon her. She was stretched flat upon her back, her long black hair in two plaits over her shoulders. Her face was waxen and shrunk, like the face of a corpse, and her pulse, when I felt it, was so faint that at first I could scarcely feel it. Her breathing was very slow and shallow and her flesh cold. I shook her, but there was no response at all. I lifted her eyelids, and noticed how the eyeballs were turned up under the upper lid, so that only the whites were visible. The touch of my finger-tip upon the sensitive ball evoked no reaction. I immediately wondered whether she took drugs.

Merridew seemed to think it necessary to make some explanation. He was babbling about the heat—she couldn't bear so much as a silk nightgown—she had suggested that he should occupy the other bed—he had slept heavily—right through the thunder. The rain blowing in on his face had aroused him. He had got up and shut the window. Then he had called to Felice to know if she was all right—he thought the storm might have frightened her. There was no answer. He had struck a light. Her condition had alarmed him—and so on.

I told him to pull himself together and to try whether, by chafing his wife's hands and feet, we could restore the circulation. I had it firmly in my mind that she was under the influence of some opiate. We set to work, rubbing and pinching and slapping her with wet towels and shouting her name in her ear. It was like handling a dead woman, except for the very slight but perfectly regular rise and fall of her bosom, on which—with a kind of surprise that there should be any flaw on its magnolia whiteness—I noticed a large brown mole, just over the heart. To my perturbed fancy it suggested a wound and a menace. We had been hard at it for some time, with the sweat pouring off us, when we became aware of something going on outside the window—a stealthy bumping and scraping against the panes. I snatched up the candle and looked out.

On the sill, the Cyprian cat sat and clawed at the casement. Her drenched fur clung limply to her body, her eyes glared into mine, her mouth was open in protest. She scrabbled furiously at the latch, her hind claws

slipping and scratching at the woodwork. I hammered
on the pane and bawled at her, and she struck back at
the glass as though possessed. As I cursed her and
turned away she set up a long, despairing wail.

Merridew called to me to bring back the candle and
leave the brute alone. I returned to the bed, but the
dismal crying went on and on incessantly. I suggested
to Merridew that he should wake the landlord and get
hot-water bottles and some brandy from the bar and see
if a messenger could not be sent for a doctor. He departed on this errand, while I went on with my mas-
sage. It seemed to me that the pulse was growing still
fainter. Then I suddenly recollected that I had a small
brandy-flask in my bag. I ran out to fetch it, and as I
did so the cat suddenly stopped its howling.

As I entered my own room the air blowing through
the open window struck gratefully upon me. I found
my bag in the dark and was rummaging for the flask
among my shirts and socks when I heard a loud, triumphant mew, and turned round in time to see the Cyprian cat crouched for a moment on the sill, before it
sprang in past me and out at the door. I found the flask
and hastened back with it, just as Merridew and the
landlord came running up the stairs.

We all went into the room together. As we did so,
Mrs. Merridew stirred, sat up, and asked us what in
the world was the matter.

I have seldom felt quite such a fool.

Next day the weather was cooler; the storm had
cleared the air. What Merridew had said to his wife I
do not know. None of us made any public allusion to
the night's disturbance, and to all appearance Mrs.
Merridew was in the best of health and spirits. Merridew took a day off from the waterworks, and we all
went for a long drive and picnic together. We were on
the best of terms with one another. Ask Merridew—he

will tell you the same thing. He would not—he could not, surely—say otherwise. I can't believe, Harringay, I simply cannot believe that he could imagine or suspect me—I say, there was nothing to suspect. Nothing.

Yes—this is the important date—the 24th of June. I can't tell you any more details; there is nothing to tell. We came back and had dinner as usual. All three of us were together all day, till bedtime. On my honour I had no private interview of any kind that day, either with him or with her. I was the first to go to bed, and I heard the others come upstairs about half an hour later. They were talking cheerfully.

It was a moonlight night. For once, no caterwauling came to trouble me. I didn't even bother to shut the window or the door. I put the revolver on the chair beside me before I lay down. Yes, it was loaded, I had no special object in putting it there, except that I meant to have a go at the cats if they started their games again.

I was desperately tired, and thought I should drop off to sleep at once, but I didn't. I must have been over-tired, I suppose. I lay and looked at the moonlight. And then, about midnight, I heard what I had been half ex-pecting: a stealthy scrabbling in the wisteria and a faint miauling sound.

I sat up in bed and reached for the revolver. I heard the "plop" as the big cat sprang up on to the window-ledge; I saw her black and silver flanks, and the outline of her round head, pricked ears and upright tail. I aimed and fired, and the beast let out one frightful cry and sprang down into the room.

I jumped out of bed. The crack of the shot had sounded terrific in the silent house, and somewhere I heard a distant voice call out. I pursued the cat into the passage, revolver in hand—with some idea of fin-ishing it off, I suppose. And then, at the door of the Merridews' room, I saw Mrs. Merridew. She stood with one hand on each doorpost, swaying to and fro. Then she fell down at my feet. Her bare breast was all stained with blood. And as I stood staring at her, clutching the revolver, Merridew came out and found us—like that.

Well, Harringay, that's my story, exactly as I told it to Peabody. I'm afraid it won't sound very well in Court, but what can I say? The trail of blood led from my room to hers; the cat must have run that way; I *knew* it was the cat I shot. I can't offer any explanation. I don't know who shot Mrs. Merridew, or why. I can't help it if the people at the inn say they never saw the Cyprian cat; Merridew saw. it that other night, and I know he wouldn't lie about it. Search the house, Harringay— that's the only thing to do. Pull the place to pieces, till you find the body of the Cyprian cat. It will have my bullet in it.

Animals

CLARK HOWARD

As Ned Price got off the city bus at the corner of his block, he saw that Monty and his gang of trouble-makers were, as usual, loitering in front of Shavelson's Drugstore. A large portable radio—they called it their "ghetto blaster"—was sitting atop a newspaper vending machine, playing very loud acid rock. The gang, six of them, all in their late teens, appeared to be arguing over the contents of a magazine that was circulating among them.

Ned started down the sidewalk. An arthritic limp made him favor his right leg. That, coupled with lumbago and sixty-two years of less than easy living, gave him an overall stooped, tired look. A thriftshop sport coat slightly too large didn't help matters Ned could have crossed the street and gone around Monty and his friends, but he lived on this side of the street so he would just have to cross back again farther down the block. It was difficult enough to get around these days without taking extra steps. Besides, he figured he had at least as much right to walk down the sidewalk as they did to obstruct it.

When Ned got closer, he saw the magazine the gang was passing around was *Ring* and that their argument had to do with the relative merits of two boxers named Hector "Macho" Camacho and Ray "Boom Boom" Mancini. Maybe they'd be too caught up in their argument to hassle him today. That would be a welcome change. A day without having to match wits with this year's version of the Sharks.

But no such luck.

"Hey, old man, where you been?" Monty asked as Ned approached. "Down to pick up your check?" He stepped in the middle of the sidewalk and blocked the way.

Ned stopped. "Yes," he said, "I've been down to pick up my check."

"You're one of those old people who don't let the mailman bring their check, huh?" Monty asked with a smile. "You know there's too many crooks in this neighborhood. You're smart, huh?"

"No, just careful," Ned said. If I was smart, he thought, I would have crossed the street.

"Hey, lemme ask you something," Monty said with mock seriousness. "I seen on a TV special where some old people don't get enough pension to live on an' they eat dogfood and catfood. Do you do that, old man?"

"No, I don't," Ned replied. There was a slight edge to his answer this time. He knew several people who *did* resort to the means Monty had just described.

"Listen, old man, I think you're lying," Monty said without rancor. "I myself seen you in Jamail's Grocery buying catfood."

"That's because I have a cat." Ned tried to step around Monty but the youth moved and blocked his way again.

"You got a cat, old man? Ain't that nice?" Monty feigned interest. "Wha' kind of cat you got, old man?"

"Just an ordinary cat," Ned said. "Nothing special."

"Not a Persian or a Siamese or one of them expensive cats?"

"No. Just an ordinary cat. A tabby, I think it's called."

"A tabby! Hey, tha's really nice."

"Can I go now?" Ned asked.

"Sure!" Monty said, shrugging elaborately. "Who's stopping you, old man?"

Ned stepped around him and this time the youth did not interfere with him. As he walked away, Ned heard Monty say something in Spanish and the others laughed.

A regular Freddie Prinze, Ned thought.

As Ned entered his third-floor-rear kitchenette, he said, "Molly, I'm back." Double-locking the door securely behind him, he hung his coat on a wooden wall peg and limped into a tiny cluttered living room. "Molly!" he called again. Then he stood still and a cold feeling came over him that he was alone in the apartment. "Molly?"

He stuck his head in the narrow Pullman kitchen, then pushed back a curtain that concealed a tiny sleeping alcove.

"Molly, where are you?"

Even as he asked the question one last time, Ned knew he would not find her. He hurried into the bathroom. The window was open about three inches. Ned raised it all the way and stuck his head out. Three stories below, in the alley, some kids were playing kick-the-can. A ledge ran from the window to a back-stairs landing.

"Molly!" Ned called several times.

Moments later, he was out in front looking up and down the street. Monty and his friends, seeing him, sauntered down to where he stood.

"What's the matter, old man?" Monty asked. "You lose something?"

"My cat," Ned said. He turned suspicious eyes on Monty and his friends. "You wouldn't have seen her, by any chance, would you?"

"Is there a reward?" Monty inquired.

Ned gave the question quick consideration. There was an old watch of his late wife's he could probably sell. "There might be, if the cat isn't harmed. Do you know where she is?"

Monty turned to the others. "Anybody see this old man's cat?" he asked with a total absence of concern. When they all shrugged and declared ignorance, he said to Ned, "Sorry, old man. If you'd let the mailman deliver your check, you'd have been home to look after your cat. See the price you pay for being greedy?" He strutted off down the street, his followers in his wake. Feeling ill, Ned watched them all the way to the corner, where they turned out of sight. Pain from an old ulcer began as acid churned in his stomach.

"Molly!" he called and started walking down the block. "Molly! Here, kitty, kitty."

He searched for her until well after dark.

Ned was up early the next morning and back outside looking. He scoured the block all the way to the corner, then came back the other way. In front of the drugstore, he encountered Monty again. The youth was alone this time, leaning up against the building, eating a jelly doughnut and drinking milk from a pint carton.

"You still looking for that cat, old man?" Monty asked, his tone a mixture of incredulity and irritation.

"Yes."

"Man, why don't you go in the alley and get another one? There mus' be a dozen cats back there."

"I want this cat. It belonged to my wife when she was alive."

"Hell, man, a cat's a cat," Monty said.

Shavelson, the drugstore owner, came out, broom in hand. "Want to make half a buck sweeping the sidewalk?" he asked Monty, who looked at him as if he were an imbecile, then turned away disdainfully, not even dignifying the question with an answer. Shavelson shrugged and began sweeping debris toward the curb himself. "You're out early," he said to Ned.

"My cat's lost," Ned said. "She may have got out the bathroom window while I was downtown yesterday."

"Why don't you go back in the alley—"

Ned was already shaking his head. "I want *this* cat."

"Maybe the pound got her," Shavelson suggested. "Their truck was all over the neighborhood yesterday."

The storekeeper's words sent a chill along Ned's spine. "The pound?"

"Yeah. You know, the city animal shelter. They have a truck comes around—"

"It was here yesterday? On this block?"

"Yeah."

"Where do they take the animals tney catch?" Ned asked out of a rapidly drying mouth.

"The animal shelter over on Twelfth Street, I think. They have to hold them there seventy-two hours to see if anybody claims them."

Too distressed by the thought to thank Shavelson, Ned hurried back up the street and into his building. Five minutes later, he emerged again, wearing a coat, his city bus pass in one hand. Crossing the street, he went to the bus stop and stood peering down the street, as if by sheer will he could make a bus appear.

Monty, having finished his doughnut and milk, sat on the curb in front of Shavelson's, smoking a cigarette and reading one of the morning editions from the drugstore's sidewalk newspaper rack. From time to time he glanced over at Ned, wondering at his concern over a cat. Monty knew a few backyards in the neighborhood that were knee-deep in cats.

Presently it began to sprinkle light rain. Monty stood up, folding the newspaper, and handed it to Shavelson as the storekeeper came out to move his papers inside.

"You sure you're through with it?" Shavelson asked. "Any coupons or anything you'd like to tear out?"

Monty's eyes narrowed a fraction. "Someday, man, you're gonna say the wrong thing to me," he warned. "Then you're gonna come to open up your store and you gonna find a pile of ashes."

"You'd do that for *me*?" Shavelson retorted.

The sprinkle escalated to a drizzle as the storekeeper went back inside. From the doorway, Monty looked over at the bus stop again. Ned was still standing there, his only concession to the rain being a turned-up collar. I don't believe this old fool, Monty thought. He goes to more trouble for this cat than most people do for their kids.

Tossing his cigarette into the gutter, he trotted down the block and got into an old Chevy that had a pair of oversize velvet dice dangling from the rearview mirror. Revving the engine a little, he listened with satisfaction to the rumble of the car's gutted muffler, then made a U-turn from the curb and drove to the bus stop.

"Get in, old man," he said, leaning over to the passenger window. "I'm going past Twelfth Street—I'll give you a lift."

Ned eyed him suspiciously. "No, thanks. I'll wait for the bus."

"Hey, man, waiting for a bus in this city at your age ain't too smart. An old lady over on Bates Street *died* at a bus stop last week, she was there so long. Besides, in case you ain't noticed, it's raining." Monty's voice softened a touch. "Come on, get in."

Ned glanced up the street one last time, saw that there was still no bus in sight, thought of Molly caged up at the pound, and got in.

As they rode along, Monty lighted another cigarette and glanced over at his passenger. "You thought me and my boys did something to your cat, didn't you?"

"The thought did cross my mind," Ned admitted.

"Listen, I got better things to do with my time than mess with some cat. You know, for an old guy you ain't very smart."

Ned grunted softly. "I won't argue with you there," he said.

On Twelfth, Monty pulled to the curb in front of the animal shelter. "I got to go see a guy near here, take me about fifteen minutes. I'll come back and pick you up after you get your cat."

Ned studied him for a moment. "Is there some kind of Teenager of the Year award I don't know about?"

"Very funny, man. You're a regular, what's his name, Jack Albertson, ain't you?"

At the information counter in the animal shelter a woman with tightly styled hair and a superior attitude asked, "Was the animal wearing a license tag on its collar?"

"No, she—"

"Was the animal wearing an ID tag on its collar?"

"No, she wasn't wearing a collar. She's really an apartment cat, you see—"

"Sir," the woman said, "our animal enforcement officers don't go into apartments and take animals."

"I think she got out the bathroom window."

"That makes her a street animal, unlicensed and unidentifiable."

"Oh, I can identify her," Ned assured the woman. "And she'll come to me when I call her. If you'll just let me see the cats you picked up yesterday—"

"Sir, do you have any idea how many stray animals are picked up by our trucks every day?"

"Why, no, I never gave—"

"Hundreds," he was told. "Only the ones with license tags or ID tags are kept at the shelter."

"I thought all the animals had to be kept here for three days to give their owners time to claim them," Ned said, remembering what Shavelson had told him.

"You're not listening, sir. Only the animals with license or ID tags are kept at the shelter for the legally required seventy-two hours. Those without tags are taken directly to the disposal pound."

Ned turned white. "Is that where they—where they—?" The words would not form.

"Yes, that is where stray animals are put to sleep." She paused a beat. "Either that or sold."

Ned frowned. "Sold."

"Yes, sir. To laboratories. To help offset the overhead of operating our department." Her eyes flicked over Ned's shabby clothing. "Tax dollars don't pay for *everything,* you know." But she had unknowingly given Ned an ember of hope.

"Can you give me the address of this—disposal place?"

The woman scribbled an address on a slip of paper and pushed it across the counter to him. "Your cat might still be there," she allowed, "if it was picked up late yesterday. Disposal hours for cats are from one to three. If it was a dog you'd be out of luck. They do dogs at night, eight to eleven, because there are more of them. That's because they're easier to catch. They trust people. Cats, they don't trust—''

She was still talking as Ned snatched up the address and hurried out.

Monty was waiting at the curb.

"I didn't think you'd be back this quick," Ned said, getting into the car.

"The guy I went to see wasn't there," Monty told him. It was a lie. All he had done was drive around the block.

"They've taken my cat to be gassed," Ned said urgently, "but if I can get there in time I might be able to save her." He handed Monty the slip of paper. "This is the address. It's way out at the edge of town, but if you'll take me there I'll pay you." He pulled out a pathetically worn billfold, the old-fashioned kind that zipped around three sides. When he opened it, Monty could see several faded cellophane inserts with photographs in them. The photographs were old, all in black-and-white except for a paper picture of June Allyson that had come with the billfold.

From the currency pocket Ned extracted some bills, all of them singles. "I don't have much because I haven't cashed my check yet. But I can at least buy you some gas."

Monty pushed away the hand with the money and started the car. "I don't *buy* gas, man," he scoffed. "I quit buying it when it got to a dollar a gallon."

"Where do you get it?" Ned asked.

"I siphon it. From police cars parked behind the precinct station. It's the only place where the cars are left on a lot unguarded." He flashed a smile at Ned. "That's because nobody would *dare* siphon gas from a cop car, you know what I mean?"

They got on one of the expressways and drove toward

the edge of the city. As Monty drove, he smoked and kept time to rock music from the radio by drumming his fingers on the steering wheel. Ned glanced at a scar down the youth's right cheek. Thin and straight, almost surgical in appearance, it had probably been put there by a straight razor. Ned had been curious about the scar for a long time. Now would be an opportune time to ask how he got it, but Ned was too concerned about Molly. She was such an old cat, nearly fourteen. He hoped she hadn't died of a stroke from the trauma of being captured and caged. If she was still alive, she was going to be so glad to see him Ned doubted she would ever climb out the bathroom window again.

After half an hour on the expressway, Monty exited and drove them to a large warehouselike building at the edge of the city's water-treatment center. A sign above the entrance read simply: *Animal Shelter—Unit F.*

F for final, Ned thought. He was already opening his door as Monty brought the car to a full stop.

"Want me to come in with you?" Monty asked.

"What for?" Ned wanted to know, frowning.

The younger man shrugged. "So's they don't push you around. Sometimes people push old guys around."

"Really?" Ned asked wryly.

Monty looked off at nothing. "You want me to come in or not?"

"I can handle things myself," Ned told him gruffly.

The clerk at this counter, a thin gum-chewing young man with half a dozen ballpoints in a plastic holder in his shirt pocket, checked a clipboard on the wall and said, "Nope, you're too late. That whole bunch from yesterday was shipped out to one of our lab customers early this morning."

Ned felt warm and slightly nauseated. "Do you think they might sell my cat back to me?" he asked. "If I went over there?"

"You can't go over there," the clerk said. "We're not allowed to divulge the name or address of any of our lab customers."

"Oh." Ned wet his lips. "Do you suppose you could call them for me? Tell them I'd like to make some kind of arrangements to buy back my cat?"

The clerk was already shaking his head. "I don't have time to do things like that, mister."

"A simple phone call," Ned pleaded. "It'll only take—"

"Look, mister, I said no. I'm a very busy person."

Just then someone stepped up to the counter next to Ned. Surprised, Ned saw that it was Monty. He had his hands on the counter, palms down, and was smiling at the clerk.

"What time you get off work, Very Busy Person?" he asked.

The clerk blinked rapidly. "Uh, why do you want to know?"

"I'm jus' interested in what kind of hours a Very Busy Person like you keeps." Monty's smile faded and his stare grew cold. "You don't have to tell me if you don't want to. I can wait outside and find out for myself."

The clerk stopped chewing his gum; the color disappeared from his face, leaving him sickly pale. "Why, uh—why would you do that?"

" 'Cause I ain't got nothing better to do," Monty replied. "I *was* gonna take this old man here to that lab to try and get his cat back. But if he don't know where it is, I can't do that. So I'll just hang around here." He winked at the clerk without smiling. "See you later, man."

Monty took Ned's arm and started him toward the door.

"Just—wait a minute," the clerk said.

Monty and Ned turned back to see him rummaging

in a drawer under the counter. He found a sheet of paper with three names and addresses mimeographed on it. With a ballpoint from the selection in his shirt pocket, he circled one of the addresses. Monty stepped back to the counter and took the sheet of paper.

"If it turns out they're expecting us," Monty said, "I'll know who warned them. You take my meaning, man?"

The clerk nodded. He swallowed dryly and his gum was gone.

At the door, looking at the address circled on the paper, Monty said, "Come on, old man. This here place is clear across town. You positive one of them cats in the alley wouldn't do you?"

On their way to the lab, Ned asked, "Why are you helping me like this?"

Ned shrugged. "It's a slow Wednesday, man."

Ned studied the younger man for a time, then observed, "You're different when your gang's not around."

Monty tossed him a smirk. "You gonna, what do you call it, analyze me, old man? You gonna tell me I got 'redeeming social values' or something like that?"

"I wouldn't go quite that far," Ned said dryly. "Anyway, sounds to me like you've *been* analyzed."

"Lots of times," Monty told him. "When they took me away from my old lady because it was an 'unfit environment,' they had some shrink analyze me then. When I ran away from the foster homes I was put in, other shrinks analyzed me. After I was arrested and was waiting trial in juvenile court for some burglaries, I was analyzed then. When they sent me downstate to the reformatory, I was analyzed. They're very big on analyzing in this state."

"They ever tell you the results of all that analyzing?"

"Sure. I'm incorrigible. And someday I'm supposed to develop into a sociopath. You know what that is?"

"Not exactly," Ned admitted.

Monty shrugged. "Me neither. I guess I'll find out when I become one."

They rode in silence for a few moments and then Ned said, "Well, anyway, I appreciate you helping me."

"Forget it," Monty said. He would not look at Ned; his eyes were straight ahead on the road. After several seconds, he added, "Jus' don't go telling nobody about it."

"All right, I won't," Ned agreed.

Their destination on the other side of the city was a large square two-story building on the edge of a forest preserve. It was surrounded by a chain-link fence with an entrance gate manned by a security guard. A sign on the gate read: *Consumer Evaluation Laboratory.*

Monty parked outside the gate and followed Ned over to the security-guard post. Ned explained what he wanted. The security guard took off his cap and scratched his head. "I don't know. This isn't covered in my guard manual. I'll have to call and find out if they sell animals back."

Ned and Monty waited while the guard telephoned. He talked to one person, was transferred to another, then had to repeat his story to still a third before he finally hung up and said, "Mr. Hartley of Public Relations is coming out to talk to you."

Mr. Hartley was a pleasant but firmly uncooperative man. "I'm sorry, but we can't help you," he said when Ned had told him of Molly's plight. "We have at least a hundred small animals in there—cats, dogs, rabbits, guinea pigs—all of them undergoing scientific tests. Even the shipment we received this morning has already been processed into a testing phase. We simply can't interrupt the procedure to find one particular cat."

"But it's *my* cat," Ned insisted. "She's not homeless or a stray. She belonged to my late wife—"

"I understand that, Mr. Price," Hartley interrupted, "but the animal *was* outside with no license or ID tag around its neck. It was apprehended legally and sold to us legally. I'm afraid it's just too late."

As they were talking, a bus pulled up to the gate. Hartley waved at the driver, then turned to the security guard. "These are the people from Diamonds-and-Pearls Cosmetics, Fred. Pass them through and then call Mr. Draper. He's conducting a tour for them."

As the bus passed through, Hartley turned back to resume the argument with Ned, but Monty stepped forward to intercede.

"We understand, Mr. Hartley," Monty said in a remarkably civil tone. "We're sure you'd help us if you could. Please accept our apology for taking up your time." Monty offered his hand.

"Quite all right," Hartley said, shaking hands.

Ned was staring incredulously at Monty. Macho had suddenly become Milquetoast.

"Come along, old fellow," Monty said, putting his arm around Ned's shoulders. "We'll go to a pet store and buy you a new kitty."

Ned allowed himself to be led back to the car, then demanded, "What the hell's got into you?"

"You're wasting your time with that joker," Monty said. "He's been programmed to smile and say no to whatever you want. We got to find some other way to get your cat."

"What other way?"

Monty grinned. "Like using the back door, man."

Driving away from the front gate, Monty found a gravel road and slowly circled the fenced-in area of the Consumer Evaluation Laboratory. On each side of the facility, beyond its fence, were several warehouses and small plants. In front, beyond a feeder road, was a state highway. Growing right up to its rear fence was the forest preserve: a state-protected wooded area.

Monty made one full circuit of the complex occupied by the laboratory and its neighbors, then said, "I think the best plan is to park in the woods, get past the fence in back, and sneak in that way."

"You mean slip in and *steal* my cat?" Ned asked.

Monty shrugged. "They stole her from you," he said.

Ned stared at him. "I'm sixty-two years old," he said. "I've never broken the law in my life."

"So?" said Monty, frowning. He did not see any relevance. The two men, one young, one old, each so different from the other, locked eyes in a silent stare for what seemed like a long time.

They were parked on the shoulder of the gravel road, the car windows down. The air coming into the car was fresh from the morning rain. Ned detected the scent of wet earth. Some movement a few yards up the road caught his eye and he turned his attention away from Monty. The movement was a gray squirrel scurrying across the road to the safety of the nearby woods. Watching the little animal, wild and free, made Ned think of the animals in the laboratory that were not free—the dogs and rabbits and guinea pigs.

And cats.

"All right," he told Monty. "Let's go in the back way."

Monty parked in one of the public picnic areas. From the trunk, he removed a pair of chain cutters and held them under his jacket with one hand.

"What do you carry these things for?" Ned asked, and realized at once that his question was naive.

"To clip coupons with, man," Monty replied. "Coupons save you money on everyday necessities."

The two men made their way through the trees to the

rear of the laboratory's chain-link fence. Crouching, they scrutinized the back of the complex. Monty's eyes settled immediately on a loading dock served by a single-lane driveway coming around one side of the building. "We can go in there," he said. "Overhang doors are no sweat to open. But first let's see if there's any juice in this fence." Keeping his hands well on the rubber-covered handles, he gently touched the metal fence with the tip of the chain cutters. The contact drew no sparks. "Nothing on the surface," he said. "Let's see if there's anything inside. Some of these newer chain-links have an insulated circuit running through them." Quickly and expertly, he spread the cutters and snipped one link of the metal. Again there were no sparks. "This is going to be a breeze."

With a practiced eye, he determined his pattern and quickly snipped exactly the number of links necessary to create an opening large enough for them to get through. Then he gripped the cut section and bent it open, like a door, about eight inches. The chain cutters he hid nearby in some weeds.

"Now here's our story," he said to Ned. "We was walking through the public woods here and saw this hole cut in the fence, see? We thought it was our civic duty to tell somebody about it, so we came inside looking for somebody. If we get caught, stick to that story. Got it?"

"Got it," Ned confirmed.

Monty winked approval. "Le's do it, old man."

They eased through the opening and Monty bent the cut section back into place. Then they started toward the loading dock, walking upright with no attempt at hurrying or hiding. Ned was nervous but Monty remained very cool; he even whistled a soft little tune. When he sensed Ned's anxiety, he threw him a grin.

"Relax, old man. It'll take us forty, maybe fifty seconds to reach that dock. The chances of somebody seeing us in that little bit of time are so tiny, man. And even if they do, so why? We got our story, right?''

''Yeah, right,'' Ned replied, trying to sound confident.

But as Monty predicted, they reached the loading dock unobserved and unchallenged. Once up on the dock, Monty peered through a small window in one of the doors. ''Just a big room with a lot of work tables,'' he said quietly. ''Don't look like nobody's around. Hey, this service door's unlocked. Come on.''

They moved inside into a large room equipped with butcher-block tables fixed to a tile floor. A number of hoses hung over each table, connected to the ceiling. As the two men stood scrutinizing the room, they suddenly heard a voice approaching. Quickly they ducked behind one of the tables.

An inner door opened and a man led a group of people into the room, saying, ''This is our receiving area, ladies and gentlemen. The animals we purchase are delivered here and our laboratory technicians use these tables to wash and delouse them. They are then taken into our testing laboratory next door, which I will show you next. If you would, please take a smock from the pile there, to protect your clothes from possible contact with any of the substances we use in there.''

Peering around the table, Ned and Monty watched as the people put on smocks and regrouped at the door. As they were filing out, Ned nudged Monty and said, ''Come on.''

Monty grinned. ''You catching on, old man.''

The two put on smocks and fell in at the rear of the group. They followed along as it was led through the hall and into a much larger room. This one was set up with a series of aisles formed by long work counters on which stood wire-grille cages of various sizes. Each cage was numbered and had a small slot containing a white card on its door. In each cage was a live animal.

"Our testing facility, we feel, is the best of its kind currently in existence," the tour guide said. "As you can see, we have a variety of test animals: cats, dogs, rabbits, guinea pigs. We also have access to larger animals, if a particular test requires it. Our testing procedures can be in any form. We can force-feed the test substance, introduce it by forced inhalation, reduce it to a dermal form and apply it directly to an animal's shaved skin, or inject it intravenously. Over here, for instance, are rabbits being given what is known as a Draize test. A new hairspray is being sprayed into their very sensitive eyes in order to gauge its irritancy level. Just behind the rabbits you see a group of puppies having dishwashing detergent introduced directly into their stomachs by a syringe with a tube attached to a hand pump. This is called an Internal LD-50 test; the LD stands for lethal dose and the number fifty represents one-half of a group of one hundred animals on which the test will be conducted. When half of the test group has died, we will have an accurate measurement of the toxicity level of this product. This will provide the company marketing the product with evidence of safety testing in case it is later sued because some child swallows the detergent and dies. During the course of the testing, we also learn exactly how a particular substance will affect a living body, by observing whatever symptoms the animal exhibits: convulsions, paralysis, tremors, inability to breathe, blindness as in the case of the rabbits there—"

Ned was staring at the scene around him. As he looked at the helpless, caged, tortured animals, he felt his skin crawl. Which were the animals, the ones in the cages, or the ones outside the cages? Glancing at Monty, he saw the younger man was reacting the same way— his eyes were wide, his expression incredulous, and his hands were curled into fists.

"We can test virtually any substance or product there

is,'' the guide continued. ''We test all forms of cosmetics and beauty aids, all varieties of detergents and other cleaning products, every food additive, coloring, and preservative, any new chemical or drug product— you name it. In addition to servicing private business, we test pesticides for the Environmental Protection Agency, synthetic substances for the Food and Drug Administration, and a variety of products for the Consumer Product Safety Commission. Our facility is set up so that almost no lead time is required to service our customers. As an example of this, a dozen cats brought in this morning are already in a testing phase over here—''

Ned and Monty followed the group to another aisle where the guide pointed out the newly arrived cats and explained the test being applied to them. Ned strained to see beyond the people in front of him, trying to locate Molly.

Finally the tour guide said, ''Now, ladies and gentlemen, if you'll follow me, I'll take you to our cafeteria, where you can enjoy some refreshments while our testing personnel answer any questions you have about how we can help Diamonds-and-Pearls Cosmetics keep its products free of costly lawsuits. Just drop your smocks on the table outside the door.''

Again Ned and Monty ducked down behind a workbench to conceal themselves as the people filed out of the room. When the door closed behind the group, Ned rose and hurried to the cat cages. Monty went over to lock the laboratory door.

Ned found Molly in one of the top cages. She was lying on her side, eyes wide, staring into space. The back part of her body had been shaved and three intravenous needles were stuck in her skin and held in place by tape. The tubes attached to the needles ran out the grille and up to three small bottles suspended above the cage. They were labeled: FRAGRANCE, DYE, and POLY-SORBATE 93.

Ned wiped his eyes with the heel of one hand. Un-latching the grille door, he reached in and stroked Molly. "Hello, old girl," he said. Molly opened her mouth to meow, but no sound came.

"Dirty bastards," Ned heard Monty whisper. Turn-ing, he saw the younger man reading the card on the front of Molly's cage. "This is some stuff that's going to be used in a hair tint," he said. "This test is to see if the cat can stay alive five hours with this combination of stuff in her."

"I can answer that," Ned said. "She won't. She's barely alive now."

"If we can get her to a vet, maybe he can save her," Monty suggested. "Pump her stomach or something." He bobbed his chin at the back wall. "We can get out through one of those windows—they face our hole in the fence."

"Get one open," Ned said. "I'll take Molly out."

Monty hurried over to the window while Ned gently unfastened the tape and pulled the hypodermic needles out of Molly's flesh. Once again the old cat looked at him and tried to make a sound, but she was too weak and too near death. "I know, old girl," Ned said softly. "I know it hurts."

Near the window, after opening it, Monty noticed several cages containing puppies that were up and mov-ing around, some of them barking and wagging their tails. Monty quickly dropped their cages, scooped them out two at a time, and dropped them out the window.

"Lead these pups to the fence, old man," he said as Ned came over with Molly.

"Right," Ned replied. He let Monty hold the dying cat as he painfully got his arthritic legs over the ledge and lowered himself to the ground. "What about you?" he asked as Monty handed down the cat.

"I'm gonna turn a few more pups loose, an' maybe some of those rabbits they're blinding. You head for the fence—I'll catch up."

Ned limped away from the building, calling the pups to follow him. He led them to the fence, bent the cut section open again, and let them scurry through. As he went through himself, he could feel Molly becoming even more limp in his hands. By the time he got into the cover of the trees, her eyes had closed, her mouth had opened, and she was dead. Tears coming again, he knelt and put the cat up against a tree trunk and covered her with an old red bandanna he pulled out of his back pocket.

Looking through the fence, he saw that Monty was still putting animals out the window. Two dozen cats, dogs, rabbits, and guinea pigs were moving around tentatively on the grass behind the laboratory. He's got to get out of there or he'll get caught, Ned thought. Returning through the opening in the fence, he hurried back to the window.

"Come on," he urged as the younger man came to the window with a kitten in each hand.

"No—" Monty tossed the kittens to the ground "—I'm going to turn loose every animal that can stand!"

Old man and young man fixed eyes on each other as every difference there had ever been between them faded.

"Give me a hand up, then," Ned said.

Monty reached down and pulled him back up through the window.

As they worked furiously to open more cages and move their captives out the window, they became aware of someone trying the lab door and finding it locked. Several moments later, someone tried it again. A voice outside the door mentioned a key. The two inside the lab worked all the faster. Finally, a sweating Monty

said, "I think that's all we can let go. The rest are too
near dead. Let's get out of here!"

"I'm going to do one more thing first," Ned growled.

Poised by the open window, Monty asked, "What?"

Ned walked toward a shelf on which stood several
gallons of isopropyl alcohol. "I'm going to burn this
son-of-a-bitch down."

Monty rushed over to him. "What about the other
animals?"

"You said yourself they were almost dead. At least
this will put them out of their misery without any more
torture." He opened a jug and started pouring alcohol
around the room. After a moment of indecision, Monty
joined him.

Five minutes later, just as someone in the hall got
the lab door open and several people entered, Ned and
Monty dropped out the open window and tossed a
lighted book of matches back inside.

The laboratory became a ball of flame.

While the fire spread and the building burned, Ned
and Monty managed to get the released animals through
the fence and into the woods. Sirens of fire and police
emergency vehicles pierced the quiet afternoon. There
were screams and shouts as the burning building was
evacuated. Monty retrieved the chain cutters and ran
toward the car. Ned limped hurriedly after him, but
stopped when he got to where Molly was lying under
the red bandanna. I can't leave her like that, he thought.
She had been a good, loving pet to Ned's wife, then to
Ned after his wife died. She deserved to be buried, not
left to rot next to a tree. Dropping to his knees, he
began to dig a grave with his hands.

Monty rushed back and saw what he was doing.
"They gonna catch you, old man!" he warned.

"I don't care."

Ned kept digging as Monty hurried away.

He had barely finished burying Molly a few minutes later when the police found him.

Ned's sentence, because he was a first offender and no one had been hurt in the fire, was three years. He served fourteen months. Monty was waiting for him the day he came back to the block.

"Hey, old man, ex-cons give a neighborhood a bad reputation," Monty chided.

"You ought to know," Ned said gruffly.

"You get the Vienna sausages and crackers and stuff I had sent from the commissary?"

"Yeah." He did not bother to thank Monty; he knew it would only embarrass him.

"So how you like the joint, old man?"

Ned shrugged. "It could have been worse. A sixty-two-year-old man with a game leg, there's not much they could do to me. I worked in the library, checking books out. Did a lot of reading in between. Mostly about animals."

"No kidding?" Monty's eyebrows went up. "I been learning a little bit about animals, too. I'm a, what do you call it, volunteer down at the A.S.P.C.A. That's American Society for the Prevention of Cruelty to Animals."

"I know what it is," said Ned. "Good organization. Say, did that Consumer Evaluation Laboratory ever rebuild?"

"Nope," Monty replied. "You put 'em out of business for good, old man."

"Animal shelter still selling to those other two labs?"

"Far as I know."

"Still got their addresses?"

Monty smiled. "You bet."

"Good," Ned said, nodding. Then he smiled, too.

The Yellow Cat

WILBUR DANIEL STEELE

At least once in my life I had had the good fortune
to board a deserted vessel at sea. I say "good fortune"
because it has left me the memory of a singular impression. I have felt a ghost of the same thing two or
three times since then, when peeping through the doorway of an abandoned house.

Now that vessel was not dead. She was a good vessel,
a sound vessel, even a handsome vessel, in her blunt-
bowed, coastwise way. She sailed under four lowers
across as blue and glittering a sea as I have ever known,
and there was not a point in her sailing that one could
lay a finger upon as wrong. And yet, passing that
schooner at two miles, one knew, somehow, that no
hand was on her wheel. Sometimes I can imagine a
vessel, stricken like that, moving over the empty spaces

of the sea, carrying it off quite well were it not for that indefinable suggestion of a stagger; and I can think of all those ocean gods, in whom no landsman will ever believe, looking at one another and tapping their foreheads with just the shadow of a smile.

I wonder if they all scream—these ships that have lost their souls? Mine screamed. We heard her voice, like nothing I have ever heard before, when we rowed under her counter to read her name—the *Marionnette,* it was, of Halifax. I remember how it made me shiver, there in the full blaze of the sun, to hear her going on so, railing and screaming in that stark fashion. And I remember, too, how our footsteps, pattering through the vacant internals in search of that haggard utterance, made me think of the footsteps of hurrying warders roused in the night.

And we found a parrot in a cage; that was all. It wanted water. We gave it water and went away to look things over, keeping pretty close together, all of us. In the quarters the table was set for four. Two men had begun to eat, by the evidence of the plates. Nowhere in the vessel was there any sign of disorder, except one sea-chest broken out, evidently in haste. Her papers were gone and the stern davits were empty. That is how the case stood that day, and that is how it has stood to this. I saw this same *Marionnette* a week later, tied up to a Hoboken dock, where she awaited news from her owners; but even there, in the midst of all the waterfront bustle, I could not get rid of the feeling that she was still very far away—in a sort of shippish otherworld.

The thing happens now and then. Sometimes half a dozen years will go by without a solitary wanderer of this sort crossing the ocean paths, and then in a single season perhaps several of them will turn up: vacant waifs, impassive and mysterious—a quarter-column of tidings tucked away on the second page of the evening paper.

That is where I read the story about the *Abbie Rose*. I recollect how painfully awkward and out-of-place it looked there, cramped between ruled black edges and smelling of landsman's ink—this thing that had to do essentially with air and vast colored spaces. I forget the exact words of the heading—something like "Abandoned Craft Picked Up At Sea"—but I still have the clipping itself, couched in the formal patter of the marine-news writer:

"The first hint of another mystery of the sea came in today when the schooner *Abbie Rose* dropped anchor in the upper river, manned only by a crew of one. It appears that the outbound freighter *Mercury* sighted the *Abbie Rose* off Block Island on Thursday last, acting in a suspicious manner. A boat-party sent aboard found the schooner in perfect order and condition, sailing under four lower sails, the topsails being pursed up to the mastheads but not stowed. With the exception of a yellow cat, the vessel was found to be utterly deserted, though her small boat still hung in the davits. No evidences of disorder were visible in any part of the craft. The dishes were washed up, the stove in the galley was still slightly warm to the touch, everything in its proper place with the exception of the vessel's papers, which were not to be found.

"All indications being for fair weather, Captain Rohmer of the *Mercury* detailed two of his company to bring the find back to this port, a distance of one hundred and fifteen miles. The only man available with a knowledge of the fore-and-aft rig was Stewart McCord, the second engineer. A seaman by the name of Björnsen was sent with him. McCord arrived this noon, after a very heavy voyage of five days, reporting that Björnsen had fallen overboard while shaking out the foretopsail.

McCord himself showed evidences of the hardships he has passed through, being almost a nervous wreck.''

Stewart McCord! Yes, Stewart McCord would have a knowledge of the fore-and-aft rig, or of almost anything else connected with the affairs of the sea. It happened that I used to know this fellow. I had even been quite chummy with him in the old days—that is, to the extent of drinking too many beers with him in certain hot-country ports. I remembered him as a stolid and deliberate sort of a person, with an amazing hodgepodge of learning, a stamp collection, and a theory about the effects of tropical sunshine on the Caucasian race, to which I have listened half of more than one night, stretched out naked on a freighter's deck. He has not impressed me as a fellow who would be bothered by his nerves.

And there was another thing about the story which struck me as rather queer. Perhaps it is a relic of my seafaring days, but I have always been a conscientious reader of the weather reports; and I could remember no weather in the past week sufficient to shake a man out of a top, especially a man by the name of Björnsen—a thoroughgoing seafaring name.

I was destined to hear more of this in the evening, from the ancient boatman who rowed me out on the upper river. He had been to sea in his day. He knew enough to wonder about this thing, even to indulge in a little superstitious awe about it.

''No sir-ee. Something *happened* to them four chaps. And another thing—''

I fancied I heard a sea-bird whining in the darkness overhead. A shape moved out of the gloom ahead, passed to the left, lofty and silent, and merged once more with the gloom behind—a barge at anchor, with the sea-grass clinging around her water-line.

''Funny about the other chap,'' the old fellow speculated. ''Björnsen—I b'lieve he called 'im. Now that story sounds to me kind of—'' He feathered his oars with a suspicious jerk and peered at me. "This McCord a friend of yourn?'' he inquired.

"In a way,'' I said.

"Hm-m—well—'' He turned on his thwart to squint ahead. "There she is,'' he announced, with something of relief, I thought. It was hard at that time of night to make anything but a black blotch out of the *Abbie Rose*. Of course I could see that she was pot-bellied, like the rest of the coastwise sisterhood. And that McCord had not stowed his topsails. I could make them out, pursed at the mastheads and hanging down as far as the cross-trees, like huge, over-ripe pears. Then I recollected that he had found them so—probably had not touched them since; a queer way to leave tops, it seemed to me. I could see also the glowing tip of a cigar floating rest-lessly along the farther rail. I called: "McCord! Oh, McCord!''

The spark came swimming across the deck. "Hello! Hello, there—ah—'' There was a note of querulous uneasiness there that somehow jarred with my remem-brance of this man.

"Ridgeway,'' I explained.

He echoed the name uncertainly, still with that sug-gestion of peevishness, hanging over the rail and peer-ing down at us. "Oh! By gracious!'' he exclaimed abruptly. "I'm glad to see you, Ridgeway. I had a boatman coming out before this, but I guess—well, I guess he'll be along. By gracious! I'm glad—''

"I'll not keep you,'' I told the gnome, putting the money in his palm and reaching for the rail. McCord lent me a hand on my wrist. Then when I stood squarely on the deck beside him he appeared to forget my pres-ence, leaned forward heavily on the rail, and squinted after my waning boatman.

"Ahoy—boat!'' he called out, sharply, shielding his lips with his hands. His violence seemed to bring him

out of the blank, for he fell immediately to puffing
strongly at his cigar and explaining in rather a shame-
voiced way that he was beginning to think his own boatman had "passed him up."

"Come in and have a nip," he urged with an abrupt
heartiness, clapping me on the shoulder.

"So you've—" I did not say what I had intended. I
was thinking that in the old days McCord had made
rather a fetish of touching nothing stronger than beer.
Neither had he been of the shoulder-clapping sort. "So
you've got something aboard?" I shifted.

"Dead men's liquor," he chuckled. It gave me a
queer feeling in the pit of my stomach to hear him. I
began to wish I had not come, but there was nothing
for it now but to follow him into the afterhouse. The
cabin itself might have been nine feet square, with three
bunks occupying the port side. To the right opened the
master's state-room, and a door in the forward bulkhead
led to the galley.

I took in these features at a casual glance. Then,
hardly knowing why I did it, I began to examine them
with greater care.

"Have you a match?" I asked. My voice sounded
very small, as though something unheard of had happened to all the air.

"Smoke?" he said. "I'll get you a cigar."

"No." I took the proffered match, scratched it on
the side of the galley door, and passed out. There
seemed to be a thousand pans there, throwing my match
back at me from every wall of the boxlike compartment. Even McCord's eyes, in the doorway, were large
and round and shining. He probably thought me crazy.
Perhaps I was, a little. I ran the match along close to
the ceiling and came upon a rusty hook a little aport of
the center.

"There," I said. "Was there anything hanging from

this—er—say a parrot—or something, McCord?'' The match burned my fingers and went out.

"What do you mean?'' McCord demanded from the doorway. I got myself back into the comfortable yellow glow of the cabin before I answered, and then it was a question.

"Do you happen to know anything about this craft's personal history?''

"No. What are you talking about! Why?''

"Well, I do,'' I offered. "For one thing, she's changed her name. And it happens this isn't the first time she's—well, damn it all, fourteen years ago I helped pick up this whatever-she-is off the Virginia Capes—in the same sort of condition. There you are!'' I was yapping like a nerve-strung puppy.

McCord leaned forward with his hands on the table, bringing his face beneath the fan of the hanging-lamp. For the first time I could mark how shockingly it had changed. It was almost colorless. The jaw had somehow lost its old-time security and the eyes seemed to be loose in their sockets. I had expected him to start at my announcement; he only blinked at the light.

"I am not surprised,'' he remarked at length. "After what I've seen and heard—'' He lifted his fist and brought it down with a sudden crash on the table. "Man—let's have a nip!''

He was off before I could say a word, fumbling out of sight in the narrow state-room. Presently he reappeared, holding a glass in either hand and a dark bottle hugged between his elbows. Putting the glasses down, he held up the bottle between his eyes and the lamp, and its shadow, falling across his face, green and luminous at the core, gave him a ghastly look—like a mutilation or an unspeakable birth-mark. He shook the bottle gently and chuckled his "Dead men's liquor'' again. Then he poured two half-glasses of the clear gin, swallowed his portion, and sat down.

"A parrot," he mused, a little of the liquor's color creeping into his cheeks. "No, this time it was a cat, Ridgeway. A yellow cat. She was—"

"*Was?*" I caught him up. "What's happened—what's become of her?"

"Vanished. Evaporated. I haven't seen her since night before last, when I caught her trying to lower the boat—"

"*Stop it!*" It was I who banged the table now, without any of the reserve of decency. "McCord, you're drunk—*drunk,* I tell you. A *cat*! Let a *cat* throw you off your head like this! She's probably hiding out below this minute, on affairs of her own."

"Hiding?" He regarded me for a moment with the queer superiority of the damned. "I guess you don't realize how many times I've been over this hulk, from decks to keelson, with a mallet and a foot-rule."

"Or fallen overboard," I shifted, with less assurance. "Like this fellow Björnsen. By the way, McCord—" I stopped there on account of the look in his eyes.

He reached out, poured himself a shot, swallowed it, and got up to shuffle about the confined quarters. I watched their restless circuit—my friend and his jumping shadow. He stopped and bent forward to examine a Sunday-supplement chromo tacked on the wall, and the two heads drew together, as though there was something to whisper. Of a sudden I seemed to hear the old gnome croaking. "Now that story sounds to me kind of—"

McCord straightened up and turned to face me.

"What do you know about Björnsen?" he demanded.

"Well—only what they had you saying in the papers," I told him.

"Pshaw!" He snapped his fingers, tossing the affair aside. "I found her log," he announced in quite another tone.

"You did, eh? I judged, from what I read in the paper, that there wasn't a sign."

"No, no; I happened on this the other night, under the mattress in there." He jerked his head toward the state-room. "Wait!" I heard him knocking things over in the dark and mumbling at them. After a moment he came out and threw on the table a long, cloth-covered ledger, of the common commercial sort. It lay open at about the middle, showing close script running indiscriminately across the column ruling.

"When I said 'log,' " he went on, "I guess I was going it a little strong. At least, I wouldn't want that sort of log found around *my* vessel. Let's call it a personal record. Here's his picture, somewhere—" He shook the book by its back and a common kodak blueprint fluttered to the table. It was the likeness of a solid man with a paunch, a huge square beard, small squinting eyes, and a bald head. "What do you make of him—a writing chap?"

"From the nose down, yes," I estimated. "From the nose up, he will 'tend to his own business if you will 'tend to yours, strictly."

McCord slapped his thigh. "By gracious! that's the fellow! He hates the Chinaman. He knows as well as anything he ought not to put down in black and white how intolerably he hates the Chinaman, and yet he must sneak off to his cubby-hole and suck his pencil, and—and how is it Stevenson has it?—the 'agony of composition,' you remember. Can you imagine the fellow, Ridgeway, bundling down here with the fever on him—"

"About the Chinaman," I broke in. "I think you said something about a Chinaman?"

"Yes. The cook, he must have been. I gather he wasn't the master's pick, by the reading-matter here. Probably clapped on to him by the owners—shifted from one of their others at the last moment; a queer trick.

Listen.'' He picked up the book and, running over the pages with a selective thumb, read:

" '*August second*. First part, moderate southwesterly breeze—' and so forth—er—but here he comes to it:

" 'Anything can happen to a man at sea, even a funeral. In special to a Chinyman, who is of no account to social welfare, being a barbarian as I look at it.'

"Something of a philosopher, you see. And did you get the reserve in that 'even a funeral'? An artist, I tell you. But wait; let me catch him a bit wilder. Here:

" 'I'll get that mustard-colored— [This is back a couple of days.] Never can hear the bastard coming, in them carpet slippers. Turned round and found him standing right to my back this morning. Could have stuck a knife into me easy. "Look here!'' says I, and fetched him a tap on the ear that will make him walk louder next time, I warrant. He could have stuck a knife into me easy.'

"A clear case of moral funk, I should say. Can you imagine the fellow, Ridgeway—''

"Yes; oh yes.'' I was ready with a phrase of my own. "A man handicapped with an imagination. You see he can't quite understand this 'barbarian,' who has him beaten by about thirty centuries of civilization—and his imagination has to have something to chew on, something to hit—a 'tap on the ear,' you know.''

"By gracious! that's the ticket!'' McCord pounded his knee. "And now we've got another chap going to pieces—Peters, he calls him. Refuses to eat dinner on August the third, claiming he caught the Chink making passes over the chowder-pot with his thumb. Can you believe it, Ridgeway—in this very cabin here?'' Then he went on with a suggestion of haste, as though he had somehow made a slip. "Well, at any rate, the disease seems to be catching. Next day it's Bach, the second seaman, who begins to feel the gaff. Listen:

" 'Back he comes to me tonight, complaining he's

being watched. He claims the Chink has got the evil eye. Says he can see through a two-inch bulk-head, and the like. The Chink's laying in his bunk, turned the other way. "Why don't you go aboard of him?" says I. The Dutcher says nothing, but goes over to his own bunk and feels under the straw. When he comes back he's looking queer. "By God!" says he, "the devil has swiped my gun!" . . . Now if that's true there is going to be hell to pay in this vessel very quick. I figure I'm still master of this vessel.' "

"The evil eye," I grunted. "Consciences gone wrong there somewhere."

"Not altogether, Ridgeway. I can see that yellow man peeking. Now just figure yourself, say, eight thousand miles from home, out on the water alone with a crowd of heathen fanatics crazy from fright, looking around for guns and so on. Don't you believe you'd keep an eye around the corners, kind of—eh? I'll bet a hat he was taking it all in, lying there in his bunk, 'turned the other way.' Eh? I pity the poor cuss— Well, there's only one more entry after that. He's good and mad. Here:

" 'Now, by God! this is the end. My gun's gone too; right out from under lock and key, by God! I been talking with Bach this morning. Not to let on, I had him in to clean my lamp. There's more ways than one, he says, and so do I.' "

McCord closed the book and dropped it on the table. "Finis," he said. "The rest is blank paper."

"Well!" I will confess I felt much better than I had for some time past. "There's *one* 'mystery of the sea' gone to pot, at any rate. And now, if you don't mind, I think I'll have another of your nips, McCord."

He pushed my glass across the table and got up, and behind his back his shoulder rose to scour the corners of the room, like an incorruptible sentinel. I forgot to take up my gin, watching him. After an uneasy minute or so he came back to the table and pressed the tip of a forefinger on the book.

"Ridgeway," he said, "you don't seem to understand. This particular 'mystery of the sea' hasn't been scratched yet—not even *scratched,* Ridgeway." He sat down and leaned forward, fixing me with a didactic finger. "What happened?"

"Well, I have an idea the 'barbarian' got them, when it came to the pinch."

"And let the—remains over the side?"

"I should say."

"And then they came back and got the 'barbarian' and let *him* over the side, eh? There were none left, you remember."

"Oh, good Lord, I don't know!" I flared with a childish resentment at this catechising of his. But his finger remained there, challenging.

"I do," he announced. "The Chinaman put them over the side, as we have said. And then, after that, he died—of wounds about the head."

"So?" I still had sarcasm.

"You will remember," he went on, "that the skipper did not happen to mention a *yellow* cat in his confessions."

"McCord," I begged him, "please drop it. Why in thunder *should* he mention a cat?"

"True. Why *should* he mention a cat? I think one of the reasons why he should *not* mention a cat is because there did not happen to be a cat aboard at that time."

"Oh, all right!" I reached out and pulled the bottle to my side of the table. Then I took out my watch. "If you don't mind," I suggested, "I think we'd better be going ashore. I've got to get to my office rather early in the morning. What do you say?"

He said nothing for a moment, but his finger had dropped. He leaned back and stared straight into the core of the light above, his eyes squinting.

"He would have been from the south of China, probably." He seemed to be talking to himself. "There's a
considerable sprinkling of the belief down there, I've
heard. It's an uncanny business—this transmigration of
souls—"

Personally, I had had enough of it. McCord's fingers
came groping across the table for the bottle. I picked it
up hastily and let it go through the open companionway,
where it died with a faint gurgle, out somewhere on the
river.

"Now," I said to him, shaking the vagrant wrist,
"either you come ashore with me or you go in there
and get under the blankets. You're drunk, McCord—
drunk. Do you hear me?"

"Ridgeway," he pronounced, bringing his eyes down
to me and speaking very slowly. "You're a fool, if you
can't see better than that. I'm not drunk. I'm sick. I
haven't slept for three nights—and now I can't. And you
say—you—" He went to pieces very suddenly, jumped
up, pounded the leg of his chair on the decking, and
shouted at me: "And you say that, you—you landlub-
ber, you office coddler! You're so comfortably sure that
everything in the world is cut and dried. Come back to
the water again and learn how to wonder—and stop
talking like a damn fool. Do you know where— Is there
anything in your municipal budget to tell me where
Björnsen went? Listen!" He sat down, waving me to
do the same, and went on with a sort of desperate re-
pression.

"It happened on the first night after we took this
hellion. I'd stood the wheel most of the afternoon—off
and on, that is, because she sails herself uncommonly
well. Just put her on reach, you know, and she carries
it off pretty well—"

"I know," I nodded.

"Well, we mugged up about seven o'clock. There
was a good deal of canned stuff in the galley, and Björn-

sen wasn't a bad hand with a kettle—a thoroughgoing
Square-head he was—tall and lean and yellow-haired,
with little fat, round cheeks and a white mustache. Not
a bad chap at all. He took the wheel to stand till midnight, and I turned in, but I didn't drop off for quite a
spell. I could hear his boots wandering around over my
head, padding off forward, coming back again. I heard
him whistling now and then—an outlandish air. Occasionally I could see the shadow of his head waving in
a block of moonlight that lay on the decking right down
there in front of the state-room door. It came from the
companion; the cabin was dark because we were going
easy on the oil. They hadn't left a great deal, for some
reason or other.''

McCord leaned back and described with his finger
where the illumination had cut the decking.

"There! I could see it from my bunk, as I lay, you
understand. I must have almost dropped off once when
I heard him fiddling around out here in the cabin, and
then he said something in a whisper, just to find out if
I was still awake, I suppose. I asked him what the matter was. He came and poked his head in the door.

" 'The breeze is going out,' says he. 'I was wondering if we couldn't get a little more sail on her.' Only I
can't give you his fierce Square-head tang. 'How about
the tops?' he suggested.

"I was so sleepy I didn't care, and I told him so. 'All
right,' he says, 'but I thought I might shake out one of
them tops.' Then I heard him blow at something outside. 'Scat, you—' Then: 'This cat's going to set me
crazy, Mr. McCord,' he says, 'following me around
everywhere.' He gave a kick, and I saw something yellow floating across the moonlight. It never made a
sound—just floated. You wouldn't have known it ever
lit anywhere, just like—''

McCord stopped and drummed a few beats on the

table with his fist, as though to bring himself back to the straight narrative.

"I went to sleep," he began again. "I dreamed about a lot of things. I woke up sweating. You know how glad you are to wake up after a dream like that and find none of it is so? Well, I turned over and settled to go off again, and then I got a little more awake and thought to myself it must be pretty near time for me to go on deck. I scratched a match and looked at my watch. 'That fellow must be either a good chap or asleep,' I said to myself. And I rolled out quick and went above-decks. He wasn't at the wheel. I called him: 'Björnsen! Björnsen!' No answer."

McCord was really telling a story now. He paused for a long moment, one hand shielding an ear and his eyeballs turned far up.

"That was the first time I really went over the hulk," he ran on. "I got out a lantern and started at the forward end of the hold, and I worked aft, and there was nothing there. Not a sign, or a stain, or a scrap of clothing, or anything. You may believe that I began to feel funny inside. I went over the decks and the rails and the house itself—inch by inch. Not a trace. I went out aft again. The cat sat on the wheel-box, washing her face. I hadn't noticed the scar on her head before, running down between her ears—rather a new scar—three or four days old, I should say. It looked ghastly and blue-white in the flat moonlight. I ran over and grabbed her up to heave her over the side—you understand how upset I was. Now you know a cat will squirm around and grab something when you hold it like that, generally speaking. This one didn't. She just drooped and began to purr and looked up at me out of her moonlit eyes under that scar. I dropped her on the deck and backed off. You remember Björnsen had *kicked* her— and I didn't want anything like that happening to—"

The narrator turned upon me with a sudden heat, leaned over and shook his finger before my face.

"There you go!" he cried. "You, with your stout stone buildings and your policemen and your neighborhood church—you're so damn sure. But I'd just like to see you out there, alone, with the moon setting, and all the lights gone tall and queer, and a shipmate—" He lifted his hand overhead, the finger-tips pressed together and then suddenly separated as though he had released an impalpable something into the air.

"Go on," I told him.

"I felt more like you do, when it got light again, and warm and sunshiny. I said 'Bah!' to the whole business. I even fed the cat, and I slept awhile on the roof of the house—I was so sure. We lay dead most of the day, without a streak of air. But that night—! Well, that night I hadn't got over being sure yet. It takes quite a jolt, you know, to shake loose several dozen generations. A fair, steady breeze had come along, the glass was high, she was staying herself like a doll, and so I figured I could get a little rest lying below in the bunk, even if I didn't sleep.

"I tried not to sleep, in case something should come up—a squall or the like. But I think I must have dropped off once or twice. I remember I heard something fiddling around in the galley, and I hollered 'Scat!' and everything was quiet again. I rolled over and lay on my left side, staring at that square of moonlight outside my door for a long time. You'll think it was a dream—what I saw there."

"Go on," I said.

"Call this table-top the spot of light, roughly," he said. He placed a finger-tip at about the middle of the forward edge and drew it slowly toward the center. "Here, what would correspond with the upper side of the companion-way, there came down very gradually the shadow of a tail. I watched it streaking out there across the deck, wiggling the slightest bit now and then. When it had come down about halfway across the light, the solid part of the animal—its shadow, you understand—began to appear, quite big and round. But how could she hang there, done up in a ball, from the hatch?''

He shifted his finger back to the edge of the table and puddled it around to signify the shadowed body.

''I fished my gun out from behind my back. You see, I was feeling funny again. Then I started to slide one foot over the edge of the bunk, always with my eyes on that shadow. Now I swear I didn't make the sound of a pin dropping, but I had no more than moved a muscle when that shadowed thing twisted itself around in a flash—and there on the floor before me was the profile of a man's head, upside down, listening—a man's head with a tail of hair.''

McCord got up hastily and stepped in front of the state-room door, where he bent down and scratched a match.

''See,'' he said, holding the tiny flame above a splintered scar on the boards. ''You wouldn't think a man would be fool enough to shoot at a shadow?''

He came back and sat down.

''It seemed to me all hell had shaken loose. You've no idea, Ridgeway, the rumpus a gun raises in a box like this. I found out afterward the slug ricocheted into the galley, bringing down a couple of pans—and that helped. Oh yes, I got out of here quick enough. I stood there, half out of the companion, with my hands on the hatch and the gun between them, and my shadow running off across the top of the house shivering before my eyes like a dry leaf. There wasn't a whisper of sound in the world—just the pale water floating past and the sails towering up like a pair of twittering ghosts. And everything that crazy color—

''Well, in a minute I saw it, just abreast of the mainmast, crouched down in the shadow of the weather rail, sneaking off forward very slowly. This time I took a good long sight before I let go. Did you ever happen to see black-powder smoke in the moonlight? It puffed out perfectly round, like a big, pale balloon, this did, and for a second something was bounding through it— without a sound, you understand—something a shade solider than the smoke and big as a cow, it looked to me. It passed from the weather side to the lee and ducked behind the sweep of the mainsail like *that*—" McCord snapped his thumb and forefinger under the light.

"Go on," I said. "What did you do then?"

McCord regarded me for an instant from beneath his lids, uncertain. His fist hung above the table. "You're—" He hesitated, his lips working vacantly. A forefinger came out of the fist and gesticulated before my face. "If you're laughing, why, damn me, I'll—"

"Go on," I repeated. "What did you do then?"

"I followed the thing." He was still watching me sullenly. "I got up and went forward along the roof of the house, so as to have an eye on either rail. You understand, this business had to be done with. I kept straight along. Every shadow I wasn't absolutely sure of I *made* sure of—point-blank. And I rounded the thing up at the very stem—sitting on the butt of the bowsprit, Ridgeway, washing her yellow face under the moon. I didn't make any bones about it this time. I put the bad end of that gun against the scar on her head and squeezed the trigger. It snicked on an empty shell. I tell you a fact; I was almost deafened by the report that didn't come.

"She followed me aft. I couldn't get away from her. I went and sat on the wheel-box and she came and sat on the edge of the house facing me. And there we stayed for upwards of an hour, without moving. Finally she went over and stuck her paw in the water-pan I'd set out for her; then she raised her head and looked at me and yawled. At sun-down there'd been two quarts of water in that pan. You wouldn't think a cat could get away with two quarts of water in—"

He broke off again and considered me with a sort of weary defiance.

"What's the use?" He spread out his hands in a gesture of hopelessness. "I knew you wouldn't believe it when I started. You *couldn't*. It would be a kind of blasphemy against the sacred institution of pavements. You're too damn smug, Ridgeway. I can't shake you. You haven't sat two days and two nights, keeping your eyes open by sheer teeth-gritting, until they got used to it and wouldn't shut any more. When I tell you I found that yellow thing snooping around the davits, and three bights of the boat-fall loosened out, plain on deck—you grin behind your collar. When I tell you she padded off forward and evaporated—flickered back to hell and hasn't been seen since, then—why, you explain to yourself that I'm drunk. I tell you—" He jerked his head back abruptly and turned to face the companionway, his lips still apart. He listened for a moment, then he shook himself out of it and went on:

"I tell you, Ridgeway, I've been over this hulk with a foot-rule. There's not a cubic inch I haven't accounted for, not a plank I—"

This time he got up and moved a step toward the companion, where he stood with his head bent forward and slightly to the side. After what might have been twenty seconds of this he whispered, "Do you hear?"

Far and far away down the reach a ferry-boat lifted its infinitesimal wail, and then the silence of the night river came down once more, profound and inscrutable. A corner of the wick above my head sputtered a little—that was all.

"Hear what?" I whispered back. He lifted a cautious finger toward the opening.

"Somebody. Listen."

The man's faculties must have been keyed up to the pitch of his nerves, for to me the night remained as voiceless as a subterranean cavern. I became intensely irritated with him; within my mind I cried out against this infatuated pantomime of his. And then, of a sudden, there *was* a sound—the dying rumor of a ripple, somewhere in the outside darkness, as though an object had been let into the water with extreme care.

"You heard?"

I nodded. The ticking of the watch in my vest pocket came to my ears, shucking off the leisurely seconds, while McCord's fingernails gnawed at the palms of his hands. The man was really sick. He wheeled on me and cried out, "My God! Ridgeway—why don't we go out?"

I, for one, refused to be a fool. I passed him and climbed out of the opening; he followed far enough to lean his elbows on the hatch, his feet and legs still within the secure glow of the cabin.

"You see, there's nothing." My wave of assurance was possibly a little over-done.

"Over there," he muttered, jerking his head toward the shore lights. "Something swimming."

I moved to the corner of the house and listened.

"River thieves," I argued. "The place is full of—"

"Ridgeway. Look behind you!"

Perhaps it *is* the pavements—but no matter; I am not ordinarily a jumping sort. And yet there was something in the quality of that voice beyond my shoulder that brought the sweat stinging through the pores of my scalp even while I was in the act of turning.

A cat sat there on the latch, expressionless and immobile in the gloom.

I did not say anything. I turned and went below. McCord was there already, standing on the farther side of the table. After a moment or so the cat followed and sat on her haunches at the foot of the ladder and stared at us without winking.

"I think she wants something to eat," I said to McCord.

He lit a lantern and went into the galley. Returning with a chunk of salt beef, he threw it into the farther corner. The cat went over and began to tear at it, her muscles playing with convulsive shadow-lines under the sagging yellow hide.

And now it was she who listened, to something beyond the reach of even McCord's faculties, her neck stiff and her ears flattened. I looked at McCord and found him brooding at the animal with a sort of listless malevolence. "*Quick!* She has kittens somewhere about." I shook his elbow sharply. "When she starts, now—"

"You don't seem to understand," he mumbled. "It wouldn't be any use."

She had turned now and was making for the ladder with the soundless agility of her race. I grasped McCord's wrist and dragged him after me, the lantern banging against his knees. When we came up the cat was already amidships, a scarcely discernible shadow at the margin of our lantern's ring. She stopped and looked back at us with her luminous eyes, appeared to hesitate, uneasy at our pursuit of her, shifted here and there with quick, soft bounds, and stopped to fawn with her back arched at the foot of the mast. Then she was off with an amazing suddenness into the shadows forward.

"Lively now!" I yelled at McCord. He came pounding along behind me, still protesting that it was of no use. Abreast of the foremast I took the lantern from him to hold above my head.

"You see," he complained, peering here and there over the illuminated deck. "I tell you, Ridgeway, this

thing—'' But my eyes were in another quarter, and I
slapped him on the shoulder.

"An engineer—an engineer to the core," I cried at
him. "Look aloft, man."

Our quarry was almost to the cross-trees, clambering
up the shrouds with a smartness no sailor has ever come
to, her yellow body, cut by the moving shadows of the
ratlines, a queer sight against the mat of the night.
McCord closed his mouth and opened it again for two
words: "By gracious!" The following instant he had
the lantern and was after her. I watched him go up
above my head—a ponderous, swaying climber into the
sky—come to the cross-trees, and squat there with his
knees clamped around the mast. The clear star of the
lantern shot this way and that for a moment, then it
disappeared, and in its place there sprang out a bag of
yellow light, like a fire-balloon at anchor in the heavens. I could see the shadows of his head and hands
moving monstrously over the inner surface of the sail,
and muffled exclamations without meaning came down
to me. After a moment he drew out his head and called:
"All right—they're here. Heads! there below!"

I ducked at his warning, and something spanked on
the planking a yard from my feet. I stepped over to the
vague blur on the deck and picked up a slipper—a slipper covered with some woven straw stuff and soled with
a matted felt, perhaps a half-inch thick. Another struck
somewhere abaft the mast, and then McCord reappeared above and began to stagger down the shrouds.
Under his left arm he hugged a curious assortment of
litter, a sheaf of papers, a brace of revolvers, a gray
kimono, and a soiled apron.

"Well," he said when he had come to deck, "I feel
like a man who has gone to hell and come back again.
You know I'd come to the place where I really believed
that about the cat. When you think of it— By gracious!
we haven't come so far from the jungle, after all."

We went aft and below and sat down at the table as we had been. McCord broke a prolonged silence.

"I'm sort of glad he got away—poor cuss! He's probably climbing up a wharf this minute, shivering and scared to death. Over toward the gas-tanks, by the way he was swimming. By gracious! now that the world's turned over straight again, I feel I could sleep a solid week. Poor cuss! can you imagine him, Ridgeway—"

"Yes," I broke in. "I think I can. He must have lost his nerve when he made out your smoke and shinnied up there to stow away, taking the ship's papers with him. He would have attached some profound importance to them—remember, the 'barbarian,' eight thousand miles from home. Probably couldn't read a word. I suppose the cat followed him—the traditional source of food. He must have wanted water badly."

"I should say! He wouldn't have taken the chances he did."

"Well," I announced, "at any rate, I can say it now—there's another 'mystery of the sea' gone to pot."

McCord lifted his heavy lids.

"No," he mumbled. "The mystery is that a man who has been to sea all his life could sail around for three days with a man bundled up in his top and not know it. When I think of him peeking down at me— and playing off that damn cat—probably without realizing it—scared to death—by gracious! Ridgeway, there was a pair of funks aboard this craft, eh? Wow—yow— I could sleep—"

"I should think you could."

McCord did not answer.

"By the way," I speculated. "I guess you were right about Björnsen, McCord—that is, his fooling with the foretop. He must have been caught all of a bunch, eh?"

Again McCord failed to answer. I looked up, mildly surprised, and found his head hanging back over his chair and his mouth opened wide. He was asleep.

The Black Cat

EDGAR ALLAN POE

For the most wild yet most homely narrative which
I am about to pen, I neither expect nor solicit belief.
Mad indeed would I be to expect it, in a case where
my very senses reject their own evidence. Yet, mad am
I not—and very surely do I not dream. But to-morrow
I die, and to-day I would unburden my soul. My immediate purpose is to place before the world, plainly,
succinctly, and without comment, a series of mere
household events. In their consequences, these events
have terrified—have tortured—have destroyed me. Yet I
will not attempt to expound them. To me, they have
presented little but horror—to many they will seem less
terrible than *baroques*. Hereafter, perhaps, some intellect may be found which will reduce my phantasm to
the commonplace—some intellect more calm, more

logical, and far less excitable than my own, which will perceive, in the circumstances I detail with awe, nothing more than an ordinary succession of very natural causes and effects.

From my infancy I was noted for the docility and humanity of my disposition. My tenderness of heart was even so conspicuous as to make me the jest of my companions. I was especially fond of animals, and was indulged by my parents with a great variety of pets. With these I spent most of my time, and never was so happy as when feeding and caressing them. This peculiarity of character grew with my growth, and, in my manhood, I derived from it one of my principal sources of pleasure. To those who have cherished an affection for a faithful and sagacious dog, I need hardly be at the trouble of explaining the nature or the intensity of the gratification thus derivable. There is something in the unselfish and self-sacrificing love of a brute, which goes directly to the heart of him who has had frequent occasion to test the paltry friendship and gossamer fidelity of mere *Man*.

I married early, and was happy to find in my wife a disposition not uncongenial with my own. Observing my partiality for domestic pets, she lost no opportunity of procuring those of the most agreeable kind. We had birds, gold-fish, a fine dog, rabbits, a small monkey, and a *cat*.

This latter was a remarkably large and beautiful animal, entirely black, and sagacious to an astonishing degree. In speaking of his intelligence, my wife, who at heart was not a little tinctured with superstition, made frequent allusion to the ancient popular notion, which regarded all black cats as witches in disguise. Not that she was ever *serious* upon this point—and I mention the matter at all for no better reason than that it happens, just now, to be remembered.

Pluto—this was the cat's name—was my favorite pet

and playmate. I alone fed him, and he attended me wherever I went about the house. It was even with difficulty that I could prevent him from following me through the streets.

Our friendship lasted, in this manner, for several years, during which my general temperament and character—through the instrumentality of the Fiend Intemperance—had (I blush to confess it) experienced a radical alteration for the worse. I grew, day by day, more moody, more irritable, more regardless of the feelings of others. I suffered myself to use intemperate language to my wife. At length, I even offered her personal violence. My pets, of course, were made to feel the change in my disposition. I not only neglected, but ill-used them. For Pluto, however, I still retained sufficient regard to restrain me from maltreating him, as I made no scruple of maltreating the rabbits, the monkey, or even the dog, when, by accident, or through affection, they came in my way. But my disease grew upon me—for what disease is like Alcohol!—and at length even Pluto, who was now becoming old, and consequently somewhat peevish—even Pluto began to experience the effects of my ill temper.

One night, returning home, much intoxicated, from one of my haunts about town, I fancied that the cat avoided my presence. I seized him; when, in his fright at my violence, he inflicted a slight wound upon my hand with his teeth. The fury of a demon instantly possessed me. I knew myself no longer. My original soul seemed, at once, to take its flight from my body; and a more than fiendish malevolence, gin-nurtured, thrilled every fibre of my frame. I took from my waistcoatpocket a penknife, opened it, grasped the poor beast by the throat, and deliberately cut one of its eyes from the socket! I blush, I burn, I shudder, while I pen the damnable atrocity.

When reason returned with the morning—when I had

slept off the fumes of the night's debauch—I experienced a sentiment half of horror, half of remorse, for the crime of which I had been guilty; but it was, at best, a feeble and equivocal feeling, and the soul remained untouched. I again plunged into excess, and soon drowned in wine all memory of the deed.

In the meantime the cat slowly recovered. The socket of the lost eye presented, it is true, a frightful appearance, but he no longer appeared to suffer any pain. He went about the house as usual, but, as might be expected, fled in extreme terror at my approach. I had so much of my old heart left, as to be at first grieved by this evident dislike on the part of a creature which had once so loved me. But this feeling soon gave place to irritation. And then came, as if to my final and irrevocable overthrow, the spirit of PERVERSENESS. Of this spirit philosophy takes no account. Yet I am not more sure that my soul lives, than I am that perverseness is one of the primitive impulses of the human heart—one of the indivisible primary faculties, or sentiments, which give direction to the character of Man. Who has not, a hundred times, found himself committing a vile or a stupid action, for no other reason than because he knows he should *not*? Have we not a perpetual inclination, in the teeth of our best judgment, to violate that which is *Law,* merely because we understand it to be such? This spirit of perverseness, I say, came to my final overthrow. It was this unfathomable longing of the soul *to vex itself*—to offer violence to its own nature— to do wrong for the wrong's sake only—that urged me to continue and finally to consummate the injury I had inflicted upon the unoffending brute. One morning, in cold blood, I slipped a noose about its neck and hung it to the limb of a tree;—hung it with the tears streaming from my eyes, and with the bitterest remorse at my heart;—hung it *because* I knew that it had loved me, and *because* I felt it had given me no reason of offence;—hung it *because* I knew that in so doing I was committing a sin—a deadly sin that would so jeopardize my immortal soul as to place it—if such a thing were possible—even beyond the reach of the infinite mercy of the Most Merciful and Most Terrible God.

On the night of the day on which this most cruel deed was done, I was aroused from sleep by the cry of fire. The curtains of my bed were in flames. The whole house was blazing. It was with great difficulty that my wife, a servant, and myself, made our escape from the conflagration. The destruction was complete. My entire worldly wealth was swallowed up, and I resigned myself thenceforward to despair.

I am above the weakness of seeking to establish a sequence of cause and effect, between the disaster and the atrocity. But I am detailing a chain of facts—and wish not to leave even a possible link imperfect. On the day succeeding the fire, I visited the ruins. The walls, with one exception, had fallen in. This exception was found in a compartment wall, not very thick, which stood about the middle of the house, and against which had rested the head of my bed. The plastering had here, in great measure, resisted the action of the fire—a fact which I attributed to its having been recently spread. About this wall a dense crowd were collected, and many persons seemed to be examining a particular portion of it with very minute and eager attention. The words "strange!" "singular!" and other similar expressions, excited my curiosity. I approached and saw, as if graven in *bas-relief* upon the white surface, the figure of a gigantic *cat*. The impression was given with an accuracy truly marvelous. There was a rope about the animal's neck.

When I first beheld this apparition—for I could scarcely regard it as less—my wonder and my terror were extreme. But at length reflection came to my aid. The cat, I remembered, had been hung in a garden adjacent to the house. Upon the alarm of fire, this garden had been immediately filled by the crowd—by some one of whom the animal must have been cut from the tree and thrown, through an open window, into my chamber. This had probably been done with the view of arousing me from sleep. The falling of other walls had compressed the victim of my cruelty into the substance of the freshly-spread plaster; the lime of which, with the flames, and the *ammonia* from the carcass, had then accomplished the portraiture as I saw it.

Although I thus readily accounted to my reason, if not altogether to my conscience, for the startling fact just detailed, it did not the less fail to make a deep impression upon my fancy. For months I could not rid myself of the phantasm of the cat; and, during this period, there came back into my spirit a half-sentiment that seemed, but was not, remorse. I went so far as to regret the loss of the animal, and to look about me, among the vile haunts which I now habitually frequented, for another pet of the same species, and of somewhat similar appearance, with which to supply its place.

One night as I sat, half stupefied, in a den of more than infamy, my attention was suddenly drawn to some black object, reposing upon the head of one of the immense hogsheads of gin, or of rum, which constituted the chief furniture of the apartment. I had been looking steadily at the top of this hogshead for some minutes, and what now caused me surprise was the fact that I had not sooner perceived the object thereupon. I approached it, and touched it with my hand. It was a black cat—a very large one—fully as large as Pluto, and closely resembling him in every respect but one. Pluto had not a white hair upon any portion of his body; but this cat had a large, although indefinite splotch of white, covering nearly the whole region of the breast.

Upon my touching him, he immediately arose, purred

loudly, rubbed against my hand, and appeared delighted with my notice This, then, was the very creature of which I was in search. I at once offered to
purchase it of the landlord; but this person made no
claim to it—knew nothing of it—had never seen it before.

I continued my caresses, and when I prepared to go
home, the animal evinced a disposition to accompany
me. I permitted it to do so; occasionally stooping and
patting it as I proceeded. When it reached the house it
domesticated itself at once, and became immediately a
great favorite with my wife.

For my own part, I soon found a dislike to it arising
within me. This was just the reverse of what I had an-
ticipated; but—I know not how or why it was—its evident fondness for myself rather disgusted and annoyed
me. By slow degrees these feelings of disgust and an-
noyance rose into the bitterness of hatred. I avoided the
creature; a certain sense of shame, and the remem-
brance of my former deed of cruelty, preventing me
from physically abusing it. I did not, for some weeks,
strike, or otherwise violently ill use it; but gradually—
very gradually—I came to look upon it with unutterable
loathing, and to flee silently from its odious presence,
as from the breath of a pestilence.

What added, no doubt, to my hatred of the beast,
was the discovery, on the morning after I brought it
home, that, like Pluto, it also had been deprived of one
of its eyes. This circumstance, however, only endeared
it to my wife, who, as I have already said, possessed,
in a high degree, that humanity of feeling which had
once been my distinguishing trait, and the source of
many of my simplest and purest pleasures.

With my aversion to this cat, however, its partiality
for myself seemed to increase. It followed my footsteps
with a pertinacity which it would be difficult to make
the reader comprehend. Whenever I sat, it would crouch

beneath my chair, or spring upon my knees, covering me with its loathsome caresses. If I arose to walk it would get between my feet and thus nearly throw me down, or, fastening its long and sharp claws in my dress, clamber, in this manner, to my breast. At such times, although I longed to destroy it with a blow, I was yet withheld from so doing, partly by a memory of my former crime, but chiefly—let me confess it at once—by absolute *dread* of the beast.

This dread was not exactly a dread of physical evil—and yet I should now be at a loss how otherwise to define it. I am almost ashamed to own—yes, even in this felon's cell, I am almost ashamed to own—that the terror and horror with which the animal inspired me, had been heightened by one of the merest chimeras it would be possible to conceive. My wife had called my attention, more than once, to the character of the mark of white hair, of which I have spoken, and which constituted the sole visible difference between the strange beast and the one I had destroyed. The reader will remember that this mark, although large, had been originally very indefinite; but, by slow degrees—degrees nearly imperceptible, and which for a long time my reason struggled to reject as fanciful—it had, at length, assumed a rigorous distinctness of outline. It was now the representation of an object that I shudder to name—and for this, above all, I loathed, and dreaded, and would have rid myself of the monster *had I dared*—it was now, I say, the image of a hideous—of a ghastly thing—of the GALLOWS!—oh, mournful and terrible engine of Horror and of Crime—of Agony and of Death!

And now was I indeed wretched beyond the wretchedness of mere Humanity. And *a brute beast*—whose fellow I had contemptuously destroyed—*a brute beast* to work out for *me*—for me, a man fashioned in the image of the High God—so much of insufferable woe! Alas! neither by day nor by night knew I the blessing of rest any more! During the former the creature left me no moment alone, and in the latter I started hourly from dreams of unutterable fear to find the hot breath of *the thing* upon my face, and its vast weight—an incarnate nightmare that I had no power to shake off—incumbent eternally upon my *heart*!

Beneath the pressure of torments such as these the feeble remnant of the good within me succumbed. Evil thoughts became my sole intimates—the darkest and most evil of thoughts. The moodiness of my usual temper increased to hatred of all things and of all mankind; while from the sudden, frequent, and ungovernable outbursts of a fury to which I now blindly abandoned myself, my uncomplaining wife, alas, was the usual and the most patient of sufferers.

One day she accompanied me, upon some household errand, into the cellar of the old building which our poverty compelled us to inhabit. The cat followed me down the steep stairs, and, nearly throwing me headlong, exasperated me to madness. Uplifting an axe, and forgetting in my wrath the childish dread which had hitherto stayed my hand, I aimed a blow at the animal, which, of course, would have proved instantly fatal had it descended as I wished. But this blow was arrested by the hand of my wife. Goaded by the interference into a rage more than demoniacal, I withdrew my arm from her grasp and buried the axe in her brain. She fell dead upon the spot without a groan.

This hideous murder accomplished, I set myself forthwith, and with entire deliberation, to the task of concealing the body. I knew that I could not remove it from the house, either by day or by night, without the risk of being observed by the neighbors. Many projects entered my mind. At one period I thought of cutting the corpse into minute fragments, and destroying them by fire. At another, I resolved to dig a grave for it in the floor of the cellar. Again, I deliberated about casting it in the well in the yard—about packing it in a box, as if merchandise, with the usual arrangements, and so getting a porter to take it from the house. Finally I hit upon what I considered a far better expedient than either of these. I determined to wall it up in the cellar, as the monks of the Middle Ages are recorded to have walled up their victims.

For a purpose such as this the cellar was well adapted. Its walls were loosely constructed, and had lately been plastered throughout with a rough plaster, which the dampness of the atmosphere had prevented from hardening. Moreover, in one of the walls was a projection, caused by a false chimney, or fireplace, that had been filled up and made to resemble the rest of the cellar. I made no doubt that I could readily displace the bricks at this point, insert the corpse, and wall the whole up as before, so that no eye could detect any thing suspicious.

And in this calculation I was not deceived. By means of a crowbar I easily dislodged the bricks, and, having carefully deposited the body against the inner wall, I propped it in that position, while with little trouble I relaid the whole structure as it originally stood. Having procured mortar, sand, and hair, with every possible precaution, I prepared a plaster which could not be distinguished from the old, and with this I very carefully went over the new brick-work. When I had finished, I felt satisfied that all was right. The wall did not present the slightest appearance of having been disturbed. The rubbish on the floor was picked up with the minutest care. I looked around triumphantly, and said to myself: "Here at least, then, my labor has not been in vain."

My next step was to look for the beast which had been the cause of so much wretchedness; for I had, at length, firmly resolved to put it to death. Had I been able to meet with it at the moment, there could have been no doubt of its fate; but it appeared that the crafty animal had been alarmed at the violence of my previous anger, and forbore to present itself in my present mood. It is impossible to describe or to imagine the deep, the blissful sense of relief which the absence of the detested creature occasioned in my bosom. It did not make its appearance during the night; and thus for one night, at least, since its introduction into the house, I soundly and tranquilly slept; aye, *slept* even with the burden of murder upon my soul.

The second and third day passed, and still my tormentor came not. Once again I breathed as a freeman. The monster, in terror, had fled the premises for ever! I should behold it no more! My happiness was supreme! The guilt of my dark deed disturbed me but little. Some few inquiries had been made, but these had been readily answered. Even a search had been instituted—but of course nothing was to be discovered. I looked upon my future felicity as secured.

Upon the fourth day of the assassination, a party of the police came, very unexpectedly, into the house, and proceeded again to make rigorous investigation of the premises. Secure, however, in the inscrutability of my place of concealment, I felt no embarrassment whatever. The officers bade me accompany them in their search. They left no nook or corner unexplored. At length, for the third or fourth time, they descended into the cellar. I quivered not in a muscle. My heart beat calmly as that of one who slumbers in innocence. I walked the cellar from end to end. I folded my arms upon my bosom, and roamed easily to and fro. The police were thoroughly satisfied and prepared to depart. The glee at my heart was too strong to be restrained. I burned to say if but one word, by way of triumph, and to render doubly sure their assurance of my guiltlessness.

"Gentlemen," I said at last, as the party ascended the steps, "I delight to have allayed your suspicions. I wish you all health and a little more courtesy. By the bye, gentlemen, this—this is a very well-constructed house,'' (in the rabid desire to say something easily, I scarcely knew what I uttered at all),—''I may say an *excellently* well-contructed house. These walls—are you going, gentlemen?—these walls are solidly put together''; and here, through the mere frenzy of bravado, I rapped heavily with a cane which I held in my hand, upon that very portion of the brickwork behind which stood the corpse of the wife of my bosom.

But may God shield and deliver me from the fangs of the Arch-Fiend! No sooner had the reverberation of my blows sunk into silence, than I was answered by a voice from within the tomb!—by a cry, at first muffled and broken, like the sobbing of a child, and then quickly swelling into one long, loud, and continuous scream, utterly anomalous and inhuman—a howl—a wailing shriek, half of horror and half of triumph, such as might have arisen only out of hell, conjointly from the throats of the damned in their agony and of the demons that exult in the damnation.

Of my own thoughts it is folly to speak. Swooning, I staggered to the opposite wall. For one instant the party on the stairs remained motionless, through extremity of terror and awe. In the next a dozen stout arms were toiling at the wall. It fell bodily. The corpse, already greatly decayed and clotted with gore, stood erect before the eyes of the spectators. Upon its head, with red extended mouth and solitary eye of fire, sat the hideous beast whose craft had seduced me into murder, and whose informing voice had consigned me to the hangman. I had walled the monster up within the tomb.

The Squaw

BRAM STOKER

Nurnberg at the time was not so much exploited as
it has been since then. Irving had not been playing
Faust, and the very name of the old town was hardly
known to the great bulk of the travelling public. My
wife and I being in the second week of our honeymoon,
naturally wanted someone else to join our party, so that
when the cheery stranger, Elias P. Hutcheson, hailing
from Isthmian City, Bleeding Gulch, Maple Tree
County, Neb. turned up at the station at Frankfort, and
casually remarked that he was going on to see the most
all-fired old Methuselah of a town in Yurrup, and that
he guessed that so much travelling alone was enough to
send an intelligent, active citizen into the melancholy
ward of a daft house, we took the pretty broad hint and
suggested that we should join forces. We found, on

comparing notes afterwards, that we had each intended to speak with some diffidence or hesitation so as not to appear too eager, such not being a good compliment to the success of our married life; but the effect was entirely marred by our both beginning to speak at the same instant—stopping simultaneously and then going on together again. Anyhow, no matter how, it was done; and Elias P. Hutcheson became one of our party. Straightway Amelia and I found the pleasant benefit; instead of quarrelling, as we had been doing, we found that the restraining influence of a third party was such that we now took every opportunity of spooning in odd corners. Amelia declares that ever since she has, as the result of that experience, advised all her friends to take a friend on the honeymoon. Well, we "did" Nurnberg together, and much enjoyed the racy remarks of our Transatlantic friend, who, from his quaint speech and his wonderful stock of adventures, might have stepped out of a novel. We kept for the last object of interest in the city to be visited the Burg, and on the day appointed for the visit strolled round the outer wall of the city by the eastern side.

The Burg is seated on a rock dominating the town and an immensely deep fosse guards it on the northern side. Nurnberg has been happy in that it was never sacked; had it been it would certainly not be so spick and span perfect as it is at present. The ditch has not been used for centuries, and now its base is spread with tea-gardens and orchards, of which some of the trees are of quite respectable growth. As we wandered round the wall, dawdling in the hot July sunshine, we often paused to admire the views spread before us, and in especial the great plain covered with towns and villages and bounded with a blue line of hills, like a landscape of Claude Lorraine. From this we always turned with new delight to the city itself, with its myriad of quaint old gables and acre-wide red roofs dotted with dormer windows, tier upon tier. A little to our right rose the towers of the Burg, and nearer still, standing grim, the Torture Tower, which was, and is, perhaps, the most interesting place in the city. For centuries the tradition of the Iron Virgin of Nurnberg has been handed down as an instance of the horrors of cruelty of which man is capable; we had long looked forward to seeing it; and here at last was its home.

In one of our pauses we leaned over the wall of the moat and looked down. The garden seemed quite fifty or sixty feet below us, and the sun pouring into it with an intense, moveless heat like that of an oven. Beyond rose the grey, grim wall seemingly of endless height, and losing itself right and left in the angles of bastion and counterscarp. Trees and bushes crowned the wall, and above again towered the lofty houses on whose massive beauty Time has only set the hand of approval. The sun was hot and we were lazy; time was our own, and we lingered, leaning on the wall. Just below us was a pretty sight—a great black cat lying stretched in the sun, whilst round her gambolled prettily a tiny black kitten. The mother would wave her tail for the kitten to play with, or would raise her feet and push away the little one as an encouragement to further play. They were just at the foot of the wall, and Elias P. Hutcheson, in order to help the play, stooped and took from the walk a moderate sized pebble.

"See!" he said, "I will drop it near the kitten, and they will both wonder where it came from."

"Oh, be careful," said my wife; "you might hit the dear little thing!"

"Not me, ma'am," said Elias P. "Why, I'm as tender as a Maine cherry-tree. Lor, bless ye, I wouldn't hurt the poor pooty little critter more'n I'd scalp a baby. An' you may bet your variegated socks on that! See, I'll drop it fur away on the outside so's not to go near her!" Thus saying, he leaned over and held his arm out at full length and dropped the stone. It may be that there is some attractive force which draws lesser matters to greater; or more probably that the wall was not plumb but sloped to its base—we not noticing the inclination from above; but the stone fell with a sickening thud that came up to us through the hot air, right on the kitten's head, and shattered out its little brains then and there. The black cat cast a swift upward glance, and we saw her eyes like green fire fixed an instant on Elias P. Hutcheson; and then her attention was given to the kitten, which lay still with just a quiver of her tiny limbs, whilst a thin red stream trickled from a gaping wound. With a muffled cry, such as a human being might give, she bent over the kitten licking its wounds and moaning. Suddenly she seemed to realise that it was dead, and again threw her eyes up at us. I shall never forget the sight, for she looked the perfect incarnation of hate. Her green eyes blazed with lurid fire, and the white, sharp teeth seemed to almost shine through the blood which dabbled her mouth and whiskers. She gnashed her teeth, and her claws stood out stark and at full length on every paw. Then she made a wild rush up the wall as if to reach us, but when the momentum ended fell back, and further added to her horrible appearance for she fell on the kitten, and rose with her black fur smeared with its brains and blood. Amelia turned quite faint, and I had to lift her back from the wall. There was a seat close by in shade of a spreading plane-tree, and here I placed her whilst she composed herself. Then I went back to Hutcheson, who stood without moving, looking down on the angry cat below.

As I joined him, he said:

"Wall, I guess that air the savagest beast I ever see—'cept once when an Apache squaw had an edge on a half-breed what they nicknamed 'Splinters' 'cos of the way he fixed up her papoose which he stole on a raid just to show that he appreciated the way they had given his mother the fire torture. She got that kinder look so set on her face that it jest seemed to grow there. She followed Splinters mor'n three year till at last the braves got him and handed him over to her. They did say that no man, white or Injun, had ever been so long a-dying under the tortures of the Apaches. The only time I ever see her smile was when I wiped her out. I kem on the camp just in time to see Splinters pass in his checks, and he wasn't sorry to go either. He was a hard citizen, and though I never could shake with him after that papoose business—for it was bitter bad, and he should have been a white man, for he looked like one—I see he had got paid out in full. Durn me, but I took a piece of his hide from one of his skinnin' posts an' had it made into a pocket-book. It's here now!'' and he slapped the breast pocket of his coat.

Whilst he was speaking the cat was continuing her frantic efforts to get up the wall. She would take a run back and then charge up, sometimes reaching an incredible height. She did not seem to mind the heavy fall which she got each time but started with renewed vigor; and at every tumble her appearance became more horrible. Hutcheson was a kind-hearted man— my wife and I had both noticed little acts of kindness to animals as well as to persons—and he seemed concerned at the state of fury to which the cat had wrought herself.

"Wall, now!" he said, "I du declare that that poor critter seems quite desperate. There! there! poor thing, it was all an accident—though that won't bring back your little one to you. Say! I wouldn't have had such a thing happen for a thousand! Just shows what a clumsy fool of a man can do when he tries to play! Seems I'm too darned slipperhanded to even play with a cat. Say Colonel!'' it was a pleasant way he had to bestow titles freely—"I hope your wife don't hold no grudge against me on account of this unpleasantness? Why, I wouldn't have had it occur on no account."

He came over to Amelia and apologised profusely, and she with her usual kindness of heart hastened to assure him that she quite understood that it was an accident. Then we all went again to the wall and looked over.

The cat missing Hutcheson's face had drawn back across the moat, and was sitting on her haunches as though ready to spring. Indeed, the very instant she saw him she did spring, and with a blind unreasoning fury, which would have been grotesque, only that it was so frightfully real. She did not try to run up the wall, but simply launched herself at him as though hate and fury could lend her wings to pass straight through the great distance between them. Amelia, womanlike, got quite concerned, and said to Elias P. in a warning voice:

"Oh! you must be very careful. That animal would try to kill you if she were here; her eyes look like positive murder."

He laughed out jovially. "Excuse me, ma'am," he said, "but I can't help laughin'. Fancy a man that has fought grizzlies an' Injuns bein' careful of bein' murdered by a cat!"

When the cat heard him laugh, her whole demeanor seemed to change. She no longer tried to jump or run up the wall, but went quietly over, and sitting again beside the dead kitten began to lick and fondle it as though it were alive.

"See!" said I, "the effect of a really strong man. Even that animal in the midst of her fury recognises the voice of a master, and bows to him!"

"Like a squaw!" was the only comment of Elias P. Hutcheson, as we moved on our way round the city fosse. Every now and then we looked over the wall and each time saw the cat following us. At first she had kept going back to the dead kitten, and then as the distance grew greater took it in her mouth and so followed. After a while, however, she abandoned this, for we saw her following all alone; she had evidently hidden the body somewhere. Amelia's alarm grew at the cat's persistence, and more than once she repeated her warning; but the American always laughed with amusement, till finally, seeing that she was beginning to be worried, he said:

"I say, ma'am, you needn't be skeered over that cat. I go heeled, I du!" Here he slapped his pistol pocket at the back of his lumbar region. "Why sooner'n have you worried, I'll shoot the critter, right there, an' risk the police interferin' with a citizen of the United States for carryin' arms contrairy to reg'lations!" As he spoke he looked over the wall, but the cat on seeing him, retreated, with a growl, into a bed of tall flowers, and was hidden. He went on: "Blest if that ar critter ain't got more sense of what's good for her than most Christians. I guess we've seen the last of her! You bet, she'll go back now to that busted kitten and have a private funeral of it, all to herself!"

Amelia did not like to say more, lest he might, in mistaken kindness to her, fulfil his threat of shooting the cat: and so we went on and crossed the little wooden bridge leading to the gateway whence ran the steep paved roadway between the Burg and the pentagonal Torture Tower. As we crossed the bridge we saw the cat again down below us. When she saw us her fury seemed to return, and she made frantic efforts to get up the steep wall. Hutcheson laughed as he looked down at her, and said:

"Goodbye, old girl. Sorry I injured your feelin's, but you'll get over it in time! So long!" And then we passed through the long, dim archway and came to the gate of the Burg.

When we came out again after our survey of this most

beautiful old place which not even the well-intentioned efforts of the Gothic restorers of forty years ago have been able to spoil—though their restoration was then glaring white—we seemed to have quite forgotten the unpleasant episode of the morning. The old lime tree with its great trunk gnarled with the passing of nearly nine centuries, the deep well cut through the heart of the rock by those captives of old, and the lovely view from the city wall whence we heard, spread over almost a full quarter of an hour, the multitudinous chimes of the city, had all helped to wipe out from our minds the incident of the slain kitten.

We were the only visitors who had entered the Torture Tower that morning—so at least said the old custodian—and as we had the place all to ourselves were able to make a minute and more satisfactory survey than would have otherwise been possible. The custodian, looking to us as the sole source of his gains for the day, was willing to meet our wishes in any way. The Torture Tower is truly a grim place, even now when many thousands of visitors have sent a stream of life, and the joy that follows life, into the place; but at the time I mention it wore its grimmest and most gruesome aspect. The dust of ages seemed to have settled on it, and the darkness and the horror of its memories seem to have become sentient in a way that would have satisfied the Pantheistic souls of Philo or Spinoza. The lower chamber where we entered was seemingly, in its normal state, filled with incarnate darkness; even the hot sunlight streaming in through the door seemed to be lost in the vast thickness of the walls, and only showed the masonry rough as when the builder's scaffolding had come down, but coated with dust and marked here and there with patches of dark stain which, if walls could speak, could have given their own dread memories of fear and pain. We were glad to pass up the dusty wooden staircase, the custodian leaving the outer door open to light us somewhat on our way; for to our eyes the one long-wick'd, evil-smelling candle stuck in a sconce on the wall gave an inadequate light. When we came up through the open trap in the corner of the chamber overhead, Amelia held on to me so tightly that I could actually feel her heart beat. I must say for my own part that I was not surprised at her fear, for this room was even more gruesome than that below. Here there was certainly more light, but only just sufficient to realise the horrible surroundings of the place. The builders of the tower had evidently intended that only they who should gain the top should have any of the joys of light and prospect. There, as we had noticed from below, were ranges of windows, albeit of medi- aeval smallness, but elsewhere in the tower were only a very few narrow slits such as were habitual in places of mediaeval defence. A few of these only lit the cham- ber, and these so high up in the wall that from no part could the sky be seen through the thickness of the walls. In racks, and leaning in disorder against the walls, were a number of headsmen's swords, great double-handed weapons with broad blade and keen edge. Hard by were several blocks whereon the necks of the victims had lain, with here and there deep notches where the steel had bitten through the guard of flesh and shored into the wood. Round the chamber, placed in all sorts of irregular ways, were many implements of torture which made one's heart ache to see—chairs full of spikes which gave instant and excruciating pain; chairs and couches with dull knobs whose torture was seemingly less, but which, though slower, were equally efficacious; racks, belts, boots, gloves, collars, all made for compressing at will; steel baskets in which the head could be slowly crushed into a pulp if necessary; watchmen's hooks with long handle and knife that cut at resistance—this a spe- ciality of the old Nurnberg police system; and many, many other devices for man's injury to man. Amelia grew quite pale with the horror of the things, but fortunately did not faint, for being a little overcome she sat down on a torture chair, but jumped up again with a shriek, all tendency to faint gone. We both pretended that it was the injury done to her dress by the dust of the chair, and the rusty spikes which had upset her, and Mr. Hutcheson acquiesced in accepting the explanation with a kind-hearted laugh.

But the central object in the whole chamber of horrors was the engine known as the Iron Virgin, which stood near the centre of the room. It was a rudely-shaped figure of a woman, something of the bell order, or, to make a closer comparison, of the figure of Mrs. Noah in the children's Ark, but without that slimness of waist and perfect *rondeur* of hip which marks the aesthetic type of the Noah family. One would hardly have recognised it as intended for a human figure at all had not the founder shaped on the forehead a rude semblance of a woman's face. This machine was coated with rust without, and covered with dust; a rope was fastened to a ring in the front of the figure, about where the waist should have been, and was drawn through a pulley, fastened on the wooden pillar which sustained the flooring above. The custodian pulling this rope showed that a section of the front was hinged like a door at one side; we then saw that the engine was of considerable thickness, leaving just enough room inside for a man to be placed. The door was of equal thickness and of great weight, for it took the custodian all his strength, aided though he was by the contrivance of the pulley, to open it. This weight was partly due to the fact that the door was of manifest purpose hung so as to throw its weight downwards, so that it might shut of its own accord when the strain was released. The inside was honeycombed with rust—nay more, the rust alone that comes through time would hardly have eaten so deep into the iron walls; the rust of the cruel stains was deep indeed! It was only, however, when we came to look at the inside of the door that the diabolical intention was manifest to the full. Here were several long spikes, square and massive, broad at the base and sharp at the points, placed in such a position that when the door should close the upper ones would pierce the eyes of the victim, and the lower ones his heart and vitals. The sight was too much for poor Amelia, and this time she fainted dead off, and I had to carry her down the stairs, and place her on a bench outside till she recovered. That she felt it to the quick was afterwards shown by the fact that my eldest son bears to this day a rude birthmark on his breast, which has, by family consent, been accepted as representing the Nurnberg Virgin.

When we got back to the chamber we found Hutcheson still opposite the Iron Virgin; he had been evidently philosophising, and now gave us the benefit of his thought in the shape of a sort of exordium.

"Wall, I guess I've been learnin' somethin' here while madam has been gettin' over her faint. 'Pears to me that we're a long way behind the times on our side of the big drink. We uster think out on the plains that the Injun could give us points in tryin' to make a man uncomfortable; but I guess your old mediaeval law-and-order party could raise him every time. Splinters was pretty good in his bluff on the squaw, but this here young miss held a straight flush all high on him. The points of them spikes air sharp enough still, though even the edges air eaten out by what uster be on them. It'd be a good thing for our Indian section to get some specimens of this here play-toy to send round to the Reservations jest to knock the stuffin' out of the bucks, and the squaws too, by showing them as how old civilisation lays over them at their best. Guess but I'll get in that box a minute jest to see how it feels."

"Oh no! no!" said Amelia. "It is too terrible!"

"Guess, ma'am, nothin's too terrible to the ex-plorin' mind. I've been in some queer places in my time. Spent a night inside a dead horse while a prairie fire swept over me in Montana Territory—an' another time slept inside a dead buffler when the Comanches was on the war path an' I didn't keer to leave my kyard on them. I've been two days in a caved-in tunnel in the Billy Broncho gold mine in New Mexico, an' was one of the four shut up for three parts of a day in the caisson what slid over on her side when we were set-tin' the foundations of the Buffalo Bridge. I've not funked an odd experience yet, an' I don't propose to begin now!"

We saw that he was set on the experiment, so I said: "Well, hurry up, old man, and get through it quick!"

"All right, General," said he, "but I calculate we ain't quite ready yet. The gentlemen, my predecessors, what stood in that thar canister, didn't volunteer for the office—not much! And I guess there was some orna-mental tyin' up before the big stroke was made. I want to go into this thing fair and square, so I must get fixed up proper first. I dare say this old galoot can rise some string and tie me up accordin' to sample?"

This was said interrogatively to the old custodian, but the latter, who understood the drift of his speech, though perhaps not appreciating to the full the niceties of dialect and imagery, shook his head. His protest was, however, only formal and made to be overcome. The American thrust a gold piece into his hand, saying: "Take it, pard! it's your pot; and don't be skeer'd. This ain't no necktie party that you're asked to assist in!" He produced some thin frayed rope and proceeded to bind our companion with sufficient strictness for the purpose. When the upper part of his body was bound, Hutcheson said:

"Hold on a moment, Judge. Guess I'm too heavy for you to tote into the cannister. You just let me walk in, and then you can wash up regardin' my legs!"

Whilst speaking he had backed himself into the opening which was just enough to hold him. It was a close fit and no mistake. Amelia looked on with fear in her eyes, but she evidently did not like to say anything. Then the custodian completed his task by tying the American's feet together so that he was now absolutely helpless and fixed in his voluntary prison. He seemed to really enjoy it, and the incipient smile which was habitual to his face blossomed into actuality as he said:

"Guess this here Eve was made out of the rib of a dwarf! There ain't much room for a full-grown citizen of the United States to hustle. We uster make our coffins more roomier in Idaho territory. Now, Judge, you jest begin to let this door down, slow, on to me. I want to feel the same pleasure as the other jays had when those spikes began to move toward their eyes!"

"Oh no! no! no!" broke in Amelia hysterically. "It is too terrible! I can't bear to see it!—I can't! I can't!" But the American was obdurate. "Say, Colonel," said he, "why not take Madame for a little promenade? I wouldn't hurt her feelin's for the world; but now that I am here, havin' kem eight thousand miles, wouldn't it be too hard to give up the very experience I've been pinin' an' pantin' fur? A man can't get to feel like canned goods every time! Me and the Judge here'll fix up this thing in no time, an' then you'll come back, an' we'll all laugh together!"

Once more the resolution that is born of curiosity triumphed, and Amelia stayed holding tight to my arm and shivering whilst the custodian began to slacken slowly inch by inch the rope that held back the iron door. Hutcheson's face was positively radiant as his eyes followed the first movement of the spikes.

"Wall!" he said, "I guess I've not had enjoyment like this since I left Noo York. Bar a scrap with a French sailor at Wapping—an' that warn't much of a picnic neither—I've not had a show fur real pleasure in this dod-rotted Continent, where there ain't no b'ars nor no Injuns, an' wheer nary man goes heeled. Slow there, Judge! Don't you rush this business! I want a show for my money this game—I du!"

The custodian must have had in him some of the blood of his predecessors in that ghastly tower, for he worked the engine with a deliberate and excruciating slowness which after five minutes, in which the outer edge of the door had not moved half as many inches, began to overcome Amelia. I saw her lips whiten, and felt her hold upon my arm relax. I looked around an instant for a place whereon to lay her, and when I looked at her again found that her eye had become fixed on the side of the Virgin. Following its direction I saw the black cat crouching out of sight. Her green eyes shone like danger lamps in the gloom of the place, and their colour was heightened by the blood which still smeared her coat and reddened her mouth. I cried out:

"The cat! look out for the cat!" for even then she sprang out before the engine. At this moment she looked like a triumphant demon. Her eyes blazed with ferocity, her hair bristled out till she seemed twice her normal size, and her tail lashed about as does a tiger's when the quarry is before it. Elias P. Hutcheson when he saw her was amused, and his eyes positively sparkled with fun as he said:

"Darned if the squaw hain't got on all her war paint! Jest give her a shove off if she comes any of her tricks on me, for I'm so fixed everlastingly by the boss, that durn my skin if I can keep my eyes from her if she wants them! Easy there, Judge! Don't you slack that ar rope or I'm euchered!"

At this moment Amelia completed her faint, and I had to clutch hold of her round the waist or she would have fallen to the floor. Whilst attending to her I saw the black cat crouching for a spring, and jumped to turn the creature out.

But at that instant, with a sort of hellish scream, she hurled herself, not as we expected at Hutcheson, but straight at the face of the custodian. Her claws seemed to be tearing wildly as one sees in the Chinese drawings of the dragon rampant, and as I looked I saw one of them light on the poor man's eye, and actually tear through it and down his cheek, leaving a wide band of red where the blood seemed to spurt from every vein.

With a yell of sheer terror which came quicker than even his sense of pain, the man leaped back, dropping as he did so the rope which held back the iron door. I jumped for it, but was too late, for the cord ran like lightning through the pulley-block, and the heavy mass fell forward from its own weight.

As the door closed I caught a glimpse of our poor companion's face. He seemed frozen with terror. His eyes stared with a horrible anguish as if dazed, and no sound came from his lips.

And then the spikes did their work. Happily the end was quick, for when I wrenched open the door they had pierced so deep that they had locked in the bones of the skull through which they had crushed, and actually tore him—it—out of his iron prison till, bound as he was, he fell at full length with a sickly thud upon the floor, the face turning upward as he fell.

I rushed to my wife, lifted her up and carried her out, for I feared for her very reason if she should wake from her faint to such a scene. I laid her on the bench outside and ran back. Leaning against the wooden column was the custodian moaning in pain whilst he held his reddening handkerchief to his eyes. And sitting on the head of the poor American was the cat, purring loudly as she licked the blood which trickled through the gashed socket of his eyes.

I think no one will call me cruel because I seized one of the old executioner's swords and shore her in two as she sat.

A Great Sight

JANWILLEM VAN DE WETERING

No, it wasn't easy. It took a great deal of effortful dreaming to get where I am now. Where I am now is Moose Bay, on the Maine coast, which is on the east of the United States of America, in case you haven't been looking at maps lately. Moose Bay is long and narrow, bordered by two peninsulas and holding some twenty square miles of water. I've lived on the south shore for almost thirty years now, always alone—if you don't count a couple of old cats—and badly crippled. Lost the use of my legs I have, thirty years ago, and that was my release and my ticket to Moose Bay. I've often wondered whether the mishap was really an accident. Sure enough, the fall was due to faulty equipment (a new strap that broke) and quite beyond my will. The telephone company that employed me acknowledged their responsibility easily enough, paying me handsomely so that I could be comfortably out of work for the rest of my life. But didn't I, perhaps, dream myself into that fall? You see, I wasn't exactly happy being a telephone repairman. Up one post and down another, climbing or slithering up and down forever, day after day, and not in the best of climates. For years I did that and there was no way I could see in which the ordeal would ever end. So I began to dream of a way out, and of where I would go. To be able to dream is a gift. My father didn't have the talent. No imagination the old man had, in Holland he lived, where I was born, and he had a similar job to what I would have later. He was a window-cleaner and I guess he could only visualize death, for when *he* fell it was the last thing he ever did. I survived, with mashed legs. I never dreamed of death, I dreamed of the great sights I would still see, whisking myself to a life on a rocky coast, where I would be alone, maybe with a few old cats, in a cedar log cabin with a view of the water, the sky, and a line of trees on the other shore. I would see, I dreamed, rippling waves or the mirror-like surface of a great expanse of liquid beauty on a windless day. I never gave that up, the possibility of seeing great sights, and I dreamed myself up here, where everything is as I thought it might be, only better.

Now don't get me wrong, I'm not your dreamy type. No long hair and beads for me, no debts unpaid or useless things just lying about in the house. Everything is spic-and-span with me; the kitchen works, there's an ample supply of staples, each in their own jar, I have good vegetables from the garden, an occasional bird I get with the shotgun, and fish caught off my dock. I can't walk so well, but I get about on my crutches and the pickup has been changed so that I can drive it with my hands. No fleas on the cats, either, and no smell from the outhouse. I have all I need and all within easy reach. There must be richer people in the world (don't I see them sometimes, sailing along in their hundred-foot skyscrapers?), but I don't have to envy them. May they live happily for as long as it takes; I'll just sit here and watch the sights from my porch.

Or I watch them from the water. I have an eight-foot dory and it rows quite well in the bay if the waves aren't too high, for it *will* ship water when the weather gets rough. There's much to see when I go rowing. A herd of harbor seals lives just out of my cove and they know me well, coming to play around my boat as soon as I sing out to them. I bring them a rubber ball that they push about for a bit, and throw even, until they want to go about their own business again and bring it back. I've named them all and can identify the individuals when they frolic in the spring, or raise their tails and heads, lolling in the summer sun.

I go out most good days, for I've taken it upon myself to keep this coast clean. Garbage drifts in, thrown in by the careless, off ships I suppose, and by the city people, the unfortunates who never look at the sights. I get beer cans to pick up in my net, and every variety of plastic container, boards with rusty nails in them and occasionally a complete vessel, made out of crumbly foam. I drag it all to the same spot and burn the rubbish. Rodney, the fellow I share Moose Bay with—he lives a mile down from me in a tar-papered shack—makes fun of me when I perform my duty. He'll come by in his smart powerboat, flat on the water and sharply pointed, with a loud engine pushing it that looks like three regular outboards stacked on top of each other. Rodney can really zip about in that thing. He's a thin, ugly fellow with a scraggly black beard and big slanted eyes above his crooked nose. He's from here, of course, and he won't let me forget his lawful nativity. Much higher up the scale than me, he claims, for what am I but some itinerant, an alien washed up from nowhere, tolerated by the locals? If I didn't happen to be an old codger, and lame, Rodney says, he would drown me like he does his kittens. Hop, into the sack, weighed down with a good boulder, and away with the mess. But being what I am, sort of human in a way, he puts up with my presence for a while, provided I don't trespass on his bit of the shore, crossing the high-tide line, for then he'll have to shoot me, with the deer rifle he now uses for poaching. Rodney has a vegetable garden, too, even though he doesn't care for greens. The garden is a trap for deer so that he can shoot them from his shack, preferably at night, after he has frozen them with a flashlight.

There are reasons for me not to like Rodney too much. He shot my friend, the killer whale that used to come here some summers ago. Killer whales are a rare sight on this coast, but they do pop up from time to time. They're supposed to be wicked animals, that will push your boat over and gobble you up when you're thrashing about, weighed down by your boots and your oilskins. Maybe they do that, but my friend didn't do it to me. He used to float alongside my dory, that he could have tipped with a single flap of his great triangular tail. He would roll over on his side, all thirty feet of him, and grin lazily from the corner of his huge curved mouth. I could see his big gleaming teeth and mirror my face in his calm, humorous eye, and I would sing to him. I haven't got a good loud voice, but I would hum away, making up a few words here and there, and he'd lift a flipper in appreciation and snort if my song wasn't long enough for his liking. Every day that killer whale came to me; I swear he was waiting for me out in the bay, for as soon as I'd splash my oars I'd see his six-foot fin cut through the waves, and a moment later his black-and-white head, always with that welcoming grin.

Now we don't have any electricity down here, and

kerosene isn't as cheap as it used to be, so maybe Rodney was right when he said that he shot the whale because he needed the blubber. Blubber makes good fuel, Rodney says. Me, I think he was wrong, for he never got the blubber anyway. When he'd shot the whale, zipping past it in the powerboat, and got the animal between the eyes with his deer rifle, the whale just sank. I never saw its vast body wash up. Perhaps it didn't die straightaway and could make it to the depth of the ocean, to die there in peace.

He's a thief, too, Rodney is. He'll steal anything he can get his hands on, to begin with his welfare. There's nothing wrong with Rodney's back but he's stuffed a lot of complaints into it, enough so that the doctors pay attention. He collects his check and his food stamps, and he gets his supplies for free. There's a town, some fifty miles further along, and they employ special people there to give money to the poor, and counselors to listen to pathetic homemade tales, and there's a society that distributes gifts on holiday. Rodney even gets his firewood every year, brought by young religious men on a truck; they stack it right where Rodney points— no fee.

"Me against the world," Rodney says, "for the world owes me a living. I never asked to be born but here I am, and my hands are out." He'll be drinking when he talks like that, guzzling my Sunday bourbon on my porch, and he'll point his long finger at me. "You some sort of Kraut?"

I say I'm Dutch. The Dutch fought the Krauts during the war; I fought a bit myself until they caught me and put me in a camp. They were going to kill me, but then the Americans came. "Saved you, did we?" Rodney will say, and fill up his glass again. "So you owe us now, right? So how come you're living off the fat of this land, you with the crummy legs?" He'll raise his glass and I'll raise mine.

Rodney lost his wife. He still had her when I settled in my cabin, I got to talk to her at times and liked her fine. She would talk to Rodney, about his ways, and he would leer at her, and he was still leering when she was found at the bottom of a cliff. "Never watched where she was going," Rodney said to the sheriff, who took the corpse away. The couple had a dog, who was fond of Rodney's wife and unhappy when she was gone. The dog would howl at night and keep Rodney awake, but the dog happened to fall off the cliff, too. Same cliff. Maybe I should have reported the coincidence to the authorities, but it wasn't much more than a coincidence and, as Rodney says, accidents will happen. Look at me, I fell down a telephone post, nobody pushed *me*, right? It was a brand-new strap that snapped when it shouldn't have; a small event, quite beyond my control.

No, I never went to the sheriff and I've never stood up to Rodney. There's just the two of us on Moose Bay. He's the bad guy who'll tip his garbage into the bay and I'm the in-between guy who's silly enough to pick it up. We also have a good guy, who lives at the end of the north peninsula, at the tip, facing the ocean. Michael his name is, Michael the lobsterman. A giant of a man, Michael is, with a golden beard and flashing teeth. I can see his smile when his lobster boat enters the bay. The boat is one of these old-fashioned jobs, sturdy and white and square, puttering along at a steady ten knots in every sort of weather. Michael's got a big winch on it, for hauling up the heavy traps, and I can see him taking the lobsters out and putting the bait in and throwing them back. Michael has some thousand traps, all along the coast, but his best fishing is here in Moose Bay. Over the years we've got to know each other and I sometimes go out with him, much further than the dory can take me. Then we see the old squaws flock in, the diver ducks that look as if they've flown in from a Chinese painting, with their thin curved tailfeathers and delicately-drawn wings and necks. Or we watch the big whales, snorting and spouting, and the haze on the horizon where the sun dips, causing indefinably soft colors, or we just smell the clear air together, coming to cool the forests in summer. Michael knows Rodney, too, but he isn't the gossipy kind. He'll frown when he sees the powerboat lurking in Moose Bay and gnaw his pipe before he turns away. When Michael doesn't stop at my dock he'll wave and make some gesture, in lieu of conversation—maybe he'll hold his hands close together to show me how far he could see when he cut through the fog, or he'll point at a bird flying over us, a heron in slow flight, or a jay, hurrying from shore to shore, gawking and screeching, and I'll know what he means.

This Michael is a good guy, I knew it the first time I saw his silhouette on the lobster boat, and I've heard good stories about him, too. A knight in shining armor who has saved people about to drown in storms, or marooned and sick on the islands. A giant and a genius, for he's built his own boat, and his gear—even his house, a big sprawling structure out of driftwood on pegged beams. And he'll fight when he has to, for it isn't always cozy here. He'll be out in six-foot waves and I've seen him when the bay is frozen up, excepting the channel where the current rages, with icicles on his beard and snow driving against his bow—but he'll still haul up his traps.

I heard he was out in the last war, too, flying an airplane low above the jungle, and he still flies now, on Sundays, for the National Guard.

Rodney got worse. I don't know what devil lives in that man but the fiend must have been thrown out of the lowest hells. Rodney likes new games and he thought it would be fun to chase me a bit. My dory sits pretty low in the water, but there are enough good days here and I can get out quite a bit. When I do Rodney will wait for me, hidden behind the big rocks east of my cove, and he'll suddenly appear, revving his engine, trailing a high wake. When his curly waves hit me I have to bail for my life, and as soon as I'm done the fear will be back, for he'll be after me again.

I didn't quite know what to do then. Get a bigger boat? But then he would think of something else. There are enough games he can play. He knows my fondness for the seals, he could get them one by one, as target practice. There's my vegetable garden, too, close to the track; he could back his truck into it and get my cats as an afterthought, flattening them into the gravel, for they're slow these days, careless with old age. The fear grabbed me by the throat at night, as I watched my ceiling, remembering his dislike of my cabin and thinking how easily it would burn, being made of old cedar with a roof of shingles. I knew it was him who took the battery out of my truck, making me hitchhike to town for a new one. He was also sucking my gas, but I keep a drum of energy near the house. Oh, I'm vulnerable here all right, with the sheriff coming down only once a year. Suppose I talk to the law, suppose the law talks to Rodney, suppose *I* fall down that cliff, too?

I began to dream again, like I had done before, when I was still climbing the telephone posts like a demented monkey. I was bored then, hopelessly bored, and now I was hopelessly afraid. Hadn't I dreamed my way out once before? Tricks can be repeated.

My dream gained strength; it had to, for Rodney was getting rougher. His powerboat kept less distance, went faster. I couldn't see myself sticking to the land. I need to get out on the bay, to listen to the waves lapping the rocks, to hear the seals blow when they clear their nostrils, to hear the kingfishers and the squirrels whirr in the trees on shore, to spot the little ring-necked ducks, busily investigating the shallows, peering eagerly out of their tufted heads. There are the quiet herons stalking the mudflats and the ospreys whirling slowly; there are eagles, even, diving and splashing when the alewives run from the brooks. Would I have to potter about in the vegetable patch all the time, leaning on a crutch while pushing a hoe with my free hand?

I dreamed up a bay free of Rodney. There was a strange edge to the dream—some kind of quality there that I couldn't quite see, but it was splendid, a great sight and part of my imagination although I couldn't quite make it out.

One day, fishing off my dock, I saw Michael's lobster boat nosing into the cove: I waved and smiled and he waved back, but he didn't smile.

He moored the boat and jumped onto the jetty, light as a great cat, touching my arm. We walked up to my porch and I made some strong coffee.

"There's a thief," Michael said, "stealing my lobsters. He used to take a few, few enough to ignore maybe, but now he's taking too many."

"Oho," I said, holding my mug. Michael wouldn't be referring to me. Me? Steal lobsters? How could I ever haul up a trap? The channel is deep in the bay. A hundred feet of cable and a heavy trap at the end of it, never. I would need a winch, like Rodney has on his powerboat.

Besides, doesn't Michael leave me a lobster every now and then? Lying on my dock in the morning, its claws neatly tied with a bit of yellow string?

"Any idea?" he asked.

"Same as yours," I said, "but he's hard to catch. The powerboat is fast. He nips out of the bay before he does his work, to make sure you aren't around."

"Might get the warden," Michael said, "and then he might go to jail, and come out again, and do something bad."

I agreed. "Hard to prove, it would be," I said. "A house burns down, yours or mine. An accident maybe."

Michael left. I stayed on the porch, dreaming away, expending some power. A little power goes a long way in a dream.

It happened the next day, a Sunday it was. I was walking to the shore, for it was low tide and I wanted to see the seals on their rocks. It came about early, just after sunrise. I heard an airplane. A lot of airplanes come by here. There's the regular commuter plane from the town to the big city, and the little ones the tourists fly in summer, and the flying club. There are also big planes, dirtying up the sky, high up, some of them are Russians, they say; the National Guard has to be about, to push them back. The big planes rumble, but this sound was different, light but deadly, far away still. I couldn't see the plane, but when I did it was coming silently, ahead of its own sound, it was that fast. Then it slowed down, surveying the bay.

I've seen fighter planes during World War II, Germans and Englishmen flew them, propeller jobs that would spin around each other above the small Dutch lakes, until one of the planes came down, trailing smoke. Jet planes I only saw later, here in America. They looked dangerous enough, even while they gambolled about, and I felt happy watching them, for I was in the States and they were protecting me from the bad guys lurking in the east.

This airplane was a much-advanced version of what I had seen in the late '40s. Much longer it was, and sleek and quiet as it lost height, aiming for the channel. A baby-blue killer, with twin rudders, sticking up elegantly far behind the large gleaming canopy up front, reflecting the low sunlight. I guessed her to be seventy feet long, easily the size of the splendid yachts of the rich summer people, but there was no pleasure in her; she was all functional, programmed for swift pursuit and destruction only. I grinned when I saw her American stars, set in circles, with a striped bar sticking out at each side. When she was closer I thought I could see the pilot, all wrapped up in his tight suit and helmet, the living brain controlling this deadly superfast vessel of the sky.

I saw that the plane was armed, with white missiles attached to its slender streamlined belly. I had read about those missiles. Costly little mothers they are. Too costly to fire at Rodney's boat, busily stealing away right in front of my cove. Wouldn't the pilot have to explain the loss of one of his slick rockets? He'd surely be in terrible trouble if he returned to base incomplete.

Rodney was thinking the same way for he was jumping up and down in his powerboat, grinning and sticking two fingers at the airplane hovering above the bay.

Then the plane roared and shot away, picking up speed at an incredible rate. I was mightily impressed and grateful, visualizing the enemy confronted with such force, banking, diving, rising again at speeds much faster than sound.

The plane had gone and I was alone again, with Rodney misbehaving in the bay, taking the lobsters out as fast as he could—one trap shooting up after another, yanked up by his nastily whining little winch.

The plane came back, silently, with the roar of its twin engines well behind it. It came in low, twenty-five feet above the short choppy waves. Rodney, unaware, busy, didn't even glance over his shoulder. I was leaning on the railing of my porch, gaping stupidly. Was the good guy going to ram the bad guy? Would they go down together? This had to be the great sight I had been dreaming up. Perhaps I should have felt guilty.

Seconds it took, maybe less than one second. Is there still time at five thousand miles an hour?

Then there was the flame, just after the plane passed the powerboat. A tremendous cloud of fire, billowing, deep orange with fiery red tongues, blotting out the other shore, frayed with black smoke at the edges. The flame shot out of the rear of the plane and hung sizzling around Rodney's boat. The boat must have dissolved instantly, for I never found any debris. Fried to a cinder. Did Rodney's body whizz away inside that hellish fire? It must have, bones, teeth and all.

I didn't see where the plane went. There are low hills at the end of the bay, so it must have zoomed up immediately once the afterburners spat out the huge flame.

Michael smiled sadly when he visited me a few days later and we were having coffee on my porch again.

"You saw it happen?"

"Oh yes," I said. "A great sight indeed."

"Did he leave any animals that need taking care of?"

"Just the cat," I said. The cat was on my porch, a big marmalade tom that had settled in already.

Time has passed again since then. The bay is quiet now. We're having a crisp autumn and I'm enjoying the cool days rowing about on the bay, watching the geese gather, honking majestically as they get ready to go south.